FINDING EMMA

FINDING EMMA

Steena Holmes

amazon publishing

Text copyright © 2012 Steena Holmes

Published by Amazon Publishing
P.O. Box 400818, Las Vegas, NV 89140
ISBN-13: 9781477800119
ISBN-10: 1477800115

ACKNOWLEDGMENTS

Finding Emma is a story dear to my heart. I am honored to donate the proceeds from each book to the Missing Children Society of Canada—an organization that focuses on reuniting families.

A special thank you to my own family for believing in me and never letting me give up on my dream. Micah, Ayla, and Judah—thank you for helping me create Hannah, Alexis, and Emma. Without you these girls wouldn't have come alive.

Thank you to my handsome and supportive husband for his never-ending supply of coffee, chocolate, and belief in me.

Sophia Paige Lewis—thank you for being Emma on my cover. You are beautiful, and I knew as soon as I saw your picture that you should portray Emma.

Jennifer Jones with Luxe Photography—without you I wouldn't have this beautiful cover.

Carmen Johnson, my editor, who believed in *Emma* enough to see its potential. I've always believed all you ever needed was one person to love a book enough, and for me—that is you!

Pamela Harty, aka Agent Awesome, thank you for believing in me. You are truly a blessing, and I'm so thankful God put you in my path.

So many wonderful women fell in love with Emma's story that it's not possible to thank each one individually—but you know who you are!

To my "circle of trust" girls who believed in me from the moment we met.

Sherri Gall, for that talk on my couch when Emma's story came to life—this is for you!

CHAPTER ONE

A child's scream shattered the peaceful silence of the Sunday afternoon.

Megan shot up from the blanket on the lawn, her heart hammering as she scanned the street in front of her. She groaned as two of her daughters squirted each other in a water-gun fight as they came up the walkway. She'd dozed off. Again. The late nights working on Peter's books had to stop. Yesterday, she'd woken up to find her third daughter, Emma, across the street at the neighbors', crawled halfway into their doghouse.

She glanced down at Emma, her youngest child, playing with a dandelion on the blanket. Thank God, she was still there. The three-year-old gazed in rapture at the sky.

"Red balloon, Momma?"

Megan twirled her fingers in Emma's tight curls.

"Later, honey."

"Red, Momma. Red balloons." Emma gestured toward the sky with her pudgy fingers. Megan turned her head and noticed the explosion of color that filled the air. Red, yellow, and blue balloons danced with the breeze, sweeping across the sky.

The annual carnival was here, just in time for the end-of-school celebration their small town always held. It was also Emma's birthday. Megan wished for time to stand still. Her baby was growing too fast.

"Mom, can we have a popsicle?" Hannah shook droplets of water over Megan's bare legs. She gasped at the coldness. Laughing, Megan jumped up and backed away from her soaked daughter only to find a giggling Emma clutched around her leg.

"Don't you come any closer." Megan had a hard time keeping the smile off her face before a sparkle of mischief lit up Hannah's blue eyes as she lunged across the blanket. Laughing, Megan scooped up Emma, ran toward the front door, and closed the screen in Hannah's face. Alexis crossed the driveway, stepping over Megan's gladioli, and aimed the almost-empty water gun at her older sister.

"Alexis Marie Taylor, if you douse your sister in more water, she'll get your half of the popsicle," Megan warned. Alexis's eyes widened as she dropped the water gun on the grass and bounded across to the porch before placing her arms around Hannah's shoulders.

"Would I do that?" Alexis tilted her head and beamed the most innocent smile Megan had ever seen.

Megan snorted. "No monkey business, you two, or Emma and I will eat your popsicles. Got it?" Megan narrowed her eyes and pursed her lips. Who knew? Maybe the serious look would work.

"Come in and get dried off. Your dad should be home soon." She opened the screen door for the girls then locked it. The past couple of days Emma had snuck outside behind Megan's back to catch some butterflies. Or try to at least.

For dinner, they were going downtown to watch the parade and eat corn dogs, candied apples, and cotton candy at the carnival. The girls were so excited. Peter had even promised the girls he'd win them each a stuffed teddy bear and Megan couldn't wait to show Emma the clowns.

"Why don't we play a game of hopscotch while we wait for your dad?" Megan called after the girls as they ran up the stairs to change. She loved being a mother, even though having three girls so close in age exhausted her. Being a mom fulfilled her in more ways than she had thought possible.

"Hey, Em? How about we make some more lemonade? This time we'll do less sugar." She'd let the girls make it just after lunch and Alexis had almost dumped the whole container of sugar in the bowl.

The phone rang just as footsteps pounded down the stairs.

"Just going out to grab my headband," Hannah yelled.

"Lock the door when you come back in," Megan called out just as the screen door slammed.

With the phone balanced between her shoulder and ear, Megan opened the fridge and rooted inside for the filtered water jug. She groaned when she realized it was empty, having forgotten to fill it after pouring a glass earlier. The automated message informed her that the Sears catalog order was in. She frowned. She hadn't ordered anything. When the automated voice repeated its message, Megan grabbed her daily calendar and flipped through the last few weeks to see if she'd written down anything. Weird. There was nothing in her notes.

A quick glance at the clock after hanging up the phone confirmed Peter should be home any minute.

"All right, pumpkin, let's go change your Pull-Up and get ready to watch the parade. Just wait till you see the clowns . . ." Megan turned toward Emma only to find herself talking to an empty room.

"Emma?" Megan walked into the living room fully expecting to find Emma in there, playing with the new ponies Peter had given her that morning.

The room was empty.

She retraced her steps and headed out to the hallway.

"Emma, are you upstairs? Girls, is your sister with you?" Megan took a step, gripped the railing, and waited to hear Emma's running footsteps. She didn't remember hearing the slam of the screen door when Hannah came back in.

"Not here," Hannah called out.

Startled, Megan took her foot off the step, glanced around, and looked at the screen door. "Hannah, did you lock the door like I told you to?" She fought to keep the panic out of her voice as she ran across the hallway to the open door.

Megan couldn't breathe.

Unlocked.

"Emma!" Megan ran outside calling her baby's name. She stopped in the middle of the driveway and scanned the area. Nothing. She wasn't chasing butterflies, pulling flowers out of the garden, or playing with dandelions. She wasn't anywhere.

Megan screamed as loud as she could and tears started to stream down her face.

Emma was gone.

CHAPTER TWO

Two Years Later

I f looks could kill, her daughter would be a goddess whose stare withered Megan into dust in the hallway. All from the glance of a ten-year-old.

"Why, Mom? Why won't you let us walk?" Alexis half-turned on the stairs, hands on her hips as she challenged a rule they had created two years ago.

Megan closed her eyes and pinched the top of her nose. Drops of water from the end of her high ponytail dripped down the back of her neck. She'd rushed through her shower.

"Alexis, you know why," she said. Her head throbbed. Great. It was only eight in the morning and she already had a headache. Megan headed to the kitchen for aspirin and water.

"But you let us walk home . . ." Alexis followed her.

"Yes, with an adult. Not alone. Sorry, but you are not walking to school by yourself. Honestly, Alex. Why do you have to push this? And today of all days." With last night's attempted abduction plastered all over the news there was no way another one of her daughters would be kidnapped. Not this time.

The afternoon Safe Walks program she'd started was going well, but she couldn't round up enough volunteers to help in the mornings. She hoped by next year she would. Until then, she would continue to drive her daughters to school. It was the least she could do.

"What's the big deal? Dad trusts us enough to walk home."

Megan swallowed the pills and leaned against the counter. "I'm not Dad."

The look of defiance on her daughter's face dissolved before she walked out of the kitchen and headed back up the stairs. Megan shook her head.

"Stop arguing and just get ready," she called over her shoulder. The thud of Alexis's feet as they stomped up the stairs sounded along the hardwood floor.

"And change into a pair of pants without holes in the knees," she said before Alexis had the chance to slam her door.

Megan grabbed her glass of water and headed into Peter's office.

His desk was a mess. Books were piled up in one corner, stacks of bills and house appraisals in the other. His laptop had been moved to the edge of his desk so he could read the morning news. Peter sat there, his fingers splayed through his hair.

"Did you know about this?" He leaned back in his chair and held up the front page for her to see.

The headline captured her attention: MISSING. A ball of steel dropped in Megan's stomach. *Oh God, please let that little girl be okay.* Her heart raced at the thought of another family having to experience their nightmare.

She pulled the paper toward her when she realized the picture wasn't of the little girl plastered all over the evening news, but of Emma.

Her baby.

"Always remembered, always loved. Emma Taylor will turn five years old today. As a town, we pray for her safe return."

"I had no idea." Megan's hand shook as she scanned the article and read about the attempted abduction beneath a recap about Emma. She handed the paper back to Peter who folded it up and let it drop to the floor before reaching for Megan.

"I was thinking we could play hooky and spend the day together. Maybe go for a drive along the beach?" Peter pulled her into his lap and ran his hand along her jawline before he cupped the back of her neck and brought her close.

Megan pulled away. "I have that assembly later this afternoon I need to get ready for."

She watched the light in Peter's eyes dim. "But, I could always pick up some coffee. . ."

Peter eyed her chest and winked. "Is there anything else on the menu with the coffee?"

Megan leaned forward and placed a tender kiss on his lips.

"Maybe," she said, her voice transformed into a husky whisper. She pulled away only to be tugged back down. This time Peter didn't settle for a small kiss. When his lips met hers, he didn't hold back. He made sure she knew what he wanted on the menu. Megan sighed. It had been so long . . .

"Argh, would you guys get a room or something? Gross." Alexis groaned from outside the door.

"Oops," Megan said while Peter rubbed at his face with his free hand. "I'll be back with coffee."

Peter's voice stopped her from leaving. "Promise?"

Megan looked at Peter. Really looked at him. She knew he meant more than just coffee. Their intimacy, or lack thereof, was starting to hurt their marriage. She could see it in his eyes.

"Yes," she said. She gave him a wink before facing her daughter.

"I was thinking we could go out for ice cream or something tonight. You know, to celebrate. . ." She listened to the silence that met her words.

She took the brush and elastic Alexis held out, spun her daughter around so her back faced her, and then pulled her hair into a ponytail high on her head.

"Are we really going to celebrate Emma's birthday?" Alexis asked.

Peter walked out of the room.

Megan swallowed past the lump in her throat as she caught the slight droop of his shoulders. "Of course we will." She kissed the top of her daughter's head before turning her around to give her a brief hug and glance down at her new outfit. Alexis had changed into a brown sundress with tiny white flowers along the hem, a soft purple cardigan over her top, and blue socks pulled high up her legs. Megan shook her head but kept her mouth shut. *This battle is not worth it.* At least she'd changed her pants.

"All right, you. Ready? How about if I drop you off at the corner this time so you can pretend you didn't get a ride to school?" Megan placed her arm around her daughter's shoulders.

Alexis shrugged. "Whatever." They both knew Megan wouldn't drive away until she knew both her children were safe inside the school. She never did.

⚜

Megan tapped her fingers against the steering wheel to the song on the radio. Something about a girl and a white horse. She didn't really listen to the song, she just liked the beat.

She pulled her phone out of her purse and scrolled through the notifications. Seven new emails and one text message. She glanced up, noticed the car in front of her still hadn't moved forward in the line for the drive-thru. She should have just gone inside and ordered, but when she compared the line of people standing at the doors to the line of cars, waiting in her vehicle won, hands down.

She clicked on the text message from her husband—*hurry home.* A smile bloomed on Megan's face. Her fingers danced across the phone's keyboard as she texted him back. The man needed to have some patience. It had been too long since they played hooky. Just the thought sent a flutter of excitement through her stomach. It had been too long indeed.

Megan glanced in her side-view mirror. With two cars behind her, it was too late for her to change her mind and suggest they just make coffee at home. She could be here a while.

She placed her phone on the passenger seat and thought back to when she dropped Alexis and Hannah off at school. A block away from the school grounds, Alexis had begged her to pull over. Up ahead were a group of kids she recognized and there was no way she was going to be caught with her mom. Megan waited as they sprinted down the sidewalk to catch up with the group. Only Hannah, her eldest, looked back to wave. True to her word, Megan didn't drive away until she knew the girls were safe inside the school yard.

Her phone buzzed. Another text from Peter. As she reached down to grab the phone, the bobbing of yellow curls in her rearview mirror caught her eye. Her heart stopped.

Emma.

She grabbed the steering wheel hard and forced herself to take a deep breath. She tried to remember the steps her counselor gave her to do the next time she thought she saw her missing daughter.

Number one: take a deep breath. Right. Megan filled up her lungs and tried to exhale only to have it catch in her throat.

Those yellow curls bobbed again, beside an outstretched hand.

Number two: count to five. One. Megan let out the air trapped in her lungs. Two. She looked in the mirror again, desperate for another glimpse. Three. She drank in the sight of the little girl. Hair in pigtails with a pink ribbon attached the elastics. She wore a spring jacket, white with large colored flowers.

Turn your head. Please turn your head.

Megan held the steering wheel tight. The counting stopped as she waited for a view of the little girl's face. With her head half turned, a tiny dimple showed as the girl beamed a huge smile up to the woman who held her hand.

Emma has a dimple.

The phone vibrated on the seat again. Megan ignored it. Her hand crept over to the door handle, her fingers grasped onto the latch, and she pulled it open. That was her daughter. She knew it. The yellow curly hair, the dimple in her cheek, she looked the same size and age. It had to be her.

She opened the door and swung her leg out, only to have her Jeep lurch forward. She jammed her foot on the brake, put the car in park, and hopped out.

The girl was gone. Despite the cars behind her, she ran across the parking lot and grabbed onto the store door as it swung shut.

Her daughter and a strange woman stood before her. Their backs were turned. She paused, listened to the gentle cadence of Emma's voice, letting it wash over her before she stepped forward and yanked her daughter's tiny hand out of the woman's. The little girl turned.

Megan sank to her knees, her vision blurred by the tears that swelled up in her eyes.

"Emm . . . a." Megan's voice faltered as she looked into the eyes of the little girl before her. They were brown. Brown. Not blue. Not the sea blue that shone when Emma was happy or the pale blue that glimmered when they were filled with tears.

Not Emma's eyes.

Megan stood and took a step back. She held her hands out in front of her.

"I'm so sorry. So sorry . . . I thought she . . . my daughter's . . . missing for two years." Megan's voice faltered. She couldn't look down at the little girl so she stared only at the woman who looked at her with a mixture of pity and anger.

"I'm so sorry," Megan whispered again.

She took another step back and something stopped her. She turned only to have her way of escape blocked by an older man who reached out to steady her. Megan brought up her arms, pushed his hands away, and rushed out of the coffee shop. Tears blocked her view and she almost stumbled off the curb.

A horn honked. She looked up and a woman in the van parked behind her scowled. Megan hurried to her Jeep, opened the door, and fumbled with her seat belt. The honking continued while her phone buzzed. Megan placed her head in her hands as sobs tore through her body.

Not Emma. All she wanted to do was curl up in her bed and succumb to the pain of what had just happened.

The van behind her honked again, this time longer. Megan put the Jeep in drive and pulled ahead. She was boxed in on all sides in the drive-thru. No way to escape, no way to get away from the woman with her child, the child who looked so much like Emma yet wasn't her.

⚜

Megan pulled into her driveway and she realized she'd forgotten all about Peter. She stared down at the now-cold coffees beside her and sighed. As if this day could get any worse. Stuck in the drive-thru, she'd managed to choke out her order for coffee. She hid her face at the window, wordlessly handed the money over and drove off before she could receive her change. She'd driven around, mindless to her surroundings. At one point, she pulled over to close her heavy eyes. She was empty of tears. Empty of emotion.

When she walked into her house, the silence slapped her in the face. Megan slipped off her shoes and headed into the kitchen. She placed the coffee on the island and read the note left by Peter:

"Broken promises hurt. Actions speak louder than words."

Megan buried her head in her hands. Little by little, their marriage was falling apart. The fact he'd leave her a note like this said a lot. Too much. Once upon a time, it wouldn't have been an issue, he would have understood. Not now. She wadded up the paper and tossed it into the recycling can beside the garbage. She glanced at the coffee, unwilling to drink it cold but also unable to heat it up.

The phone rang. Megan closed her eyes and tried to ignore its incessant ringing. She walked into the living room and sank into the chair closest to the large bay windows. With her head leaned back against the cushion, Megan relaxed her body, another step her counselor suggested she try. Empty herself of all thoughts, will the tension to release out of her shoulders, imagine her feet grounded, and push all the negative energy out, starting from the top of the head to the tips of the toes.

Her counselor said something about a tree with roots and focusing on the depths of those roots, but that seemed too new age for her. Her mother wanted her to pray, but all her prayers went unanswered, so she settled for something in-between. She took a deep breath and counted to five before she released it. Her body deflated as the air escaped out of her lungs.

As she sank into the chair, she opened her eyes and focused on a picture on the wall ahead of her. Emma. The Christmas before she was taken. Her cute little chubby cheeks with the dimple in the middle.

Detective Riley, the officer in charge of Emma's case, had warned them that her cheeks would have thinned out since that Christmas but that the dimples would never leave. That wasn't the only change they should expect. Those adorable curls would have been cut off, her hair would be short. She might've even been made to look like a little boy, for the first bit. Megan shuddered at the thought. Most kidnappers will do what they can to alter a child's appearance right after they've been taken so the general public would pass them over. They would be looking for a little girl, not a boy. But it had been over two years now and her hair would have grown. No matter how she looked, Megan knew she would recognize her daughter.

Like I knew it was her today?

Megan shook her head as shame flooded through her. Her heart squeezed as her lungs constricted. She gasped as the realization of what had happened washed over her. Her counselor warned her about this. She had to stop looking for her daughter. There were consequences to her actions. She knew she scared that little girl today and probably terrified the mother. She acted like a madwoman. Deranged. Out of her mind. Out of control.

Megan bowed her head. That's what was happening to her. She was losing her mind. Everything her mother, Peter, and even her best friend, Laurie, were worried about was coming true. She couldn't tell Peter. He would be livid with her for doing this, again. She could call her counselor but she already knew what she would say. Medication.

Megan shook her head in denial. She would not be medicated. The memory of those first few months after Emma had disappeared was a fog because of the medication. She wouldn't go through that again. Losing her child was not an illness. Trying to find her, never giving up, that wasn't something to medicate.

The phone rang again. She counted each ring, waiting for it to stop. She knew it might be Peter, but she couldn't speak to him. Not right now. Not after what happened this morning. All she wanted to do was hide.

Without Emma she was a shell. A shell of a mother, of a wife, of a woman. No matter how hard she tried to maintain the calm and collected persona everyone knew and trusted, it was all a ruse. After today, she wasn't sure if she could keep it up.

Megan reached for the blanket she'd knit last Christmas and wrapped it around her. She stared out the front window, mesmerized by the sway of the grass in the gentle breeze. She imagined the feel of the breeze in her hair, the tickle of a dandelion held in the tight grip of a toddler as it brushed against her cheek.

A sob ripped through Megan's body. She'd tried so hard not to think about that day.

⚜

The persistent knocking startled Megan and she stumbled off the chair and made her way to the front door.

"I knew when you didn't answer the phone, something was wrong." Laurie Dunlop, her best friend, pushed past her and headed to the kitchen.

"I hate to say this, girlfriend, but you look like crap." Laurie held out a cup of coffee she'd brought and shoved it into her hands.

Megan curled her fingers around the hot paper cup. She was so cold.

"Why aren't you dressed?" Laurie dug into her purse she'd placed on the counter and slapped down the Kinrich newspaper.

"I am." Megan refused to look at the paper and instead glanced down at the jeans and black T-shirt she wore. What was wrong with her outfit?

Laurie shook her head. "Meg, I love you and I know today is a difficult day for you, but you cannot wear that to the assembly."

Megan sagged against the counter and stared at Laurie in shock. She'd forgotten all about the assembly. The coffee sloshed around in the cup as she brought her shaking hands to her lips.

"You forgot, didn't you?"

Megan bit her lip. This assembly meant so much to her. She'd specifically planned it for today on Emma's birthday. She wanted Emma to be in everyone's thoughts. How could she have forgotten?

"That's not like you. Did something happen?"

Megan glanced over at the clock. Only a half hour before she needed to be at the school. She shook her head and headed toward the stairs.

"Meg, are you okay?" Laurie followed her and paused at the foot of the stairs.

Megan bit her lip. She couldn't tell her. Not yet. She couldn't afford to fall apart and that's what would happen. Tears welled in her eyes before she blinked them away.

Her shoulders sagged as she dragged her body up the stairs. She had ten minutes to pull herself together. Ten minutes to reassemble herself into the strong woman everyone believed her to be.

CHAPTER THREE

Megan reached for the cold metal handle and stopped. Her hand shook like an addict's body in withdrawal. *Get a grip, woman.* She'd faced larger giants than the pint-sized ones beyond the gymnasium door. One. She took a breath. Two. The muffled roar of the crowd echoing through the empty corridors of the school surged toward her. An explosion of panic threatened to overwhelm her as tiny dots clouded her vision.

Not now. Please, God, not now. Not again.

Over one hundred children waited inside the gymnasium for her. This was not the time for a panic attack to hit. Megan took a deep breath; her nostrils flared as she wrestled to calm herself. She reached for the handle again, only to have her hand slip off. It was drenched in sweat. If she didn't step through those doors, she'd hate herself forever. One more thing to add to the guilt. Through gritted teeth she yanked open the door and plastered a smile on her face. Jill Maguire, Meadowvale Elementary's principal, stepped forward and pulled her into a crushing hug.

"I saw today's paper. I'm amazed at your strength," she whispered.

Strength had nothing to do with it. The attempted abduction plastered all over the news last night had only fueled the fire and determination already in Megan's heart.

She wiped her sweaty palms on her thighs as a round of applause filled the gymnasium. Megan gave a slight wave to the kids who watched her with bright eyes.

She counted the steps to the podium. Counting de-stressed her—at least that's what her counselor said. It also made her look like a fool when she forgot to count under her breath.

As the noise in the room receded, Megan cleared her throat and opened her notebook. She had already warned Jill about her opening. This wasn't the time for fairytale stories and pats on the back. There was a sexual predator in their community and she refused to stand on the sidelines while he attempted to kidnap another girl.

"Hi, guys." Megan waved as she looked down over the podium. "It's good to see you again. Johnny, you should leave Becky's hair alone." The crowd laughed. She knew these kids. They lived on her street, took part in her Safe Walks program, and invited her daughters to their birthday parties.

"Last night, a man came into our town and tried to take a girl away from her family. They were out shopping and the girl ventured away from her parents and was approached by a stranger." She looked over the crowd and realized that all eyes were on her and the room had quietened. She gripped the sides of the podium and squared her shoulders. An instant calm settled over her.

"We all know what to do when a stranger approaches, right?"

"Yell for help!" the cry echoed through the gymnasium. Megan's fist pumped the air in response.

"What if that stranger wants to take you someplace?" The excitement level in the gymnasium sizzled and she loved the feeling. The kids were listening.

"Don't go!" the audience cried out in unison.

"Do you know what that little girl did, even though the man told her he was a police officer? She yelled for help and her parents came running right away. But the man got away. And he's out there, somewhere, waiting for another boy or girl to trust him. I'm here today to make sure that doesn't happen."

The room burst into applause while Megan choked back a sob. Tears pooled in her eyes and she blinked past them. When the noise quieted down, Megan walked away from the podium and stepped closer to the crowd.

She held up the town's newspaper for all to see. It was good to know she wasn't alone in this fight.

"You all know my story. But let me make it real for you." Tears rolled down her cheeks, gathered at her chin, and then fell to the floor. Megan swiped the tears away from her eyes before she continued.

"The headline for today's paper holds a picture of my youngest daughter. You've all seen this before. Today is Emma's birthday. It's also the day she was taken from us, by another stranger in our town. Emma didn't have the opportunity to yell for help. But you do. If I could have one birthday wish for Emma, other than for her to come home today, it would be for each and every one of you to yell as loud as you can if you ever meet a stranger who wants to take you somewhere with them without your parents' permission. That would be my wish."

⚜

Megan stepped into Emma's room and was barraged by the emotions she'd tried so hard to keep at bay. It was here, in her baby's room, that the walls surrounding Megan's heart crumpled. To most people, Megan was a pillar of strength. A fighter. Only Peter knew the truth. Here, in Emma's room, Megan was only a mother with a broken heart.

What would she look like today?

Megan crossed the room to Emma's single bed and stroked the picture of her youngest daughter on the nightstand. Emma's sweet smile captured her heart.

Is her hair still as fair? Megan picked up the frame as tears welled up in her eyes. *Would she still look like me as a child or would she have outgrown that, like Alexis when she turned five?*

She glanced down at the envelope clenched in her hand. Her eyes burned as she read the bold cursive writing that contrasted against the white paper.

Happy Birthday, Emma. Love, Daddy.

A car door slammed outside. With a sigh, Megan stood from Emma's bed and edged toward the window. Peter was home early. She hugged herself in an attempt to warm up. From the moment she'd slipped out of bed, her body felt like it had been encased in ice. It wore her down. The assembly had drained her today. More than she cared to admit.

Tired of being strong for everyone else in her life, of trying to prove she was okay and not a basket of nerves, Megan needed some time alone, time to wallow in her self-pity and loneliness before her girls came home and she had to be strong. Again.

Megan leaned her head against the window and watched Peter enter the house. It would get easier, she was told, by those who didn't understand. Easier for whom? For those who forgot? For those whose child was still safe in their arms? Life didn't get easier. It wasn't fair.

The heavy tread on the stairway announced her husband's presence.

"You got her a card," Megan said, her voice a mere whisper against the silence in the room. She counted the steps it took for Peter to walk toward her. Her body relaxed as his arms wrapped themselves around her. Her body trembled as the sobs she worked so hard to rein in escaped.

Megan's breath caught in her throat as Peter took the card he'd left in the room from her hand. He leaned to the side and placed the card down on the bed. Face up. Megan couldn't look away from it. A chill had settled deep within, freezing her body until the flow of her blood slowed. She waited for his warmth to seep into her bones.

"The little girl on the card reminded me of Emma. I had to buy it." The roughness of his voice filled the room. One hand stroked her back.

Megan pulled her head back and saw tears fall from her husband's crystal blue eyes. She could count on one hand the amount of times she'd seen him cry. She touched a tear with her finger and used the pad of her thumb to brush away the rest.

"It's perfect." She rested her head against his chest again. She stood there for what felt like years but could only be minutes before Peter took hold of her arms and leaned back to look in her eyes.

"How was the assembly?"

"It was . . . okay. Hard, but I dealt with it. After what we heard on the news last night, I couldn't reschedule. Not today. Even if all I did was remind those kids of the steps they can take if something ever was to happen. It was worth it." She stepped away and stood by the bed.

"Worth killing yourself over?" A sad smile covered Peter's face.

"That's a bit melodramatic, don't you think? I'm not killing myself. I may be tired, but I just need more sleep. I'll be fine."

"Until you fall apart. I just want you to be careful. Last year . . ." Peter took a step toward her but Megan backed away.

"I'm fine."

When Peter's shoulders slumped, she knew he didn't believe her. She expected him to argue, to insist that he knew better, that he knew the signs. When he didn't, she shrugged her shoulder. Some victories didn't deserve bragging rights.

"About this morning . . ." She hated the small arguments that became a regular routine in their busy lives.

"I figured something came up." Peter rubbed his hands down Megan's arm. "You're freezing. Why don't you go have a bath?"

Megan sank down onto Emma's bed. She knew she should tell him about the little girl this morning, but she couldn't. Instead, she smoothed the covers, fluffed the pillow, and righted the stuffed lamb that rested on its side.

"I will in a minute." She waited until Peter's footsteps left Emma's room before her shoulders hunched over and she bowed her head. Her eyes remained dry. Two years' worth of tears had already been spilled in this room.

"I miss you, baby. I'm so sorry I lost you. I should have paid better attention."

❧

Megan pulled back the curtain and searched the sidewalk outside.

"They'll be home soon. Relax. I made some tea." Peter crossed the living-room floor and handed her a steaming cup.

She gave him a brief smile before she turned her attention back to the view outside.

"Why haven't they called? If they're running late, they know to call. I should have picked them up." She bit her lip.

"Megan. Stop. They'll be home." Peter sat down in the corner chair, picked up his latest home-building magazine, and flipped through the pages.

She took a sip from her tea before setting it down on the coffee table. How could Peter be so relaxed?

After another glance outside, Megan headed to the front door. She'd just wait for them outside, maybe head toward the school, and meet them somewhere in between. *They can't be that far away, right?*

"Where're you going?" The annoyed tone in Peter's voice stopped her.

"I'll wait for them outside." She placed her hand on the doorknob, opened the door, and listened for the computerized voice to announce that the front door was ajar. Even after two years of listening to the installed alarm system, Megan still worried it would one day stop working.

"You need to let them grow. They're old enough now to walk home by themselves."

This was the first time since the inception of her Safe Walks program that her children had no adult supervision. Megan counted to three. One. Deep breath. Two. This wasn't working. Three. She needed to devise another method of calming. She didn't want to go back to the psychiatrist.

"Wait for me. I'll walk with you," Peter said as the telltale creak in the chair let Megan know he'd stood up. She also heard the sigh in his voice.

She pulled the door open and held it for Peter. He knew her so well.

⚜

"Mrs. Temple walked us to the corner but then we saw a little puppy all by himself so Hannah wanted to see if it was lost but then I told her we were late as it is." Alexis, their nine-year-old, skipped beside Peter as Megan held her eldest daughter Hannah's hand. They'd met the girls at the end of the block. It was all Megan could do to keep her emotions together and not lose it.

Hannah squeezed her hand three times, their silent message in their family. *I. Love. You.* Megan glanced down and smiled. The worried look in Hannah's eyes was still there.

"What have we told you girls about stray dogs?" Peter looked over his shoulder at Hannah, a frown on his face.

Hannah's head dropped down to her chest and her feet shuffled along the sidewalk.

"I thought it was old Mr. Patterson's dog. Honest. I didn't go near it," she whispered. She glanced up at Megan. "Not like last time."

Megan rubbed her thumb over the scars on Hannah's hand as her daughter tightened her grip.

"I know. We were just worried. Did you thank Mrs. Temple for walking you so far?" Megan made a mental note to write her a thank-you note.

"I did. She said not to worry about it and that today was difficult enough and that you didn't need to be worried about us walking home alone." Hannah bit her lip and readjusted the backpack slung over her shoulder.

"That was nice of her," Megan said as they walked up the driveway. Peter and Alexis had already entered the house, but Hannah continued to drag her feet.

"What's up, kiddo?"

"Nothing." Hannah stared at the ground as her feet shuffled against the pavement.

"Are you sure?" Megan placed her arm around her daughter's slender frame and squeezed. Today was a hard day for everyone.

"Mom, I . . ." Hannah's shoulders slumped. "Can we talk in private?"

Megan's heart sank at the worry in Hannah's voice. "Sure we can. Let's go sit on the swing in the back."

Alexis stuck her head out the front door and held the cordless phone up high.

"Grandma's on the phone."

Megan sighed. Talking to her mom wasn't something she wanted to deal with right now.

"Tell her I'll call back," she called out.

Alexis shook her head. "Nope. Grandma says she wants to talk to you. No excuses this time either."

Megan's eyebrow rose as she glared at her daughter. "Excuse me?"

Alexis shrugged her shoulder. "That's what Grandma said to say."

Megan closed her eyes and groaned. For a woman who drilled into her children always to respect your elders, she wasn't doing too good of a job of teaching the same message to her grandkids.

"We'll talk after, okay?" Megan leaned down and placed a kiss on top of Hannah's head.

Hannah rolled her eyes and Megan had to purse her lips to keep from snapping at her. She grabbed the phone out of Alexis's hand instead and watched Hannah swing her backpack off her shoulder and drag it on the ground.

Megan waited until the kids were inside the house before she sat down on one of the front-porch chairs and raised the phone to her ear.

"Well, it's about time. How are you holding up, Megan? Your dad and I are thinking of you today."

"We're fine, thanks for asking." Megan leaned back in the chair.

"Well, I just didn't want you to think we forgot Emma's birthday."

"I know you wouldn't have. Why don't we do lunch this week?" Megan asked. "It's been a while and I'm in the mood for some good Chinese food."

"It's only been a while because you never call anymore. Nor do you return any of my emails or comment on that new fancy webpage you set up for me on that book thing."

"Facebook, Mom. It's called Facebook." An intense pounding started in Megan's head.

"I'm worried about you. You run yourself ragged trying to do everything. Just don't fall back into old habits. You know, get depressed and everything again." Sheila whispered *depressed* as though the word itself was evil.

Megan wanted to laugh. If only her mother knew.

"I'm not depressed."

"Are you sure? I'm worried," Sheila said. Again.

"Yes, I'm sure." A wave of heaviness settled over Megan's body as she said good-bye and hung up the phone. Peter opened the front door and stuck his head out.

"What'd she want?"

Megan shook her head, stood from the chair. "Nothing important."

Of course, Emma would come home. That wasn't even a question. Megan's whole purpose in life was to make sure their daughter came home. It's why she organized assemblies, handed out flyers, and wrote for online media outlets about missing children. To bring her daughter home. She knew the statistics, better than she should. Over 800,000 children are reported missing every year and the majority of those children are never found and presumed dead. Megan refused to believe her daughter was a statistic.

She couldn't be. Emma was still alive, she knew it. A mother's heart would know if her child was dead or not. There was a special connection, a bond. That bond was still there.

Megan stood up on shaking legs.

So, why didn't she feel the connection anymore?

CHAPTER FOUR

"Hey, Mom."

Megan forced a smile as she entered the large, sunny kitchen.

Hannah and Alexis were perched at the island bar. Alexis sat with her bar stool tipped backward so her chest met her knees whereas Hannah sat straight as a rod on hers. The two girls were so opposite of each other in looks and in temperament, yet they were only sixteen months apart. Alexis nibbled on her brown shoulder-length hair, an annoying habit Megan couldn't stand. She stood behind them and placed her hands on both backs.

With Alexis, she added a bit of strength, forcing her stool back onto four feet. When Alexis glanced up, Megan raised her eyebrow and waited for her daughter to sit properly on her stool. Megan wouldn't even begin to count the number of times Alexis had tipped that stool over because she leaned too far back. One hospital trip and five stitches to the head was enough for one lifetime.

"So, tell me, how was school?" She peeked over their shoulders. Alexis worked on a science assignment, a subject she found difficult, and Hannah doodled on a math worksheet.

"Boring." Alexis bit on the end of her pencil while her head was tilted backward. "Can't wait till it's over."

"So, who walked the other group of kids home today? Do you know?" The first school to implement Megan's Safe Walks program was the girls'. There were five parent volunteers so far to help with the routes.

"Erica's mom," Alexis muttered. Megan knew from the tone that Alexis didn't like her. For some reason Alexis didn't get along with Mrs. Johnston, but the woman had a heart of gold.

"Nice outfit." Megan crossed her arms as she took in Alexis's black skull shirt and short skirt.

Alexis glanced down at her clothing and red stained her cheeks. What? Did she not think Megan would say anything?

"I like it," Alexis mumbled.

"It's not what you had on this morning, is it? Did you think I wouldn't notice? You kind of stood out in the crowd, Alex, with your bright lime-green sweater."

Alexis folded her arms across her body and sulked.

"It's only clothing, Mom. Besides, Grandma says I'm unique and I need to show the world that I'm an original."

"And did Grandma tell you it was okay to disobey your parents, go behind their backs, and change clothes at school?" If Sheila dearest were here right now, she'd realize her worries about depression were overrated. Anger? Now that would be a different story.

At least her daughter had the decency to lower her head in shame.

"No."

"Didn't think so," Megan said. She squeezed Alexis's shoulder before turning. Hannah's gaze never left her science paper. Megan placed her arms around Hannah's body and pulled until she rested against her chest. It took a moment, but Hannah relaxed her hard posture and melted against her body.

Megan placed her cheek against Hannah's hair.

"Hard day?"

Hannah nodded. Megan glanced up at Peter who stood with his back against the stove. He shrugged his shoulder.

"I ordered pizza on my way home," Peter said. No one answered. Pizza was Emma's favorite meal.

"Maybe we could go get some ice cream later?" Megan walked over to the sink. Breakfast dishes still sat in the cold, murky water. The mundane task seemed easy to follow, anything to keep her mind off what today signified. She held her cold fingers under the flow of hot water, and listened to the quiet chatter of her daughters as they worked through their homework.

A hand settled on her shoulder.

"Want help?" Peter held a tea towel in his hand.

"Thanks," she said.

"Argh." Hannah's voice caught her attention.

Megan turned and faced her daughter. Hannah had pushed her books away and held a pencil in her hand. Her long blonde hair framed against her face and her big blue eyes shimmered with tears.

Hannah's chin wobbled.

"What's the matter?"

"Stupid math." Hannah's shoulders slumped. Megan crossed the room, grabbed the book, and scanned it.

"It's the same question as the one above it, just worded differently." She looked into her daughter's eyes and moved to give her a hug.

Hannah swiveled her stool so she faced outward and held out her arms. Huge sobs racked her body as she clung to Megan.

"Hannah, honey, it's okay. Shhh, it's going to be okay," said Megan, her voice soft as she held her eldest daughter in her arms.

The doorbell rang. When Peter left the room, Megan pulled away and lifted Hannah's chin so she could look in her eyes.

"What's wrong?"

Hannah's body jumped as she hiccupped through her tears. Alexis, who still sat on the stool beside Hannah, giggled. Megan gave her a look and nodded her head toward the living room. After Alexis jumped down and ran to the other room, Megan grabbed the stool and pulled it close to her child. Hannah, with a tentative reach, touched Megan's hand and grabbed hold.

"I miss her."

Hannah's voice was so low Megan almost didn't catch the words. Her heart lurched as she took in her daughter's demeanor. While Megan felt broken, Hannah looked it. Hannah shrunk inside herself, shoulders hunched forward, chest slouched, and dark circles hung under her eyes.

"I really miss her, Mom."

"So do I, honey, so do I," Megan said. Their whole family hurt. Emma's disappearance created crevices deep within their souls.

"But it's my fault. Mom, it's my fault Emma's gone."

Megan bit her lip. They'd gone over this time and again. Hannah refused to accept that it wasn't her fault. Maybe it was time to take her back to the family counselor.

⚜

"I knew this was a mistake," Peter grumbled as they pulled into the crowded parking lot of the local ice-cream parlor. Lights blazed through the windows and the tables were filled with others on a quest for the best ice cream in town.

"So was the pizza. But you didn't hear anyone complain, did you?" Megan said.

"Yes! Mackenzie's here."

Megan glanced in the back of the Jeep. Alexis bounced in her seat. Megan knew that the moment the vehicle stopped Alexis would be out the door.

"Tone it down, chum. She's not going anywhere," said Peter.

Megan almost jumped when Peter's hand touched hers. In the midst of taking her seat belt off, she glanced up and saw the worry in his eyes.

"We're not staying long, right?"

Megan shook her head.

"Long enough to enjoy our ice cream. Why?"

Peter grabbed her hand and entwined his fingers with hers.

"I'm just not in the mood to socialize."

Megan furrowed her brows at him. Neither was she, but that's not why they came. She glanced into the parlor and saw couples they were friends with, people they had over for coffee and barbecues and shared picnics with during Alexis's soccer tournaments and Hannah's swim meets.

"Then don't."

Megan climbed out of the Jeep and left Peter there alone.

Inside the store, Megan stopped at the first booth, where an elderly couple known as Grandma Kathy and Grandpa Herb shared a banana split.

"How are you doing, dearie?" Kathy reached her hand out and patted Megan's arm.

The couple was so sweet, sitting in the booth, across from each other, making eyes at each other.

"I'm good. Thanks for asking." Megan beamed a bright smile and hoped Kathy was too high on sugar to notice the false ring to her voice.

"You know, Herbie and I were just thinking about your family. How hard today must be. But don't you be giving up hope, you hear? Your sweet baby will come home. I feel it in my bones." Kathy nodded her head while Herb pounded the table in agreement.

"That's right. And you know if Kate here feels it in her bones, then God's speaking to her. Mark her words, that little girl will be home before you know it." Herb grunted before he spooned a big glob of ice cream into his mouth.

"Of course she will," said Megan. A shiver tiptoed across her back and she shuddered. *From their lips to God's ears, that's how the saying went, wasn't it?*

Megan took a few steps before she found herself at the back of the line. She glanced around for her daughters and a momentary flight of panic gripped her heart before she found them seated beside friends in the booth by the corner.

It was good to see them smile. Both girls had been sullen throughout dinner, but Megan couldn't blame them. Was celebrating Emma's birthday this year the right thing to do? Maybe Peter had been right. There wasn't much to rejoice about. Emma wasn't here to blow out her candles or even to make a wish. Did she even know it was her birthday today? Was she happy?

Megan choked back a sob before she remembered where she was. In a crowded store where everyone stared at her, waiting to see if she would break.

She stiffened her shoulders and straightened her back before she noticed the small tug on her purse. When she glanced down, Johnny, from the assembly this afternoon, stood there with a bright smile on his face.

"Mrs. Taylor?" His toothless grin beamed up at her. The ice in her heart started to melt. How could it not, with a grin like that?

"Mrs. Taylor, it's my birthday today, did you know that?"

Johnny's words surprised her. She had no idea the boy shared Emma's birthday.

She bent down to his level and gave him a gentle hug.

"Happy birthday, Johnny. May all your wishes come true," she whispered into his ear.

Johnny pulled away and his face flushed.

"They did. Now it's your turn. My mom said I could give you this."

Megan glanced down at the chubby hands covered in chocolate ice cream. Carried in his palm was a white candle.

He pushed his hand closer toward her face until the candle was right beneath her nose.

"You gotta wish on it, Mrs. Taylor," he said with a serious face.

Megan stared at the tiny white candle. There was nothing special about it. Ten to one his mom bought it at the grocery store. Yet he believed it was a magic candle.

She glanced over to where Johnny's family sat in a booth. They all stared at her. The people of Kinrich had such good hearts, she was proud to call this town home.

"I will. I promise." She ruffled his shaggy hair before he took off back to his ice cream.

"Promise what?"

Peter stood behind her.

"That I will wish on this magic candle for Emma to come home." Megan held out the candle for him to see.

"Like that's going to work." Peter's gaze swept over the innocent candle in her hand before he peered into the floor display filled with tubs of ice cream.

Megan fisted the candle and placed it in her pocket. She should have just brought the girls and left him at home.

No matter what Johnny's wish was, it came true because his parents were determined to see him happy. Who knows? Maybe Megan's wish would come true too, then. God still answered prayers, right?

CHAPTER FIVE

Whe took you so long?" Laurie jogged in place at the entrance to the town park in the middle of downtown where she and Megan met every morning. A strand of blonde hair fell over her eyes. She blew it away and tapped her wristwatch.

Megan shrugged her shoulders before she passed her friend. Victoria Park was halfway between their houses and right across from the harbor. Most mornings she enjoyed the colorful display as the sun rose over the water, the reflection that danced among the waves as she ran through the park and down to the beach. Kinrich was known for its gorgeous sunrises. But this morning all she had wanted was a hot cup of coffee. It had taken a couple nudges from Peter before she worked up the energy to get out of bed.

"Hey, wait up," Laurie called out.

Megan shook her head. Now that she was up, she knew that running could help work off the steam that still boiled inside. Last night's emotional roller coaster had carried over to today. Peter had refused to speak to her the rest of the night after he had seen her holding the candle. Their marriage hadn't been the same since Emma's disappearance. She thought they'd been doing so well. Sure, there'd been rough spots but they'd managed to get through them. She hoped this time wasn't any different.

Megan glanced to her left. Laurie had caught up. They made it to the other side of the park in silence, but as they waited for the crosswalk light, Laurie passed her and stopped directly in her path. Her eyes shot daggers not even Megan could match on her worst days. A glare from Laurie was never a good thing. For one, it made Laurie's face bunch up into an ugly scowl, and if there was anything Laurie hated, it was to look ugly. For another, Laurie was honest to a fault. Sometimes too much. Megan wasn't sure if she really wanted to hear what her best friend was about to say.

"What's going on?"

Megan shook her head and looked to the side.

"How did last night go?"

Megan pursed her lips. She wished the light would change so they could continue their run down to the beach. The thought of running on the sand and the muscle exhaustion that would set in afterward set her pulse racing.

The illuminated walking man flashed white across the street. Megan sidestepped Laurie, ran across the road, turned right, and passed a coffee shop that had just opened. The aroma of fresh-ground beans wafted through the open window and followed Megan as she continued down the street.

The pounding of Laurie's running shoes as she increased her pace pushed Megan faster. If she could outrun Laurie, maybe she could ignore the emotional overload sure to follow once Laurie cornered her and demanded answers.

"Stop."

Megan ignored Laurie's plea and continued her pace. The corner was just ahead. Once she turned left, it was a straight line down to the beach.

"Megan, please, STOP!"

Megan glanced over her shoulder. Laurie leaned against a metal bench outside of a florist shop. Her arms were crossed against her chest and a frown had settled on her face. Megan stopped. She glanced toward the beach and then back at her friend. Not once in the past year since Laurie began to run with her in the early mornings had Megan left her friend to run alone.

Megan stopped, turned her back on the gentle calling of the beach sand, and walked toward her best friend. "Sorry. I just . . ."

Laurie raised her hand.

"Don't apologize. I know yesterday wasn't the best of days for you. But don't shut me out, okay?"

Megan dropped her head and fixed her gaze on her running shoes. Laurie was right.

"You're right. I'm sorry." She lifted her face and noticed the twinkle in her friend's eyes.

"I know. I usually am," Laurie said.

A bell jingled over the coffee shop door as they passed by on their way back.

"I donated to the Missing Children Foundation yesterday. As a birthday gift to Emma," Laurie said.

Tears filled Megan's eyes.

"Thank you. That means a lot."

Megan squeezed Laurie's arm. She swallowed back the tears and did her best to ensure a smile was planted on her face.

"What would I do without you?"

As they stood at the crosswalk, waiting to cross the street and head back into the park, Laurie unwound her arm from Megan's and placed it around her waist.

"Thank God, we'll never find out."

At the park, Megan enjoyed the silence. While she hadn't run like she wanted to, she did feel a lot better. Without Laurie, she'd be lost.

"You're fine, though, right? Nothing you want to share with me, your best friend, that you haven't told anyone else?"

Megan stared at Laurie in silence. *You've got to be kidding me? Not her too.*

"I'm fine. I'm not hiding anything from you or anyone else, for that matter. Stop worrying, okay?"

Megan fingered the card Laurie slipped into her hand earlier this morning as they said good-bye.

When life hands you lemons, choose chocolate. It always works. Love, Laurie.

By eleven in the morning, Megan couldn't handle the silence in the house any longer. She grabbed the keys from off the counter and let them dangle in her hand. She toyed with the idea of dropping by Peter's office as a surprise. Maybe he'd have time to sneak away for an early lunch. With the summer holidays looming ahead and a summer full of kid activities, Megan's free time was almost up. She might as well take advantage of it.

As she pulled into the driveway of his office, she admired the brownstone that Peter leased for his real-estate company. Situated on a corner lot, it was considered a prime location. Only three main roads led into the small town of Kinrich. When the lease on the historic building on the corner of the main street had come up, Peter grabbed it. It was an investment, but they both agreed it was worth it.

The bell over the door jingled as Megan walked through.

"Hi, Mrs. Taylor."

Dana, the petite receptionist, a young twenty-something with an attention span that could be measured by the minute, greeted her. She sat at her desk, legs crossed, with a nail file in her hand. Megan didn't understand why Peter kept her on staff.

"Dana, love the color of your nail polish." Megan tempered the sarcasm in her voice. Not that it would matter.

"You do?" Dana's eyes widened with delight. She held out her fingers and admired her bright purple nails. "You know, purple is the new black. It's the must-have color for the summer." Dana smiled. The illuminated whiteness of her teeth shone. Megan winced. Too white.

"Is Peter in?"

"Oh." Dana, flustered, glanced down at her appointment book. "No, he just left. Like, *just* left." Her dainty little shoulder shrugged.

Surprised, Megan glanced out the front door. Peter's car sat out there. So, where did he go?

"Oh, he went with Sam," Dana said. A coy smile crept on her face.

Megan bit her lip. *Her. He's out with her.*

Samantha Grayson. Peter's beautiful business partner. Devil incarnate in a miniskirt. Samantha had started to work with Peter as a real-estate agent just after Emma had been born. Maybe it was the postpartum depression, or the fact the baby weight had taken its time to melt off, but the first time Megan laid eyes on the woman, she was labeled HER.

Samantha was everything Megan was not. Tall, with the body of a model—her whole persona exuded mystery. Everything a man could want, wrapped up in a package complete with stiletto heels and tight skirts.

"Do you know when he'll return?" Megan swallowed back the remark she wanted to make.

Dana shrugged her shoulders and continued to file her nails.

Megan bit her lip before she squared her shoulders and plastered the warmest smile she could fake on her face.

"Let him know I dropped by, will you?"

"Oh, of course. He's quite busy today, though. His calendar is booked. There's a new client they're trying to land." Dana twirled her chair until she faced the computer, her fake fingernails poised over the keyboard.

Megan grabbed the doorknob and squeezed it. She counted to three.

"Thank you, Dana," Megan said through clenched teeth. *The little brat.*

She pulled open the door with too much force and the doorknob slipped out of her hand. As the door swung open, Peter walked in, his head down as he spoke on his cell phone.

"I don't know what I'd do without you. Some days I wonder . . ." Peter stuttered when Megan grabbed onto his arm before he pushed her over. "I'll see you in a few minutes, Sam."

Megan watched her husband, the way he slid his phone in his pants, the slight redness that crept up from his neck to his cheeks. She turned her face away slightly as he placed an awkward kiss on the corner of her mouth.

"I didn't expect you here." He shuffled his feet in the entryway.

Megan shrugged. "I thought I'd see if you have time for coffee or maybe an early lunch." She readjusted the purse strap on her shoulder and waited. She wasn't sure how to take what she'd just heard.

"I, ah . . . I'm actually running late for a meeting. I forgot the contract . . ." He jiggled the briefcase in his hand as if she was to know the contract wasn't in there.

Megan lifted her eyebrow and glanced behind him at Sam's brand-new hybrid.

Peter sneaked a look over his shoulder. "Oh, Sam stayed with the new client. You know, create a connection, land the deal. I need to get back there."

Megan counted to three, smiled, and stepped to the side. "Of course you do." Her cheeks hurt from keeping lips curved. "Maybe I'll bake a cake to celebrate landing the contract."

"Oh, but we don't have it yet." Peter glanced at his watch again.

This time she had no trouble keeping the smile on her face. "Knowing Sam, I have no doubt she'll create a connection with your new client. She always does."

She took a step forward, stood on her tiptoes, and placed a gentle kiss on Peter's cheek. She read the surprise in his eyes.

Megan paused for a moment, a brief moment, before she walked out the front door to her Jeep. She didn't even glance up to see if Peter watched her. She knew he wasn't.

Once upon a time, Megan had been considered an active partner with Peter in his business. When Emma had been born, they decided Megan would take a step back from work for a short time and focus on their family. She'd never really stepped back in.

When Emma disappeared, they both agreed that Megan would put all of her focus and energy into finding their daughter. They had not anticipated it, but Megan's absence from the company had made it necessary for Samantha to step up and become a partner. Megan rued the day that Samantha's presence had become necessary. Whether fairly or not, Megan didn't trust her. Not only did Megan feel like Samantha had somehow stolen her place in the company, but Megan was quite sure Samantha was out to steal her husband as well.

CHAPTER SIX

The sun shone down on Jack's bald head and beads of sweat pooled together until tiny rivers flowed into the crevices of his neck. His eyes stung from the droplets hanging from his eyelashes, while his fingernails were stained with the dark soil of his flowerbeds. Jack wiped his gnarled hands on his old overalls.

Shielding his eyes from the bright glare, he smiled. His back ached from bending over for such a long time, his fingers swollen at each joint, and his knees cracked whenever he straightened them, but it was all worth it. The perfect June day to work in his garden.

"Emmie, sweetheart, can you get Grandpa another glass of water?"

Emmie, only five years old, heaved a huge sigh as she stood from her spot on the porch. Her long braided blonde hair swung back and forth as she moved. She wore a dress that barely reached her knees. Dottie should take her shopping. Emmie loved her dresses; nothing else would suit her.

"Okay, Papa," she said in her singsong voice.

She skipped across the porch to open the screen door. He waited for the slam of the door against the old wood frame. When it came, he winced. He hoped Dottie would sleep through all the commotion sure to ensue with Emmie in the house. He should have gone in himself.

Jack walked along the stone pathway he'd created years ago, cracked and chipped in countless places. He used to worry Emmie would fall and hurt herself when she first came to live with them. He counted each step until they ended at the stairs. One of the steps sagged. Another thing that needed fixin'. He looked up at the place he called home.

An old-fashioned farmhouse, out on a countryside road, its yellow paint faded over the years, with whitewashed wooden shutters. The years had taken their toll on the old house. It seemed like just yesterday he'd picked the yellow paint at the store. But that was years ago, back when he had come home from the war. *Add paint to the list.*

He stopped as he came to the steps leading up to the deck. Emmie's puppy lay in his path.

"All right, Daisy, up and at 'em."

Jack used the handrail to hoist himself up each step. It hurt to lift his leg high over the mess Emmie left on the floor, but he did so with a grunt, and then sat in one of the white wicker chairs that graced the wraparound porch. The screen door opened and Emmie held a glass of water in her hands.

"Got it, Papa. I was quiet too." A wide smile spread across her face as she handed him the glass.

Jack drank the water in one gulp and wiped his mouth with his sleeve.

"Thanks, sweetheart. Is Grandma still sleeping?"

"Yep." Emmie twirled across the porch and plopped down next to her crayons and papers. "See the picture I made? It's you in your garden." Emmie waved the paper with one hand. "And there's Daisy sleeping on the grass. She sleeps a lot. Like my flowers, Papa?"

Emmie stretched out as far as she could and handed the paper to Jack. With the appropriate noises, he marveled at her picture.

She drew him as a skinny stick man, which suited him just fine. In the middle of his body, she drew a large red heart.

"Do you like my flowers, Emmie?" Jack leaned back in the chair and closed his eyes. Some days he wished he were twenty years younger.

"Can I go smell them?"

Jack opened one eye. As soon as Emmie saw his smile, her face lit up and she skipped her way down the porch stairs. With his eyes closed, Jack waited. Emmie loved flowers. He hoped she'd find the weeds he'd overlooked.

"Papa."

"Emmie."

"Can Daisy eat your flower?" Emmie's sweet voice called out. "DAISY!"

If that dog messes with my flowers . . .

The patter of Daisy's nails against the pathway rang out as she ran toward him. Before he could sit up, the bundle of energy jumped into his lap and licked his face. Squeals of laughter rang out as Emmie ran up the porch steps to join the fun.

He swooped his granddaughter into his lap, tilted his head down, and gave her a whisker rub. Emmie only laughed, reached up with her two small hands, and pulled his head forward to give him a nose kiss.

"Whatcha thinkin', Papa?"

Jack cuddled her close and rested his head on top of hers. Her hair smelled like strawberries.

"I'm thinking a nap would be good. You were pretty quiet earlier, princess. What were you thinking?"

Emmie twisted herself on his lap until she was in a more comfortable position. Her elbow jammed him in the ribs a few times while she squirmed. She rested her head against his chest and began to sing to herself in a quiet voice.

"Emmie?"

"I miss Mommy." A slurping, sucking noise met Jack's ear. She must be sucking her thumb again. "When is she coming? Why doesn't she come and get me?"

Jack tightened his arms around her.

"Tell you what, princess. How about you and me go have a tea party?" What he wanted to do was have a nap, but he couldn't stand to see his little girl so sad. Her mom was never going to come and get her.

"Can I draw her a picture?" Emmie looked up at him with a sad look in her eyes.

The last thing he wanted to do was break her heart.

"Of course you can, sweetie. You draw such nice pictures. Can you make me one too?"

Emmie climbed off his lap, scooped up Daisy, and headed into the house. Jack thought about all the other pictures Emmie had drawn for her mom.

Pictures all stored in a drawer, hidden away from Emmie so she'd never know they were never sent.

⚜

If there was one place Jack felt uneasy within his own home, it was in Emmie's room. Dottie had worked a miracle when Emmie came to stay with them, transforming the attic into a dream room fit for any princess.

The once spider-web-filled attic was now a soft pink, stuffed-animal-filled room. Emmie's bed sat in the middle of the room, a long white lace curtain suspended by wire along the posts of her bed. Dottie had found shag carpet to keep Emmie's toes warm in the mornings.

To the right of Emmie's bed sat an old comfy chair that Jack had lugged up the stairs. At night, either he or Dottie would sit in that chair, Emmie cuddled on their lap where they would read her a story until she fell asleep. On the other side of her bed sat a wooden table with tiny chairs Jack originally built for Emmie's mom when she was a little girl.

Squished into one of the chairs, Jack sat with an assortment of dolls. Emmie told him their names but a doll was a doll to him. Daisy sat at Emmie's feet, waiting for morsels of food to find their way out of Emmie's hands into her mouth. Jack's knees banged against the table each time he squirmed in his chair, forcing droplets of tea to spill from their cups onto the plates.

"Papa, your crown is falling off."

Jack's bald head didn't fit the crown very well and it often slipped off.

"This isn't my crown, it's too small. Who made this?" Jack grumbled as he readjusted the paper crown so it would sit on his head.

A giggle erupted from his granddaughter's little body as she covered her rosebud mouth with her fingers.

"Silly Papa, you did."

Jack erupted in a playful growl, which produced more laughter from Emmie. He struggled to keep a smile off his face, focusing on the stuffed animals seated on the other chairs and pretending to tickle them. Daisy joined in the fun, her barks sounding like yaps, which made Emmie fall over with laughter. Daisy jumped on her when she hit the floor.

"Papa, help!" Emmie said as her body doubled over.

Jack loved to hear her laughter. When she first arrived, holding on to Dottie's hand, she was such a quiet little girl. Jack never thought Emmie would be able to deal with losing her mom like she did. To have her smile and giggle meant the world to Jack.

"What's going on in here?" A furious voice filled the room.

The room got quiet. Daisy was hunkered on the floor, her head hidden beneath her two paws. Emmie stood, her head hung low. Jack turned and couldn't believe his eyes.

"I said, what's going on?"

Dottie stood in the doorway with a fierce frown on her face. It took all her effort to keep the scowl in place. She cracked a smile when Jack winked at her, but wiped it off her face before Emmie noticed. She hunched her shoulders, kept her hands locked on her hips, and took long heavy steps toward her granddaughter. She wondered how long it would take Emmie to keep from laughing.

Bending down, she moved her face in close to Emmie's. Just as her nose was about to touch Emmie's forehead, her granddaughter giggled, lifted her arms, and almost pulled Dottie to the ground with a bear hug. Not long at all.

"Grandma!"

"Can't a woman get any peace and quiet around here? You woke me up with all your laughter." Dottie smoothed the wisps of hair around Emmie's forehead.

"We're having a tea party. See?" Emmie swept her arms around, twirling as Dottie looked on.

"I see. I also see Daisy eating cookie crumbs off the table. Emmie, you know we don't want Daisy doing that."

A pout appeared on Emmie's face.

"Oh no you don't, little girl. Come on, I think Daisy needs to go outside." Dottie reached for Emmie's hand as Jack picked up Daisy and they headed to the kitchen.

Dottie puttered around in her kitchen while Jack headed outside with the dog. Emmie reached into the basket Dottie kept on the table full of crayons, books, Play-Doh, and some doll furniture for Emmie to play with. She watched as Emmie brought out the doll furniture and two dolls.

"Emmie, do you want to help me make scones?" Dottie pulled her apron off a hook on the wall and wrapped it around her body.

"Grandma, we already made scones. This morning," said Emmie. She never lifted her head, intent on her dolls and arranging the furniture on the table.

Dottie looked at her kitchen cupboard. Her glass platter, which contained her scones, muffins, and buns, stood empty. Dottie rubbed her forehead. She didn't remember baking today. A headache had hit her mid-morning so she went to lie down.

"Emmie, we haven't baked anything today. But we did make muffins yesterday, honey, remember?" Dottie pulled out her large mixing bowl and opened her pantry to retrieve the flour and sugar.

"No, Grandma, Daisy made me drop the flour and it made a mess all over the floor. 'Member?" Emmie cocked her head as she looked up.

Dottie turned away and looked out the window over her sink. She didn't remember that. All she remembered was the headache. Those horrible headaches she'd been getting all too often.

Jack walked into the house and poured himself a glass of water. She looked up into the face she'd loved for years. She'd memorized the wrinkles long ago, knew when each one appeared and the reason behind them. She loved his bald head, always did. This was her soul mate, her life partner.

"Emmie says we made scones today?"

A tender smile filled Jack's face. She saw the sadness in his eyes, and knew her memory betrayed her once again.

"You did, sweetheart. Emmie was helping you clean up the flour when you were hit with one of your headaches. I told you to lie down. It's my fault. I didn't realize the scones were in the oven and they burnt. I had to throw them out."

Exhaustion filled Dottie's soul. Some days were harder to get through than others. With Emmie around every day, it was hard to pretend all was well.

"Well, princess, why don't we go take Daisy outside and tucker her out. You go grab her ball and we'll see if we can teach her how to fetch. I think Grandma here needs a hot cup of tea," Jack said. When he leaned down to kiss Dottie on the cheek, she raised her hand, stroking the stubble on his chin.

"Thank you."

Dottie waited until the screen door slammed behind Jack and Emmie. She headed over to the kitchen table, cleaned up Emmie's mess of toys, and sank down in the seat, only to jump up when the teakettle whistled. She poured the water into the teapot. Her knitting lay in the rocking chair in the front room and she veered toward it. She gathered up the sweater she was kitting for Emmie and wound the wool around her fingers. Knit one, purl two.

The tea and her family forgotten.

CHAPTER SEVEN

"Help!"

Sherri jumped up. In her haste, she jarred the patio table and her glass of water spilled, soaking into the open magazine. She picked it up and fanned it as she scanned the yard. With so many voices screaming, she wasn't sure which child the cry came from. She jammed her feet into her flip-flops and headed out across her yard.

"Help me! Somebody help me!"

Sherri raced past the group of children playing in the sandbox and headed down the gentle slope in her yard, beyond her pathetic vegetable garden, and stopped in her tracks. She shielded her eyes with her hand against the bright glare of the sun and frowned.

In Sherri's acreage, a small hill sat off to the side. The children in her day care liked to play at the foot of the hill. From their height, three feet and under, they didn't think they could be seen. Little did they know that Sherri, who stood over five feet, could see them fine.

"David Jackson, what do you think you're doing? Get off of Travis this minute!"

"We just playin', Sherri." David scrambled up and dusted off the grass from the knees of his jeans. Even from this distance, Sherri could see the stains. Great, his mother was going to flip. Again.

Travis stayed seated, his face pale as he struggled to take a deep gulp of air.

"Travis, do you need your puffer?"

Travis raised his hand, his asthma inhaler clutched tight in his fist. He inserted the tube into his mouth and Sherri watched until she knew he was okay.

She headed back toward the patio and mentally counted heads as she passed by each group of children. Five, six, seven . . . seven . . . who am I missing? She looked over at the sandbox, the play set, and the group of girls coloring pictures at the picnic table.

Sherri's eyes stopped at the swing set. A child with a pixie haircut pumped her legs back and forth.

"Tonya, where is your sister? Where is Sarah?"

"'S'over there." Tonya pointed to Sherri's side fence. "Can you push me?"

Relieved, the tightness in Sherri's chest disappeared. Thank God, Sarah was okay. Over toward the fence, Sarah sat close to the wood boards, her legs crossed as she twirled a dandelion between her fingers. Eight. Sherri closed her eyes and took a deep breath. Of all the children to lose sight of . . .

"Sure can, hon." She pushed Tonya and watched the child throw herself backward on the swing before she pumped her legs out and swung higher than before.

Sherri meandered over to the fence. The day was filled with laughter, excited chatter, and a gentle wind that carried the children's voices. She soaked in the sun, her face tilted to the sky as she enjoyed the feel of new grass tickling her toes while she crossed the yard. Sarah sat at the fence and when she saw Sherri, her face beamed. Sherri couldn't help but smile back.

"Hey, Sarah, why are you over here by yourself?" Sherri sank into the grass and crossed her legs. She picked up a discarded dandelion and tickled Sarah's chin with it. Sarah leaned forward and tried to tickle Sherri's chin, but her arm wouldn't cross the distance.

"No alone," Sarah said as she stuck a finger into the space between two fence boards. Sherri leaned to the side. The silhouette of a little figure showed through the space between the boards.

"Well, hello there."

"'S'my friend," Sarah said. Her wide and slanted eyes sparkled as she slurred the words together. Of all the children Sherri took care of, Sarah held a special space in her heart. Only three years old, Sarah had Down syndrome.

A soft "hi" was whispered through the boards. Sherri leaned closer. A little girl was on the other side of the fence. *So, Sarah has a new friend then.* Sherri stood and leaned over the fence. The little girl looked up at her and gave a shy smile.

"See?" Sarah said. "My friend."

"I see." Sherri smiled. "Nice to meet you, Sarah's friend. I'm Sherri."

Sherri looked across the yard and waved as her elderly neighbor stood in her garden and frowned. *Uh-oh.* Sherri waved again, hoping to come across as friendly as the woman walked toward the fence. A nervous flutter took root in her stomach. She'd been meaning to walk over and introduce herself to the neighbors.

"Emmie, come here, honey."

Sherri glanced up. The little girl, Emmie, uncurled her legs and stood, dandelions clutched in the hand that she held out to her grandmother. The woman kneeled down once she reached the girl, clutched her close, and whispered into her ear.

"Hi there, I'm Sherri. I've meant to come over and introduce myself since we moved in, but the days just aren't long enough." Sherri took a step closer to the fence and stuck out her hand. She waited for her neighbor to move toward the fence, take her hand, and greet her.

The woman grabbed Emmie's hand and pulled her behind her. Sherri struggled to keep the frown off her face. Talk about friendly neighbors.

"Dorothy. This is my granddaughter, Emmie. I hope she wasn't disturbing you," she said as she removed the garden glove and placed her hand in Sherri's. Dorothy's hand was soft, albeit a little wrinkly. Emmie poked her head from behind her grandmother.

"Of course not." Sherri smiled at Emmie. "Actually, would she be able to come over and play with Sarah?" Sherri reached down and hoisted Sarah up so she could see over the fence. "I believe the girls have become friends."

"I'm sure that would be lovely, but another day perhaps. It's time to get ready for dinner, and Emmie is my little helper." Dottie nodded her head, then turned and placed her hand on Emmie's shoulder. "What do you think, Emmie, time to check on our bread and make dinner?"

Sherri held Sarah close as Emmie and Dorothy walked away. "My friend," Sarah said, her head snuggled close to Sherri's neck.

"She sure is. We'll have her over to play, okay?" Sherri said as she placed Sarah back on the grass, held her hand, and walked her back to the other children.

Sarah looked up, her eyes wide with delight. "'Morrow?" she asked.

Sherri glanced back toward the fence. Her new neighbor had disappeared into the house. Sherri wasn't used to being rebuffed. "I hope so, honey, I hope so."

⚜

"Can I have chocolate milk?" Emmie ran over to the fridge and struggled to grab the milk jug.

Dottie glanced out the kitchen window to her garden and thought of the new neighbor, Sherri, with a crowd of kids. Just what she wanted—a day care next door. Good thing their houses were a fair distance apart, otherwise the screaming and yelling of the children would annoy her. One child was enough. Any more than that and her patience level plummeted.

"Grandma?"

Dottie turned. Emmie kneeled on the chair, hands on her hips, and frowned.

"Grandma?" Emmie's voice, insistent this time.

"Just a minute," Dottie said as she poured the hot water into her teacup. A chair scraped across the floor.

"Emmie, I said just a minute." Dottie finished pouring the water, turned, and found Emmie on her tiptoes on one of the table chairs with her hand inside the cupboard. The chair tipped forward with Emmie's weight. Dottie rushed across the kitchen and caught hold of Emmie's body as she began to sway on the chair. She helped Emmie down and pushed the chair out of the way.

"Can we have a party, Grandma?"

"What for, child?" Dottie didn't understand how her grand-daughter's mind worked sometimes.

"For me." Emmie's face broke out in a smile while she brought her hands together, fingertip to fingertip.

"Please, Grandma. With cake?" Her head tilted to the side as she pleaded.

Dottie pretended to ponder the thought as she enjoyed watching Emmie, a smile planted on her face as she waited for an answer.

"Oh, I think we could do that."

A twinkle sparkled in Emmie's eyes. "Mommy's cake?"

Ever since Emmie had found out that chocolate coconut had been Mary's favorite cake, that's all she ever wanted. Anything to feel closer to her.

"I miss Mommy. I wish she could come to my party. Do you think she has parties in heaven, Grandma?"

CHAPTER EIGHT

Jack swiped his hands on his jacket as he walked across the yard. Dottie would skin him alive if he walked into the house with sawdust on his hands. He shrugged out of his jacket and noticed his pants were also coated in the dust. Oh well, in for a penny, in for a pound, as his dad used to say. He stomped his boots on the back deck. A waft of dust billowed up under his feet.

Jack sniffed the air. The mouthwatering aroma of fried onions drifted through the screen. Excited chatter greeted him as he walked through the door. Emmie sat at the kitchen table, her face covered with smears of chocolate while she held a plastic kid's knife in one hand and a bowl of frosting in the other.

"Papa!"

Jack planted a kiss on top of his granddaughter's head and rubbed her cheek with his whiskered face. Emmie tucked her head to her shoulder as she beamed a smile up at him.

"Oh Papa, you're silly."

He kissed her red cheek before he headed over to Dottie. He leaned over her shoulder and kissed her weathered cheek.

"Jack, you're all dirty. Go get changed before you come near my food," Dottie said.

She smelled of onions, garlic, and soil. He smiled as he gave her rounded frame a squeeze.

"Yes ma'am," he said as he grabbed a glass out of the cupboard and filled it with water. His parched throat welcomed the water as it washed away the tiny particles of dust he could feel in his throat.

"I'm hungry, woman. What's for dinner?" Jack stopped on his way up the stairs and bellowed down. He waited until he received the response he knew he'd get before heading up to the washroom.

"Just you never mind, old man. Go get washed up and dinner will be on the table. Hurry up now."

The sound of Emmie's laughter followed him up the stairs as he reached the bathroom. *Ah, it's good to be home.*

The glow of candles illuminated the kitchen as Jack descended the stairs. Their plain wooden table was decked out in Dottie's special linen. Jack hesitated; did he forget a special day? It wasn't their anniversary, Dottie's birthday, or even Emmie's. Both of his ladies sat at the table.

Emmie wore a crown on her head—the same one from the tea party he had been forced to participate in. Two candles sat in glass holders in the middle of the table, among Dottie's china place settings. A nervous flutter settled in his stomach. Dottie's china only came out for special occasions.

Jack rubbed his hands together as his girls beamed at him. He should have felt reassured. *Should have, would have, could have*—those words don't count when it came to the women in the house, something Jack learned years ago. Anything could be up. Jack pulled out his chair and winced as it scraped along the floor. He waited for

Dottie to say something like "Oh for pity's sake, Jack, would you lift up the chair and use your manners?" but she remained silent.

Emmie giggled. Her fingers covered her mouth and her eyes were round saucers, but the giggles didn't stop. Dottie's face cracked a smile. Jack let out the breath he didn't know he had been holding and reached for his cup of water. He expected to grab hold of the large cup he always used. The one Emmie had given him as a Christmas gift, complete with pink sparkles with tiny red words that said *I Love You.*

A snicker sounded beside him. He glanced at Dottie before looking down at the table. A small teacup sat in the place of his large cup. A small teacup.

"Whose bright idea was this?" he asked, waving his finger in the air.

Emmie giggled as he pointed his finger toward her. She raised her hand, inching its way up into the air.

"Yours?" Jack smiled inwardly as her head bobbed up and down.

"Emmie wanted to have a grown-up party tonight," said Dottie as she unwound her napkin from its ceramic holder and placed it on her lap.

Jack looked down at his own napkin. *Oh, come on.* Emmie cleared her throat and held up her napkin. She looked so cute sitting there with her napkin in the air, her little eyebrow raised as she waited for him. *Oh, for Pete's sake.* Jack grabbed the napkin, unwound it from the ceramic holder, and with pomp and ceremony, unfurled it and placed it on his lap.

"What's a man gotta do to eat around here, huh?" Jack made sure his grumble was loud enough to be heard.

Jack smiled at Dottie, and felt like he'd been sucker punched in the gut. Her eyes sparkled with life, her face beamed with happiness. This was the Dottie he married, the woman he fell in love with all those years ago. Lately the only thing he'd seen in her eyes was sadness. He reached across the table, wound his fingers through hers, and squeezed.

When the table had been cleared of all but the candles, Dottie brought over the semi-iced cake on its stand. Emmie clapped her hands and climbed onto her chair, excited for cake. Jack received an extra-wide slice, exactly how he liked it. He took a bite of cake and smacked his lips.

"Well, I think this party was perfect. Good idea, sweetie." Jack clapped his hands. Emmie scrambled off her chair and spun a pirouette before she held her dress out in a pretty bow.

Jack stood and took his plate over to the sink. Dottie leaned her hip against the kitchen counter, a soft smile on her face, as she watched Emmie dance along the kitchen floor, singing a song about sunshine. He placed his arms around her waist and pulled her close. Dottie swayed in his arms as they danced to Emmie's song.

Jack leaned close and whispered into Dottie's ear. "Can I take Emmie to town with me tomorrow? The boys at the coffee shop would like to meet her. It's been over two years. They think I'm making her up."

Dottie's body stiffened in Jack's arms.

"No."

Jack sighed.

"I don't understand. Her life revolves around this farmhouse and us. She needs to get out. What harm can it do?"

"I said no, Jack. Leave it be."

Jack pulled away from Dottie. She could be so stubborn at times. He didn't understand what the harm could be. Dottie coddled her too much. In the beginning, he understood, but to continue? It baffled his mind. The child needed interaction. She needed friends. She needed a life outside this house, even if it were only for an hour or two.

He didn't want to make the same mistakes with Emmie that they'd made with Mary.

⚜

"But I'm not tired, Grandma." Emmie poked her hands into the top her grandmother held for her and wiggled her head through the opening. She shivered as a cool breeze tickled her stomach before her pajama shirt covered it.

"I know you're not, Emmie, but Grandma is. That party wore me out. Now, let's dry your hair so Papa can come up to tuck you in, okay?"

The princess lights in Emmie's room twinkled on as Grandma flipped the switch. A soft glow filled the room. She loved her bedroom.

Emmie winced as Grandma unwound the towel from her hair. She always pulled when she did that.

Grandma moved over to the bed and sat down with her legs tucked under her. She patted the bed. Emmie flopped to the floor and wouldn't budge. She grabbed her pink lion beside her and hugged it close. Pinky didn't like getting her hair combed either.

"Sorry, love. Here, come sit down in front of me."

Emmie stood and sighed. Papa would be here soon and he wouldn't read her a story until her hair was dry.

"There, that's it," Grandma said.

Emmie tucked her legs underneath her, just like Grandma.

"Do you promise to be gentle?" Emmie held the comb tight in her hand.

"Remember that conditioner we put in your hair, the one that smells like coconuts? That takes all the tangles away, Emmie." She held out her hand. "Now, hand me the comb, please."

Emmie remembered the bottle with the furry animal on it. Grandma called it a koala bear. She closed her eyes as the comb went through her hair. A few times her head jerked backward, but so far it didn't hurt. Grandma hummed a song; it sounded nice.

"Mommy used to sing me that song too when she brushed my hair. I like it," Emmie said. The comb stopped and she couldn't hear Grandma hum anymore.

"Well, are we ready for a story yet?"

Emmie jumped. Papa's voice startled her.

"Oh, Jack, her hair isn't dry yet," Grandma said. Emmie's shoulders sank. "Just wait, love, let's put it in a braid tonight, okay?"

Grandma ran the comb through her hair again. Emmie's head jerked back a couple of times as it was braided, but she kept her eyes focused on Papa. He gave her a smile.

"Can I pick a story, Papa?" Emmie asked. Papa had pulled out a book from her shelf but it wasn't the right one. Emmie had a special book for tonight.

She leaped off her bed once Grandma was done braiding her hair and ran over to the shelf. Down on her knees, Emmie searched through the books, looking for the one with the pink cover. When she found it, she pulled it out and held it up.

"This one."

Papa scrunched his nose then tapped his fingers against the book. When he bent down and looked Emmie in the eyes, she grabbed the book out of his hands and held it close to her chest.

"How come that book, sweetheart?" Papa said.

Emmie lifted one hand and rubbed his cheek. It tickled from the prickly hair. Papa placed his hand over the top of hers.

"'Cause it's my special book." Emmie looked into his eyes. "Can we read it tonight?"

When Papa reached out and pulled her close, she snuggled in tight. She loved it when he held her. With the book wedged tight between them, Emmie placed her arms around his big body and tried to squeeze as hard as she could. Sometimes she tried to see if she could touch her fingers together. Not yet, but one day, when she was bigger, she would.

"Of course we can. Come on," Papa said.

Emmie squealed as he scooted his arms underneath her legs and tossed her into the air. Her tummy squirmed and she was afraid Papa would drop her.

"Tell me why you like this book so much, Emmie," said Papa as he dropped her onto her bed. Her blankets puffed up around her as she sank into the mattress. Her body bounced a few times as she giggled.

She waited for him to sit down on the edge of her bed with her special book in hand. He opened it and placed his finger underneath the first word. Emmie stared at the picture on the page.

"'Cause that's where Mommy is."

CHAPTER NINE

The house was awash in silence. The only sound was the slap of a card as it hit the kitchen table. A soft glow from the dimmed lighting covered the table, light enough for Jack to see the hand he was playing, but dark enough that when the sun peeked over the hill in front of his kitchen window, he'd be able to watch.

He was on his third game of solitaire and his second cup of honey-sweetened tea when the pitter-patter of tiny feet sounded on the stairs. He glanced at the watch he'd laid on the table. She was early. He continued his game; another card slapped against the table before Emmie climbed onto a chair beside him.

"Morning, Papa," Emmie said before a yawn escaped her mouth. She rubbed her eyes and laid her head down on her crossed arms, her sleepy eyes barely able to stay open. Tendrils of hair had escaped from her braid; the fuzzy pieces covered her head like a blanket.

"Morning, sweet pea." Jack noticed the toes that peeked out from under Emmie's pink housecoat. They wiggled as if to say hi.

"Where are your slippers? You know it's too cold for your feet in the morning."

Another yawn escaped from Emmie's mouth.

"They still sleepin', Papa."

Jack reached over and ruffled her hair. "Just like you should be, princess. It's too early to wake up yet. See?" He gestured toward the darkened window. "The sun is still sleeping."

Jack raised his mug of tea to his lips and grimaced when the cold liquid met his lips. With a groan, he worked his way out of his chair. His knees cracked as he leaned on the table for support.

As he poured more water into his cup, Emmie's sleepy voice piped up behind him.

"Can I have tea, Papa?"

He dunked his tea bag into the hot water a few times before he poured water into the other cup, already waiting on the counter. It was the same routine every morning. He carried both cups over to the table, dipped his spoon into the honey, and swirled it around in his cup. Emmie then did the same. She swirled the spoon first clockwise, then counterclockwise, just as Jack did every morning. He ducked his head to hide his smile.

Jack picked up his deck of cards and was about to pull out the top card without looking at the row of cards on the table, when a tiny snicker sounded. He lowered the card in his hand and squinted his eyes at his granddaughter before he glanced down at the table. He scanned each row a few times before he noticed the trick she'd pulled. She had mixed his cards around.

The little stinker.

"Shhh," Jack said, "you don't want to wake Grandma up."

Emmie covered her mouth with her hands and quieted down. Her eyes still held their twinkle. Jack rearranged his cards.

"I did have a secret to tell you, but I think I'll wait now." With his head down, he peeked out the corner of his eye to see Emmie's reaction.

Her tiny lips pursed tight. Jack grinned. Such a good little girl. Her fingers tapped the table as she waited. Just like Mary.

His heart ached as he thought of his daughter. He missed her. The last time he spoke to her was over two years ago. He'd begged her to come home, to leave the streets and the life she lived. But she refused. Even though it was killing her, she wouldn't come home. He often wondered where he went wrong. What did he do for her to run away and never come home? Was he that bad of a father? Did he not pay enough attention to his little girl?

When Dottie brought Emmie home, he swore he wouldn't make the same mistakes. This time he'd do it right. He owed Mary that much.

"Papa." Emmie's voice broke through his reverie. She reached her hand over and touched his. He looked up and saw her smile. No one could smile like Emmie. So bright, so full of life. His own little ray of sunshine.

"I can keep a secret. Promise. I can," Emmie said. She held up her two fingers and crossed them. He laughed and reached across to uncross her fingers.

"You can, can you?" he said. She bobbed her head.

"Well . . . I have a special surprise, but you have to wait a few more days. It's a secret." Jack set another card down.

"Papa, please?" Emmie tipped her head to the side; her dimples appeared as she pleaded.

Jack shook his head. "You'll just have to be a good little girl." He placed another card down on the table. Silence fell in the kitchen, broken only by the slurping noise Emmie made as she sipped her honey-sweetened water.

"Look, Papa."

Jack looked up. The sun was rising. Myriad colors shone over the dew-covered grass. The sky, crystal blue with white fluffy clouds, embraced the rising sun. Jack gathered up his cards and wrapped an elastic band around them.

"So, I hear someone wants their very own swing, huh?" Jack said. Emmie's head turned.

"Well, I think I might just have your mom's old tree swing somewhere in the garden shed. Think you want to help me look for it later?"

Emmie jumped up. "Can I?"

Before Jack could respond, footsteps sounded on the stairs. Emmie sat down in her chair and Jack gathered the two cups and walked to the counter.

"Can she what, Jack? What can Mary do?" Dottie said as she entered the kitchen.

Jack stopped and looked at her. Dark circles stood out from under her eyes and her hair looked like a rat's nest. She hugged her tattered housecoat tight against her body.

"Dottie?" Jack said. He walked toward her and placed his arms around her. She leaned into him. "Did you have a good sleep, sweetheart?"

A tired haze filled Dottie's eyes and she shrugged.

"Papa?" Emmie's voice whispered through the kitchen. He turned his head to look at her. Emmie sat in her chair, dwarfed by the table. She looked so small. Her eyes were large, round saucers as she stared at Dottie.

"What is Mary going to do, Jack?" Dottie grabbed hold of his shirt with her fists. She stared into his eyes. *What was going through her head?*

Jack rested his head against Dottie's head. He closed his eyes.

"Emmie. Not Mary, Emmie." Jack's voice broke when he whispered Mary's name.

"Emmie?" Dottie's eyes closed as she said the name. "Where's Mary? Jack, where is Mary?" Dottie's voice pitched up an octave, her fingers white from the grip she held on his shirt. Jack pulled away. His heart broke as he did so. Seeing Dottie like this hurt. It wasn't fair. His bright, cheery wife was slowly becoming a shell in front of his eyes.

Jack ran his hands along Dottie's rough housecoat. He mustered a smile and hoped Dottie couldn't see past it.

"Honey, Mary isn't here. Her daughter is. Emmie. Emmie is here," Jack said. He looked over at his granddaughter and smiled at her. "This is Mary's daughter. We were going to look for that swing later, remember?"

No one spoke. Dottie shrugged Jack's hands off her arms and took a step backward. She glanced at Emmie only to turn her head away.

"I'm tired, Jack. I want to go back to bed."

Jack's shoulders sank. His hands fell to his side. He took a step backward and bumped into the corner of the counter. Silence hung heavy over the kitchen. No one moved. Until Emmie's tiny voice shattered the stillness.

"Grandma," she said, her eyes filled with tears. "I miss my mommy."

CHAPTER TEN

The incessant beeping from her oven timer jerked Megan from her reverie as she lay on her deck lounger. The gorgeous weather had called to her, enticed her to bask in the sun as her chocolate almond scones baked in the oven. Her lethargic body betrayed her as it drank in the warm rays of the sun. She could have fallen asleep, would have, if it weren't for the scones.

She enjoyed the quiet of the day. It didn't happen very often, but her calendar was empty. No meetings, no one she needed to call. An empty slate. It should have been a welcome reprieve, an enjoyable break, but it drove Megan nuts. Without having something to focus on, memories resurfaced. Of Emma. Of the little girl at the donut shop. Of Peter's phone call with Samantha.

So, she baked.

As she pulled the scones out of the oven, the phone rang. Megan looked at the time. Two hours before school was out. She pulled the oven mitt off her one hand, grabbed the phone, and hooked it in the crook of her shoulder.

"Hey, darlin', just calling to check to see if I'm on for the walk today. I can't remember." Laurie's cheery tone placed a smile on Megan's face.

"Did you not look at the schedule I emailed at the beginning of the month?" Megan sighed. Why did she even ask? Laurie didn't have the best memory for things like this.

"Um, I think I deleted it without printing it off?"

"Why am I not surprised?" She transferred the scones onto the cooling racks and then headed over to the corkboard on the wall by the calendar.

"Yes, you are on. Today and then Friday, same route as normal." Both Megan and Laurie took two shifts a week at the school. Most other parents only took one day every two weeks.

"Cool. I had a feeling I was on. So, what are you doing?"

"Baking."

"Why, what's wrong?" Laurie knew her so well, too well sometimes.

"I can bake without there being something wrong, you know," Megan said.

Laurie snorted into the phone. "Yeah, just like I go running every morning with you 'cause I enjoy the torture. You only bake when something is wrong. So, what gives?"

Megan took off the other oven mitt, placed both in the drawer, and leaned against the cupboard. "Just one of those days." She stared out the window.

"They'll get better soon; they have to."

Megan just shook her head. If only she knew. She didn't reply. Instead, she took out the now-cold coffee she'd made this morning, poured it into a glass, added some ice cubes and cream, and headed outside back to her lounger.

"Megan?" Laurie broke the silence.

Megan placed her glass down on the wood bench beside the lounger and sighed. Tears slid down her cheeks.

"What else happened, hon?"

"Oh Laurie," Megan whispered into the phone. She couldn't believe she was crying. Again. She thought for sure she'd emptied herself out this morning.

"Okay, now you're scaring me. Did something happen to one of the girls? Is it about Emma?"

Megan choked back a sob. She didn't want to do this.

"I thought I saw Emma the other day," she said. Admitting that, saying it out loud, hurt. But if anyone could understand, it would be Laurie. The one friend who stuck with Megan through thick and thin.

Megan waited for Laurie to say something. Anything. Something like "Oh sweetie, you're okay," but instead, she got silence. A long stretch of nothingness. Megan's heart quickened. *Does she think I'm going crazy too?*

"Does Peter know?" Laurie's voice was low and soft.

"No," Megan said. She was afraid to tell him, although she wouldn't admit that to Laurie. She couldn't. That was between her and Peter.

"Did you call the counselor? You still have her private number to call in case of emergencies, don't you?"

Megan sighed. Calling the shrink was the last thing she wanted to do. She did not want to go back on the medication.

"Megan?" Laurie must have heard the sigh.

"No, I didn't call, but yes, I still have the number. You know what will happen if I tell her. I do not want to go on any crazy drugs, Laurie." Megan took a deep, calming breath. In and out. In and out.

"They're not crazy drugs, Meg, just ones to calm you down a bit."

Megan bit back a retort. If one more person told her she needed medication, she'd scream. She was *not* overwhelmed. Call it a bad day. Tomorrow would be better. There was nothing to worry about.

"Okay, listen. You and Peter need some time alone tonight to talk about this. Let me take the girls. I'll pick them up from school and treat them to a trip to the mall . . ." Laurie said.

Megan interrupted her before she could finish.

"No, that's all right. We'll be fine."

A frustrated sigh came across the phone.

"Would you let me finish?"

Megan closed her eyes. She wasn't sure what Laurie was going to say, but she couldn't imagine it'd be any worse than what she already said and what Megan already thought. Self-condemnation was the worst form of punishment.

"I'll take the girls so you and Peter can spend some time alone. You need to tell him, Megan. You promised you would if it ever happened again. And you don't need the stress of the girls around when you tell him," Laurie said.

Megan nodded, but cleared her throat when she realized Laurie couldn't see her.

"The girls will like that. Thanks."

She placed the phone on her lap and raised her face to the sun. All she wanted was to feel warm again. Somehow, though, the chill in her body seemed permanent.

⚜

She held the phone in her hand. The numbers were already dialed, all that was left was to hit the connect button. So, why did she hesitate? She stood on her deck and looked out over her yard. Jump ropes lay discarded on the grass along with a blown-up beach ball the girls had received at a birthday party the weekend before, and dandelions decorated the yard.

Megan smiled as she pictured Emma on her first birthday. She had just started to walk but hated to wear any type of shoe or slipper on her feet. As soon as Megan had set her down on the grass, she began to cry. She didn't like the prickly sensation of the grass on her delicate feet. Peter scooped her up and called her a princess. She didn't stop crying until she saw the dandelions. Megan took a picture of Emma seated on the grass, her lap covered with dandelion heads she picked. Peter sat beside her and stuck one of the weeds behind Emma's ear. A princess indeed.

Megan took a deep breath and hit the connect button on the phone. Her stomach gave a queasy turn as she listened to the ringing. The skin on her arms tingled, as if tiny ants were marching single file to her shoulder as she waited. A voice inside her head screamed at her to hang up. She had almost given in and hung up when a voice came on the line.

"Detective Thompson speaking."

Megan gulped. Peter made her promise not to call the detective overseeing Emma's case unless he knew about it. Too bad for Peter that her daughter came first.

"Hello? This is Detective Riley Thompson, how can I help you?"

Megan glanced at dandelions, pictured her daughter sitting there on the grass, and answered.

"Riley, it's Megan. Megan Taylor," she said. She knew she didn't need to introduce herself, he probably recognized her voice, but it was habit. It kept their relationship on a professional level.

"Mrs. Taylor, it's been a while. How are you?"

The warm familiarity of his voice washed over her; the butterflies in her stomach stilled. Calling was the right thing to do.

"Have you heard anything? Have there been any sightings or phone calls about Emma?" If she kept their conversation focused on Emma and nothing else, Peter couldn't object. Right?

"Actually, Meg . . . Mrs. Taylor, I was about to call you," he said.

Megan's heart leaped to her throat. She caught the mistake the moment he started to say her name. She sat down on the deck steps, leaned forward, and stroked the petals of the petunias she had planted in a pot.

"There is a forensic artist who works with our department. I know Emma's birthday is coming up, so I requested an updated sketch."

"Yesterday," Megan whispered into the phone.

"I'm sorry?"

"Yesterday," Megan said again. "Emma's birthday was yesterday." There was a pause on the phone. A slight rustling of papers could be heard in the background.

"Right, yesterday. I'm sorry, I knew that. I wanted to let you know that I have new age-progressed sketches of Emma. I can drop them by if you like? Her picture has already been updated on the national website. The new circulation of her photo on the next set of flyers will also start." More paper shuffles sounded. "Yesterday, actually."

Megan stood and walked down the stone pathway to the back of the yard. Years ago, she'd planted a flower garden along the fence. There were a few stragglers that persisted in blooming. Maybe she should think about buying some plants this year. A good summer project for Alexis.

"You mean sketches of how she would look now, right?" Megan asked. When Emma had first disappeared, they'd placed her photo everywhere. Bulletin boards, telephone poles, storefront windows. They'd received a lot of phone calls, but nothing that could pinpoint where Emma was. Maybe this time would be different. At the very least, it was nice to know she wasn't the only one trying to find her daughter.

"Right. Would you and Peter be available this evening? I could drop them off for you to look at."

Megan's hand shook with a slight tremor. She started to count to three. One—breathe in. Two—breathe out. Three—open your eyes.

The tempting thought of seeing her daughter's face, of how she would look today, pulled at her. Would she have made the same mistake at the donut shop if she'd already seen the pictures? That little girl's face, the expression in her eyes haunted Megan. She should have known better. She should have made sure, really sure, that it was Emma before she grabbed the little girl's hand.

But then she thought of what was in store for tonight. How she needed to be honest with Peter. Having the man she almost turned to for comfort come over, when she had to break the news to Peter that she'd broken another promise, probably wasn't a smart move.

"No, Riley, I'm afraid tonight's not a good night."

CHAPTER ELEVEN

"Pretty little dandelion all dressed in yellow, let's make a necklace for the pretty princess," Emmie sang. Dandelion heads filled her lap as she made a chain to go around her neck. Such pretty flowers. Papa called them "those pesky weeds," but she thought they were cute. She had one chain already made. Daisy had it around her neck. She should make one for Grandma. That might make her happy.

Daisy barked, and her little yaps increased as she fought to take off the chain.

"Shh, Daisy. Shhhh. Don't wake up Grandma." She leaned forward to grab Daisy, but her hands ended up empty. *Oh, Daisy.*

Emmie glanced around the yard. A big tire leaned against a tree. Papa promised he'd make her a swing. Maybe when he was home. She looked out to the driveway and down to the road, but Papa's truck wasn't there. Emmie's body wilted under the warm sun. *I wish Papa would hurry*, she thought.

"Pssst, little girl!"

Startled, Emmie jumped. The dandelions fell out of her lap and she squished a few under her feet as she stood. She looked around. Who called her?

"Hey, friend, over here!"

A hand waved to her through the fence behind Grandma's garden. Her friend!

"Shhhhh," Emmie called out, her voice just above a whisper. She didn't want Grandma to hear. Emmie skipped over to the fence, and the grass tickled the bottoms of her feet along the way. She stopped at the edge of the garden. Daisy barked hello. Emmie sank to her knees, grabbed Daisy, and hugged her close. Daisy licked Emmie's face. Emmie giggled as Daisy's wet tongue tickled her nose and cheeks. Holding Daisy was hard; she kept squirming in her arms.

"Hi, friend!" A hand stuck out of the fence and waved to her.

Emmie stuck her face close to the fence boards and smiled. Her friend looked pretty today. Emmie liked her dress—it was a bright yellow with pink dots all over. Emmie glanced down at her own dress. Pink with yellow flowers. They matched. Emmie giggled. Her friend giggled too. Daisy dropped out of her arms and stuck her nose through the fence.

"Friend, I got you this," the little girl said. She stuck a popsicle through the fence. It dripped down the handle. Emmie wrinkled her nose before she took the treat. Daisy jumped up, licked it, then sat. She looked so cute with her head tilted like that. Emmie squealed in delight. *Daisy sat!* "Good girl, Daisy. Good girl!" Emmie kneeled down and let her lick the popsicle as a reward.

"Your puppy is cute."

Emmie looked up to find her new friend reaching to pet Daisy, so she pushed her closer, but Daisy didn't want to move.

"Friend, can you come play? We can go on the swings. They're fun. Please?"

Emmie stepped to the side so she could look through the fence without her friend being in the way. Their backyard looked like fun. A picnic table, a sandbox, and swings. Emmie glanced behind her to the tire swing propped up against the tree and then back to the

who used to bug Jack in the summer, had grown into a Mr. Hot-shot. Not so skinny anymore. The boy's girth had expanded as the years passed after he took over the store from his dad, who had died of a stroke out in the cornfield. Jack doubted he even lent a hand to his mom and brothers on the farm. The only thing good enough for this boy was money. Just like the rest of his generation.

He tossed the coiled rope into the box and watched as a puff of dust billowed into the air. His old Ford might not be as shiny and new as Mr. Hotshot's, but it worked just fine. His old Ford had seen more, driven farther, and pulled more than its share of weight in the years since Jack bought it. They don't build them like this anymore. No sirree. Jack banged the side and grunted. The only thing ole Bet-ty needed was a good scrubbin'. Maybe he'd do that before supper.

He looked across the lot toward the donut shop. Only a hand-ful of vehicles littered the parking area. He didn't see any of the boys' trucks there. Guess he'd missed them. Still he drove over to grab a box of donut holes he'd promised his grandbaby. Emmie loved the tasty treats, especially the chocolate- and strawberry-filled ones. He drove around to the other side to the drive-thru entrance and found the missing trucks. He shook his head. He pulled into an empty stall and went inside.

"Wondered when you'd get here, the boys are getting impa-tient," the waitress at the counter said as Jack entered the store. The tiny bells above the door jingled as the door closed behind him.

"Well, I can't be that late if they stuck around, now can I?" Jack watched her pour him a cup of black coffee. He gestured to the donut holes sitting on the bottom shelf. "I'll take some of those too when I leave."

Jack looked at the far booth in the corner. Both the boys, Doug and Kenny, were slouched over their coffees as they stared at him. He'd known the men since childhood. They were closer to him than his own brothers. Jack made a trip into town once a week just to have coffee with them. Doug tapped the watch on his hand. Jack shrugged his shoulder and turned back to the counter.

"I might as well get a donut too. Can't let those boys eat alone."

"Where've you been? Figured you weren't comin' into town this week. Dougie and I have been sittin' here like a herd of cows mowin' down on the grass," said Kenny as Jack set his coffee and plate down on the table. He pulled a chair over from one of the other tables and sat down.

Jack grunted. "Workin' on the honey-do list. Thought you boys would have been long gone by now."

Jack took a sip of his coffee and peered over the rim. His was the only full cup. Black circles rimmed the other two empty cups on the table.

He looked at Doug. With his salt-and-pepper hair all over the place, he looked old.

"So, when are you going to bring that grandbaby of yours in with you?" Doug asked as he leaned back in his chair and tilted his head down to look over the top of his glasses at Jack.

"Yeah, thought you were bringing her in today. Otherwise, I would have left long ago. I got fish to catch, you know." Kenny played with the empty cup in front of him.

Jack shrugged his shoulders. Dottie had been steadfast in her refusal to let him bring Emmie today. She never let that girl out of her sight. Didn't make sense to him. Little girls need more than just tea parties and play dates with teddy bears and dolls.

"Dottie still protective?"

Jack glanced up at Doug, surprised he'd figured it out so fast. Shouldn't have been, though. Doug knew Dottie almost as well as Jack did. Almost. And it was a fact Jack didn't like.

"Said she had plans to make cookies with her today. Maybe next week."

Unsure of why he felt the need to protect Dottie, Jack was even more surprised to find himself lying. Doug only nodded, which irritated him for some odd reason. No doubt, Doug knew he was lying.

"You takin' her to the Hanton Fair this weekend? Heard the Ferris wheel was new," said Kenny.

Jack had forgotten all about the fair. Living out in the country with no paper delivery, it was easy to forget life carried on around you. He had wanted to take Emmie last year but it never happened. Something about Emmie having a cold and not feeling well. Jack never heard her cough, but Dottie knew best. He'd mentioned the fair to her a few weeks ago when the posters first started coming out but she didn't seem too interested, so Jack pushed it out of his mind. Until now.

"Thinkin' about it. It's been a while since we made our way over there. We never made it last year."

Doug grunted beside him and stretched his arms up over his head. "Well, time for me to go find a wife to feed those animals of mine. I'm getting old, you know, and all this hard labor is wearin' me down." The wrinkles in his face widened as he smiled and showed his side gold tooth.

Kenny laughed. "Headed to bingo, are we? Is Ms. Hot Pants going to be there?"

Jack smirked as he watched Doug's face go from a grin to a frown. Single his whole life, it wasn't until a few months ago Doug decided to get over his lost love and find someone else before it was too late. About time too. He'd better hurry; old men like them don't often find love in their old age.

"That's Mrs. Weatherall to you." Doug pointed a finger at Kenny. "And at least I'm doing something instead of complaining all day about how hard bachelorhood is." Doug pursed his mouth the moment he said that. He'd just crossed the line, and they all knew it.

Kenny stood up, grabbed his cup and plate, and walked away. Jack looked at Doug whose eyes followed Kenny. He looked lost. Jack turned and watched Kenny hand his dirty dishes to the waitress at the counter and walk out, never once looking back at his two friends. He shook his head. Not good.

"Aww, man, that was stupid. Why did I say it?" Doug muttered as he watched Kenny climb into his truck and drive away. Jack felt sorry for him. "I blew it, didn't I?" Doug sank into the chair, his shoulders fell with a dejected air.

"Nah, nothing that can't be fixed," Jack said. He cleared his throat and took a swig of his warm coffee. The donut sat there untouched. "Guess today wasn't a good day for him. Anything happen?"

Doug glanced up. "Nothing out of the ordinary. His mind is going, his body is getting old, and there's nothing he can do about it. Guess his doctor wants him to go on some new type of medication, but Kenny's not going for it. He outlived everyone else in his family and figured if it's his time to go, then it's time. I told him I wasn't ready." Doug shrugged his shoulders. "There's not many left of the old gang. You barely come into town anymore, and life at the old lodge isn't what it used to be. One can only play bingo for so long."

Jack nodded his head. He understood what Kenny was going through. With Dottie's dementia, the doctor kept forcing all these new pills on her. If it wasn't for Emmie . . . Losing a child does strange things to a mother's mind. Jack thought about Dottie and how she kept mixing up Emmie's name. Too many times she'd call her Mary. Sure, she looked like Mary as a child, but still. Ever since she brought Emmie home, her memory continued to slip. It scared him. He didn't want to end up alone, with a small child to raise.

Jack took another drink of his coffee, emptying the cup of every last drop.

"Well, I should go. Got a tire swing to hook up for Emmie today," he said. "Could use some help if you need somethin' to do." Jack kept his gaze on the table.

It was the first time in a long time he'd invited Doug to the farm. A long time ago he swore he'd shoot him with his shotgun if he ever stepped foot on his land. A lifetime ago. Doug never had. They rebuilt their friendship, but it was only over coffees and fishing trips. Never at the house.

"Nah, I should drop by Kenny's place and see where he's at," Doug said. His voice quivered a bit. Jack grunted. Probably a good thing he didn't come. Some bridges are too old to fix.

Jack grabbed his dishes and headed over to the counter as Doug sat at the table. He didn't look back.

The gal already stood there with his box of donut holes. She opened the container and added his uneaten donut while she shook her head. "See ya tomorrow, boys."

Jack wanted to get home, see how Dottie was feeling, and hang up that tire swing for Emmie.

CHAPTER TWELVE

Upstairs in the bedroom, Megan stood in front of a mirror. She leaned over so her long brown hair fell in waves across her face. She tried to clasp her necklace behind her neck, but kept missing the eye. Once attached, she positioned the chain on her chest to see where it laid. Not as low as she would like, but it would do. She lifted her head and gazed at the woman before her. She didn't recognize her.

The woman in the mirror looked old, haggard even. There were bags under her eyes and no amount of makeup could hide the dark circles. She looked down, at the jeans that once were snug against her hips. She twisted her waist and looked again. They looked good on her, a bit loose in areas, but better than before. The running helped.

She gathered her hair together in her hands and pulled it into a high ponytail. She should have washed it. Peter liked her hair up—only so he could take it down again. She closed her eyes and imagined the sensation of his hands on her neck, the way it felt to have him hold the weight of her hair in his hand.

Her head jerked back as the elastic in her hair tugged loose. She opened her eyes to find Peter standing behind her, a grin on his face before he buried it into the back of her neck. His lips whispered promises against her skin, his hands worked their magic until she was enthralled. She leaned back into his solid body and breathed a gentle sigh.

"This is a surprise."

Megan turned her body until she stood face to face with her husband. She laid her hands on his chest, looked into his eyes and smiled. "Laurie picked up the girls for a night out. Which means we are alone."

"And you're dressed. Why?" Peter's curved eyebrow rose; a suggestive smile lingered on his face as his gaze traveled along her body.

"Because I thought we could have a nice dinner. It's been a while since we've spent time alone together." She leaned forward and placed a soft kiss against his lips. "Maybe we could go to the Silver Rose?"

Megan turned back to the mirror. All she needed were earrings and some heels and she'd be ready to go. A tiny seed of excitement sprouted in her heart. She was actually looking forward to a night out. She'd keep her promise to Laurie, but it could wait until after dinner.

Then she saw the pout on Peter's face. Her tiny sprout withered. If she were to make up for this morning, maybe she needed to give in a bit.

"Or we could order in?" Megan said. Something like a smile flirted with her lips. Her eyes twinkled back to herself in the mirror.

Hope sprang in Peter's eyes. He bent his head to kiss the back of her neck.

"I like how you think, Mrs. Taylor." Peter wiggled his hips in a suggestive dance that brought a blush to Megan's face.

Watching this dance of seduction play out in the mirror added a new dimension to the experience. Despite being fully clothed, Megan might as well have been naked, vulnerable to Peter's desire.

His tie now off, he began to unbutton his shirt, slowly. Megan placed her hands on his chest and pushed him. He took a few steps back until his legs met the edge of the bed. She pushed again. He fell onto the bed, his arms spread out while a grin remained fixed on his face.

Passion took over Megan's body. With nimble fingers, she pulled her top up, exposing her stomach before sliding it up over her head. The shirt dropped to the floor as she edged closer to the bed. Peter's eyes lit up. When her legs were between his feet, she stopped. Her response to the desire in Peter's eyes shocked her and at the same time, excited her. It had been a long time since she played this role. She hoped it served her well. When Peter found out she broke another promise, this scene might be erased from any future scripts forever.

⚜

Relaxed, Megan leaned back against the couch in the family room and waited for Peter to join her. The moo shu pork they had ordered was delicious. Then Peter found the scones she had baked earlier and offered to make coffee to go with the treat. The coffee's aroma wafted through the house as it brewed.

She curled her feet under and picked up the magazine Laurie had dropped off when she picked up the girls: *Home & Garden Ultimate Dessert Magazine*. Laurie stuck bright yellow Post-it arrows on her favorite recipes. Laurie couldn't bake, so apparently this was her way of asking Megan to do it for her. Nice one.

She studied a coconut vanilla cake recipe as Peter entered into the room with a tray. Two cups of coffee sloshed over their rims with each step he took. Megan put the magazine down on her lap and took hold of her coffee as her husband stood before her. She didn't touch the scone.

"Find anything good?" Peter asked as he gestured to the magazine.

"Maybe." She shrugged her shoulders. Megan turned it over and showed Peter the delectable picture of a white cake with coconut icing. Everything depended on how their conversation went tonight.

Peter sipped his coffee and pulled the magazine off her lap.

She waited for him to speak, but he continued to flip through the pages. An edgy silence filled the room. Megan knew she should say something but wasn't sure how to begin. She glanced down at her wristwatch. The girls would be home in a few hours. She concentrated on her coffee cup, listening to the rattle of paper as Peter turned each page.

"So, what's wrong?"

Megan looked up and found Peter's eyes on her. Her heart gripped with fear, her stomach knotted together with sharp pains. *He knows.* The thud of the magazine as it closed startled her.

She held the coffee mug tight in her hands. Its warmth didn't impact the sudden numbness in her fingers. She took a deep breath, held it to the count of three, and exhaled. She could do this. He would forgive her. He'd understand, he had to understand.

"The other day, when I went to get coffee . . ." She struggled with the words. Her fingers pushed the coffee cup around the palms of her hand.

"You already apologized," said Peter, his voice devoid of any emotion.

"I know." Megan took a deep breath. "I was in the drive-thru and I saw her." Megan shook her head. "Emma. I thought I saw Emma walking across the parking lot."

There, she'd said it. She made no excuses, didn't even try to explain. It would be pointless. It was always the same, every time it happened. Whether she saw the top of Emma's head in a crowded mall, or heard her voice in a busy park, it always ended the same. She left the area alone, devastated that she'd gotten her hopes up. Nothing Peter could say would hurt as bad. Nothing.

The steady tick-tick-tick of the wind-up clock that sat on a bookshelf filled the silence in the room. It had been a gift from Peter when they first started dating. Megan picked at her fingernails, her head bent down to avoid her husband's gaze. *Why doesn't he say anything?* She glanced out of the corner of her eye and found him staring at his own hands. The look on his face shattered her heart into tiny pieces.

"Peter?" Megan winced. She sounded like she was begging. What if that little girl had been Emma? Would she be asking for his forgiveness then? No, it would be the other way around. Why couldn't he understand?

"What did you do?"

Megan whipped her head up. Peter's voice was so low, Megan almost asked him to repeat what he'd said.

"I, uh . . ." She couldn't say it. Not to him. He already knew. Why did he even have to ask?

Peter brought his head up and stared at the wall straight ahead.

"You what, Megan? What did you do? Did you just watch her until you realized it wasn't our daughter? Did you get out of your Jeep and grab her? Did you follow her into the store?" Peter's voice rose in cadence as he barraged her with his questions.

"What exactly did you do?"

A tear slid down Megan's cheek as she tried to form the words Peter wanted to hear. She opened her mouth, but there was nothing to say.

Peter jumped off the couch and headed to the fireplace, where a multitude of family photos stood on display across the mantle. Even though his back faced her, his anger confronted her. His shoulders were tight, his legs stiff. The muscles on his back protruded against his white T-shirt. She couldn't see what he was doing, but she knew. He stood in the same spot she favored. Directly in front of Emma's birthday picture, taken just before she was kidnapped.

"Peter, I . . ." Megan shuddered as her husband's shoulders dropped. He leaned his elbows against the mantel and his body shook. What had she done?

"I miss her too." Peter's voice cracked. "More . . . more than you can imagine. I dream about her, I wake up to the sound of her laughter. I see her too." Tremors racked his body. "Just out of my reach, her curly blonde hair—always out of my reach."

Megan perched on the edge of the couch, unsure if she should go to him to offer comfort. *Is this what our marriage has come to?* Peter turned, his bright blue eyes flooded with tears as he looked at Megan. She didn't move.

"But I know it's not her. I know the difference between my dreams and reality, Meg. Do you?" His eyes dared her to argue with him, to try to prove her innocence. She knew she shouldn't, but she did anyhow.

"What if, Peter? What if that was her? What if it was Emma? Do you want me to just give up and give in? Is that what you want?" Megan stood and crossed her arms. *Please let him say no.*

The silence in the room was deafening. All it would take was one word to shatter the precarious silence. *Please don't let him say it. I won't choose. I can't.*

"Of course not. But, you promised Meg. You made a promise and broke it. To me." Peter walked over to chair opposite the couch and sank down.

Megan didn't know what to say. She didn't know what words he needed to hear.

"I can't keep doing this. We can't keep doing this," Peter said. He rested his elbows on his knees and buried his head in his hands. "We need closure. We can't keep our lives on hold waiting"—he took a deep breath—"waiting for something that will never happen."

"What are you saying?" Megan worked hard to keep her voice level. Inside, her whole being shook. She clenched her hands. She wanted to shout at him, rail at him, but he wouldn't even look her in the eye.

"Maybe it's time to move on." His voice, a mere whisper, shattered whatever hope Megan held for them.

"Never." Venom filled her voice, full of hatred and anger. She didn't care. How dare he.

Peter lifted his head, tears rimming his eyes. "Not give up, I didn't mean that."

"Well, praise God. For a moment I thought you meant to believe our daughter was dead." She spit the words out at him, dumbfounded that he would even assume they should move on without Emma. She held her hands up in exasperation. Her whole body vibrated with anger. "Don't you dare tell me to give up. Not on Emma. I will never accept that she's not coming home. Never." She headed to the doorway afraid if she walked away, she wouldn't come back. Not to this.

Peter's voice stopped her.

"Each time you see her yet come home empty-handed, my heart breaks all over again. Except it was never whole to begin with. I don't want to accept that she's gone forever, but I don't know what else to do. We have two other children who need us, Meg. There won't be anything left for them if my heart keeps breaking."

Megan grabbed onto the trim of the door, an anchor to her trembling body. She turned to find Peter behind her. He reached his arms out but she stepped to the side. His hand brushed against her arm. She walked to the fireplace and grabbed hold of a picture on the mantel.

"It's because of our other children that I won't give up on Emma. If I let her go, I let her down. You talk of broken promises, Peter. But I'm not the only one who's broken them. What of the one we made to our girls? That they would always be safe? Oh, wait. You blame me for that one too."

Megan held on to that picture, her fingers white from the grip. A family picture when they were whole, complete. Now they were only broken, splintered into pieces that were forever lost. Megan didn't know how to fix it. Peter was supposed to be the key, the glue that held them all together while she held on to the hope of her daughter's return.

Megan's throat constricted as she tried to swallow her anger. It took a few tries before she could speak without spewing the anger that consumed her being.

"I need you, Peter. I need you to believe in me, to believe in Emma. Everything that I have done has been for her. You asked me earlier if I was having a relapse. Trying to find our daughter is the only thing keeping me sane. The *only* thing. But I can't do this alone. You talk of your heart breaking, but have you ever thought of what I go through? Do you think I enjoy the agony? I literally die inside every time, Peter. Without Emma, I'm nothing. *Nothing.*"

Sobs ripped through Megan's body as she crumpled to the floor. The picture frame tumbled out of her hand. Megan grabbed for the frame but missed. It smacked into the fireplace, the glass shattered from the impact.

She stared at the splintered glass, at the jagged lines that ripped across the surface. It's how their family lived now, cracked at the core. She picked up the frame. She could replace the glass and no one would ever know. There was no easy fix for her family, though. No way to ever hide the damage.

She looked up but found she was alone. Megan struggled to walk the distance to the couch. The steady cadence of the clock filled the silence. She pulled an afghan across her body and curled into a ball underneath it. She watched the empty doorway, praying Peter would come back. He couldn't have left. Not like this. Their marriage stood on shaky ground, but was a landslide inevitable? She couldn't believe that this would be the catalyst.

She leaned her head against the couch, her eyes closed. This could be the end of their marriage. Even at the thought, no tears came. There was nothing left within her to grieve. Maybe it would hit her tomorrow when she woke up alone in their bed.

Minutes passed as she sat there, her mind numb. She should move, but her body betrayed her with its lethargic response. So, she waited. Waited for the numbness to take over.

A slight pressure of a hand on her shoulder forced her to open her eyes. Peter came back. He stood before her, tears flowing down his face as he held a book in his hand. She glanced up at the book, puzzled.

"I do care," Peter whispered as he laid the book in her lap. He bent down, placed a tender kiss on her forehead before he left her alone, again. Confused, Megan held the book in her hands, turned it over, unsure of what it meant.

The book itself was plain. No writing covered the front or spine of the book. She opened it and her hand shook. Peter's handwriting covered the front page.

To my darling Emma. Not a day goes past without you in my thoughts. My baby. My princess. My dream is to one day hand this journal to you and explain to you the words I have written inside. I love you, Emma Wynn Taylor. I always will.

With tender care, Megan turned the page. The thin paper rustling beneath her shaking hand didn't escape her notice. Nor did she miss the now-dry wet marks, which covered the first few pages of the journal. Peter's words. Peter's tears. She held each page between her fingers with gentleness. With one glance, this book became a precious treasure, one that deserved her utmost care. Each page was dated. The words rolled together until they formed a love letter, from a father to his missing daughter.

Tears rolled down Megan's face as Peter's heart was laid out before her. Naked to the core. Peter managed to do what she had never thought to do. Could never do.

CHAPTER THIRTEEN

If all mornings could be like this, I'd die a happy man. Jack whistled as he slapped another card down on the table. He'd woken up beside a woman who still had the ability to make his heart jump with a touch. He smiled. Happy man indeed.

Emmie sat beside him at the table. While he relaxed and played his game of solitaire, she colored. She'd slept in today—a rare experience for Emmie. It had taken her a bit to settle down last night. Jack must have read close to six stories before she fell asleep. He laid down another card as he watched her. Clad in the pink puppy-dog pajamas Dottie had sewn, her hair a rat's nest of curls, she looked cute. Emmie leaned over the table as she concentrated on her picture, the tip of her tongue showing through her lips as she drew yellow flowers all over a green field.

"That's a pretty picture, Emmie."

The kitchen felt a little stuffy. *Gonna be a scorcher today.* Jack walked to the kitchen door and opened it halfway, enough to let in the early morning breeze, but not too far as to chill his granddaughter.

He rubbed her hair as he sat back in his chair. "Is that you?"

Emmie drew a picture of a little girl in a pink dress. He recognized it as the dress she wore yesterday. He waited to see if she drew a picture of Daisy, but she surprised him by drawing another girl. He smiled to himself. Little girls and their imagination.

Jack stared down at the row of cards in front of him. He'd lost another round. That was three rounds today. He normally won. He peeked at Emmie, surprised at her tenacity. His grandbaby was a flutter bug, flitting from one thing to another. But this morning she sat without making a peep, intent on her picture.

His stomach rumbled as Emmie tilted her head to look at him. He covered his mouth with his hand and acted surprised. She giggled at him. He loved that sound. It reminded him of his daughter.

Jack looked at the clock. Dottie would be up soon. Maybe he'd surprise her with breakfast. "Are you hungry yet, munchkin? How does french toast sound?"

A smile lit Emmie's face. Her favorite breakfast.

"French toast it is."

Jack rummaged around in the cupboard for the cinnamon. About to ask Emmie if she wanted to help him, he turned, but she wasn't at the table. He spun around and found her standing behind him, holding her picture.

"Can I tell you a secret, Papa?"

Her face held a grave look to it. The sparkle in her disappeared at the word. Jack knew she was serious, so he squatted until he was eye level with her and made sure the smile that fought to show itself stayed tucked away.

"Of course. You can tell me anything."

Emmie cocked her head to the side, pursed her lips, and stared straight into his eyes.

"You can't tell Grandma. Promise?"

Jack thought about it for a moment then shook his head. His knees started to ache, his back screamed at him to straighten, but this was important.

"Emmie," said Jack as he took one of her hands in his, "you know I don't keep secrets from Grandma. But I will promise you this." He held up two fingers. "If it's something I don't think Grandma needs to know, then we can keep it between us. Okay?"

Emmie bent her head to her chest. She wouldn't look him in the eye. He'd give her a few minutes to think about what he said. He'd learned the hard way with Mary that promising to keep secrets from his wife did more harm than good.

She kept her head bent. Jack noticed she wouldn't look him in the eyes. This must be bad. He placed his finger underneath her chin and gently tilted her head up until she looked at him. Her lips trembled.

"I have a friend, Papa," she said. Her eyes sparkled as she told him her secret. Jack bit back his smile.

"You do?"

He took his hand out of hers and placed it on the counter. With a groan, he used it as leverage to help him stand. Emmie stepped forward and offered her hand, which he took. He grunted as his back screamed in agony and his knees locked together.

"What's her name?"

"Friend."

Her answer took him aback. *Friend? What kind of name is that?* Maybe Dottie found one of Mary's old porcelain dolls and gave it to her. But why would she want this to be a secret?

"She wore a yellow dress, Papa, just like the flowers on my dress. And she gave me a popsicle too. But Daisy ate it. Well, she licked it. But then she sat. Papa, she *sat*. And my friend, she likes Daisy. She says she's a good puppy." Emmie's face beamed with happiness as the secret burst out of her.

Jack looked at her picture again. At the two little girls in a field of yellow flowers and Daisy sitting beside them. This must be the age of imaginary friends. Jack tried to remember if Mary ever went through this stage, but he didn't think she had.

Jack turned back to the ingredients on the counter. It had been a while since he last surprised his girls with a homemade breakfast, but if memory served, french toast wasn't that hard.

"Can I play with her, Papa?" His shirt tugged at the back. He looked over his shoulder and saw Emmie's hand had a firm hold on his shirt.

"Of course you can. Any friend who likes Daisy is a good one." No harm in that. He'd read an article in one of those parent magazines he bought Dottie for Christmas. A child's imagination is a powerful tool.

"Now?"

About to crack open an egg, Jack stopped. *Now?*

"Well, if you want to. But be quiet, okay, Grandma's still sleeping."

He expected to hear her footsteps scurry up the stairs, but instead it was the sound of the screen door as it slammed into its frame that shocked him. Dottie had been after him to fix the hinge on that door, but right at this moment, he was glad he hadn't.

Jack dropped a half-cracked egg into the bowl and hurried over to the door. Emmie, halfway across the yard, was skipping up the hill to the fence that separated their property from the neighbors.

"Emmie!"

She stopped mid-skip and turned. He could see the confusion on her face. He blinked his eyes. *So, not an imaginary friend?* He motioned with his hand for her to come back and waited. She didn't skip back. She took tiny steps with her head bent as she held the picture in her one hand, while the other trailed to the side. When she reached the porch, he held out his hand and waited for her to take it.

"Emmie, you still have your pajamas on. You can't go out to play in those."

His granddaughter looked up at him; hope filled her eyes.

"After?"

He didn't know how to respond. He thought she was talking about an imaginary friend, not the kids from next door. But when she looked up at him with those big baby-blue eyes, saying no wasn't an option. He ruffled her hair a bit.

"Tell you what, princess, after breakfast we'll talk to Grandma and see what she has to say."

The moment Emmie's eyes clouded over and her bottom lip stuck out in a royal pout, he knew he'd said the wrong thing. Seemed like Dottie had been a tad bit overprotective lately. He watched as Emmie stared at the picture she held in her hands. He might be an old man with a waning memory, but he could still put two and two together. His baby girl had found a new friend; 'bout time too.

"You know, having friends is never a bad thing. I know Grandma agrees too. That there picture in your hand is pretty nice and you spent a lot of time making it for your friend, didn't you?"

Emmie nodded her head; her mishmash of curls bounced all over the place.

"Then there's no reason why you can't give it to your friend later. Okay? But first, it's time for . . ."

"BREAKFAST!" Emmie shouted before her hands flew up to her mouth in shock. "Oops, sorry."

Jack chuckled. It was time for Dottie to get up anyway, and he apparently had breakfast to make.

Dottie waved the oven mitt in front of her face. The breeze from that action cooled her down. Why she decided to bake this afternoon was beyond her. It was too hot out.

She poured herself a glass of cold water and held it against her neck.

The phone rang on the little desk by the kitchen table. Dottie sighed as she waddled across the kitchen to answer it.

"Hello?"

"Dottie? It's Doug," a voice croaked through the phone to her.

Dottie paused. It had been a long time since she'd heard Doug's voice. A long time indeed. She could hear his age when he said his name. But then, they had both grown old, hadn't they?

"I know who it is. Supposin' you want to talk to Jack," Dottie said. She swore she'd never forgive him. A good Christian woman always kept her word.

"How are you?" The hesitation in his voice came through loud and clear. He wanted to talk to her. She sighed. It had been too long. Time didn't always heal old wounds.

"I'm fine, Doug. But then you know that, don't you? You spend enough time with my husband."

"He forgave me a long time ago. I was hopin' you'd do the same." Doug's voice was low.

"And what exactly would I be forgiving you for? For trying to take my husband's place in this house? For telling me he was dead? For taking on the role of father to my daughter? For trying to steal my heart?" Dottie swallowed the ache in her chest. No sense crying over spilled milk now. Took her and Jack too many years to try to patch up what Doug had wanted to break.

"That was a long time ago. Everything I did was with pure intentions. You know that. Don't be making it out to be more than it was. I don't recall you pushing me away either."

Dottie pulled the desk chair out and sat down. He was right. She didn't pull away. Doug was there for her when she was more alone than she'd thought possible when Jack had joined the army. She didn't like to think about that time. Alone, with a small child while her husband needed to do his duty as a man and shoot men he didn't know. She'd been weak. Alone and weak.

"You were his best friend." Dottie's voice cracked.

"I thought I was yours too."

Dottie shook her head, only to realize he couldn't see her.

"No, Doug. You were my husband's best friend. That was it. That's all you will ever be to me."

That section of her heart that she'd locked away all those years ago crumbled into fine dust at the words. Too many years had passed.

She hung up the phone without saying good-bye.

⚜

The creak of the old wood porch swing filled the air as Jack held a glass of iced tea in his hand. Sweat beads formed under his hat, trickling their way down his forehead, cheeks, and the back of his neck. He surveyed his world below and let out a contented sigh.

He took a swig of tea and wiped his mouth with the back of his hand. Nothing better than sitting in the shade on a hot day. The breeze cooled him down somewhat. It had to be cooler out here than it was inside the house. Why Dottie insisted on baking a loaf of bread and muffins on such a hot day was beyond him. He had offered to go into town and pick up some bread from the store, but she had balked at the idea. She was in a funny mood today.

Emmie's screams filled the front yard. Daisy must have splashed her again with water. He'd pulled the pool out of the garden shed after breakfast, given it a good rinse, and set it under the maple tree in the front yard. At least Emmie had one friend, even if it was a dog. Little girls need to laugh, giggle, and scream with delight every now and then. Maybe he'd pick her up a few more water toys next time he ran into town. Some of those containers of soap bubbles too. He liked to watch her twirl around on his grass with those wands.

The front screen door screeched on its hinge as Dottie pushed it open with her back. She carried the pitcher of iced tea in one hand and held glasses in the other.

"Here, let me take that." He set the iced tea down on the little table he'd made a few years back. The paint was chipped in spots and peeled in others. Time for a fresh coat. Another project to add to the list. One that grew no matter how hard he worked to shorten it. He'd like to meet the person who thought up the term *retirement*. There was nothing retiring about it.

"Did I hear the phone ring?" he asked.

Dottie stood at the porch steps with her back to him. Jack wasn't sure if she heard him or not.

"Girl sure does like that dog," she said. A faraway look had settled in her eyes when she turned.

Jack patted the cushion beside him. He waited until she was settled before he placed his arm around her shoulders and pulled her toward him. She leaned in with a sigh before she placed her head on his shoulder.

"Baking all done?" Jack pushed his feet against the floorboards and started a rocking motion with the swing.

"On the counter to cool."

Jack drew lazy circles on Dottie's arm with his fingers. He enjoyed the comfort, the security of this moment. He leaned his head back, closed his eyes, and smiled.

"Thanks for breakfast," Dottie said.

He heard the laughter in her voice. There was a reason why he didn't make breakfast that often. Emmie's yell might not have woken her up, but the smoke alarm sure did. She'd thrown on her housecoat and was still tightening the sash around her waist when she made it down the stairs. Emmie stood on a chair and waved a kitchen towel in the air, while Jack coughed as he stood over the stove trying to find a flipper to rescue the poor piece of french toast burning in the pan. Dottie poured a glass of water, handed it to Jack, and pushed him out of the way while she rescued breakfast, Emmie's squeals of laughter ringing in their ears.

"At least I tried," Jack mumbled. His face blazed red. If anything, that debacle should earn him brownie points for later on.

Emmie's laughter drifted along with the late morning breeze. A smile wreathed her face as she danced along the grass. When she reached the porch, she plopped down on the top step and waited for Daisy to catch up to her. Dottie pulled away from him to pour Emmie a glass of iced tea. Emmie gulped it down and drained every drop before handing it back.

"Thanks, Grandma. Can Daisy have some too?" A cheeky smile took place on her face as she waited for another glass.

"Your dog can drink out of that pool, thank-you-very-much. I'm not wasting my tea on any animal that would lap it up with her tongue." Dottie set the pitcher of tea back on the table and folded her arms.

"Like this?" Emmie stuck her tongue in her glass and tried to imitate her puppy.

Dottie scowled while Jack just laughed. He shooed her away before she could get into more trouble and pulled Dottie back in the swing until she rested back against his arm. Dottie shook her head.

"That girl . . ." she said.

Jack rubbed her arm. "Oh, leave her be. That puppy is her only playmate. She needs to be around other kids; having that dog as her only friend can't be all that good for her. What about when she goes off to school?"

Dottie's body stiffened in his arms. She pulled away from his body and sat up straight.

"Now, Dottie . . ." Jack said.

Dottie turned and looked at him, the fury evident from the darts her eyes shot at him. Back in the day, she used to be pretty good at darts. Guess she hasn't lost the eye for it.

"Don't you 'now, Dottie' me, Jack Henry! Are you telling me how to raise our granddaughter?" Dottie bristled under the imagined accusation.

If Jack didn't know better, he'd swear he saw steam coming out of her ears. He made it a point to keep his tone down, steady and calm, just like one would when about to corner a skittish colt. He patted her hand and didn't flinch when she moved it away. Instead, he grabbed her hand and entwined his fingers with hers. She jerked a bit but settled down when he wouldn't let go.

"All I'm sayin', Dottie-mine, is that our little girl is growing up and she needs other playmates than just two old biddies tinkering around the house. She'll head to school in another year and then what? That little girl is itchin' to spread her wings. She needs to find other girls to do the same."

Emmie pranced around the yard, in and out of the kiddie pool with Daisy following after her. His little angel. He smiled as he watched her and glanced at Dottie, sure she would be smiling too. Except she wasn't.

"Jack, I . . ." Dottie stopped, pursed her lips and wouldn't continue.

Jack waited, gave her space to compose her thoughts, but when he realized she wasn't going to budge, he decided to continue.

"The boys want to meet her too. I think Doug is a bit hurt that I haven't brought her around yet."

Dottie didn't look at him. The topic of Doug was one they tried to avoid. While it took years for Jack to forgive what happened, he knew Dottie would never forgive herself. Or Doug. When Jack returned from the war, he found out that Doug had taken his promise of watching over Dottie quite literally. He'd fallen in love with her. Jack knew he'd never recovered. It's why he was still single. His heart was already taken.

"Too bad for Doug," Dottie muttered. Jack bit his lip. Years of silence on the subject didn't mean it went away.

Emmie flopped herself down on the front lawn. Jack chuckled as he watched Daisy jump all over her.

"She's lonely, Dot," Jack said. "Don't you remember Mary at this age? Why, we couldn't keep her home long enough to brush her hair. And if she wasn't over at Jenna's house, then Jenna was here, badgering us."

The memories of the friendships they'd built over the years, the neighbors who'd lived next door through the course of their lives, and the friends Mary used to bring home filled his heart. He squeezed Dottie's hand, wanting to share the happiness with her, but her hand remained still. He sighed. And things had been looking on the bright side this morning.

"Mary was a little older than Emmie," Dottie whispered into the gentle summer breeze. Jack almost didn't hear her.

"How is Mary? Have you heard from her?"

He was desperate to hear about his daughter but squashed the pain in his heart down. Jack looked down and noticed Dottie's hand was white. He unlaced his fingers from hers and began to rub the circulation back. Dottie didn't notice, she just sat there, still; only the rise of her chest let him know she was still breathing.

"No."

"No? No, what?" Jack asked.

A deep sigh escaped out of Dottie's mouth. Her shoulders slumped as if the weight of that word, *no*, was too hard to bear.

"No, Jack, I haven't heard from Mary. She's dead to me, to us. She died the moment we got Emmie."

Jack turned and stared at her in shock. He didn't know the woman who sat beside him. *Dead to her? Our daughter?* Jack pulled his hand away from hers. He watched as her hand fell to the cushion, a dead weight.

"Emmie is all that matters now. Don't you understand? She's our second chance." Dottie's voice broke. Tears filled her eyes before trickled down her wrinkled cheeks.

Jack brushed them away with his thumb. He waited. This was the woman he knew and loved. Where she went moments ago he had no idea, but he'd do his best to ensure she never went back there.

A bee buzzed by the front porch and landed in the hanging baskets. Jack watched as it whisked its way through the flowers. Emmie's laughter echoed through the yard. He thought back to the days when Mary was a little girl. They didn't have a pool, but she loved to jump through the sprinkler.

"Okay. As long as she stays close by and doesn't go anywhere without one of us knowing." Dottie exhaled long and hard.

It hurt Jack's heart to know how tough that was for Dottie. For her to give up control. It shouldn't have been.

"Just the neighbor. We can go over and introduce ourselves, just like the old days. What do you say?"

Dottie angled her body until she faced Jack on the bench. He pushed his foot down so they stopped rocking. A pained look filled her eyes as she grabbed onto Jack's hands. Her grip surprised him. He felt her nails dig into the palm of his hand. He searched her face as he tried to understand the reason for the sudden desperation.

"I've already lost one daughter, Jack, I can't lose another. Emmie is all that matters. Jack, promise me. Promise me you won't lose her too," Dottie pleaded with him.

Jack was stunned into silence. *What is going on?*

With a flick of his wrist, Jack managed to loosen the grip Dottie held. He took her ice-cold hands into his and rubbed them. He swallowed, shaken by Dottie's words. Jack's perfect domain crumpled like a stack of cards. Emmie played in the pool, oblivious to the cracks in the facade of their perfect family. Jack took in the face of the woman who sat beside him. The face of the woman he didn't recognize. A sad smile settled on his lips and his voice cracked as he tried to echo the promise Dottie needed from him.

"I promise, Dottie-mine. I will do whatever it takes to keep the girls of my heart safe. I promise."

CHAPTER FOURTEEN

The house was quiet. Too quiet.

Dottie had coaxed Emmie into having a nap with her, which left Jack to fend for himself. He puttered around in the yard, dragged the pool to the backyard since he knew a certain little miss would want to splash in there later, and made himself a peanut butter sandwich.

Without thinking, he cut the crust off the bread and sat down to eat it at the kitchen table. It wasn't until he took a bite of the crustless sandwich that he realized what he'd done. Mary would only eat her sandwiches if the crust was off. It used to be a battle of wills between her and Dottie.

Jack set the sandwich back down on the plate. He missed his daughter. Emmie did a lot to fill that empty hole in his heart, but it wasn't enough. So many years had passed since he'd last spoken to her. Even more since he'd last seen her.

He pushed the plate away and walked into the front room. One wall was covered in framed pictures. Many of them were of Mary as a child. Jack stared at his favorite photo, taken on a summer day. Jack carried Mary on his shoulders, her smile wide as she clung to the sides of his head. He could still hear her laughter, how it rang out across the park. They'd been having a picnic. It was a good day.

He lifted the photo off its hook on the wall and carried it to the old desk by the back door. Dottie normally kept a little phone book there, but it was covered in pictures Emmie had drawn, receipts, and odd lists Dottie would make.

Jack pulled out the drawer and searched inside, pushing aside pens, pencils, and rulers, but didn't find the phone book. He pushed the drawer back in and grunted. Where was that phone book?

Jack walked back into the front room. Their old china cabinet sat against the wall. Sometimes Dottie kept papers in those drawers. He once found their wills shoved in there. That was at the beginning of this new phase with Dottie. Her forgetfulness. Now he never knew where to find things. Emmie called it Grandma's hide-and-seek game. Hide and seek, indeed.

Jack grumbled under his breath. Receipts from years ago cluttered the drawers. Seriously. He grabbed a wad and fingered through them before he tossed them in the trash can beside the cabinet. Why keep such senseless junk around? Dottie used to be so fastidious about stuff like this.

He spied Dottie's knitting bag. Hmmm, sometimes she hides things in there she didn't want Emmie to find. Jack crouched down and rifled through the bag. At the very bottom lay the phone book. He opened the tab that contained Mary's phone number, the only link to Mary they had. But it had been crossed out with black marker.

Jack scratched his head. Why would Dottie mark out Mary's phone number?

He tried to recall what the numbers were. He could barely make out a few of them, but not enough. He flipped through the book; they had to have the number of that place Mary would stay.

He glanced at the kitchen table where his crustless sandwich sat. What he was about to do felt taboo. Dottie was the go-between them and Mary, never Jack. Mary would take his money but not his calls. With a grumble under his breath, Jack ambled over to the desk in the kitchen, pulled out the stool, and sat down. If a father wanted to call his daughter, there was no reason why he shouldn't. No reason indeed.

He opened the book, found the number, and punched in the numbers. After the third ring, he was about to hang up. But someone answered.

"Martha Dover House, how can I help you today?" A soft, sweet voice answered the phone. Not what he expected from a halfway house located in the inner city of Seattle.

"Yeah, um, I'd like to speak to Mary Henry, please." Jack cleared his throat. He pulled out a pen from a jar on the desk and began to doodle on a pad of paper.

"Is she a resident, sir?"

Jack glanced behind him again. He should have just gotten Dottie to call.

"Sir?"

"A resident? She stays there off and on, I believe. Is she there now?" The way the sweet voice said the word *resident* made Jack feel like it was a hospital or something.

"I'm sorry, I don't recognize the name. May I place you on hold while I go through our files?"

Did they have a lot of residents? He remembered it being littered with druggies and messed-up kids, much like Mary, but were there too many to recognize his daughter's name? He'd been sending money there for years.

The first and only time he'd been to the Martha Dover House was after Mary ran away, at sixteen. He still carried the note she left him in his wallet.

Gone to live my own life. You'll always be my knight in shining armor, but I don't need to be rescued. I love you, Daddy. Love, your princess.

Jack didn't believe her. She was too young and had no idea what it meant to live your own life. Of course she needed to be rescued. That's what fathers did. Except she was nowhere to be found. He'd managed to trace her to the halfway house, but when he arrived in his pickup, she hadn't been seen for over a week.

He remembered thinking there was no way his daughter would be living at a halfway house, especially not among the unseemly crowd that loitered around the front yard. Mary had been raised differently, not like these kids. A little girl from a small lake town didn't do drugs. Or so he thought.

"Sir, I'm sorry for the delay. I found your daughter's file. I have Dr. Shepherd, our counselor here at Martha's House, who would like to speak to you about your daughter. May I transfer you?" The voice didn't sound so sweet anymore.

Even before he could reply, the elevator music came on. Jack groaned and swiped at his bald head. He just wanted to talk to his daughter, not some counselor.

The last time he had seen Mary was at a coffee shop. Dottie arranged for them to meet. She was supposed to have been there too, but bowed out last minute. Something about a hair appointment. Mary was livid when she saw him alone in the pickup. She almost left, turned her back on him, and walked down the sidewalk. She would have walked away without a backward glance too, if Jack hadn't called her name. When she turned, the greeting he'd been about to give caught in his throat.

That wasn't his daughter, it was just her shell. Gone was the vibrant little girl, so full of life and laughter. In her place stood a strung-out teenager, hair limp and tattered, her face shrunken and her body half its size. Her clothes hung on her, her girlish curves vanished. Dottie had warned him she was addicted to drugs, but he didn't believe her. Didn't want to.

"Come have a cup of coffee with me. It's been too long."

Jack begged Mary to spend time with him. He was her father. Her knight in shining armor. Why did she keep him at arm's length? All he wanted to do was pull her into his arms and never let her go.

He took a step toward her, but she stepped back, as if she couldn't bear to be seen close to him. Jack walked into the coffee shop and prayed that Mary would follow him. He didn't look behind him until he was at the counter and ordered his coffee and muffin. Mary ordered a hot chocolate and cookie before she turned away from him and walked to a table. Jack bought two cookies and plunked them down in front of his starving daughter.

She ate the first cookie in three bites before she even touched her hot chocolate. Jack drank in the sight of her face, her eyes, the shape of her nose, and waited to see if she would begrudge him a smile. She never did. He didn't know what to say, how to break the silence that stretched between them. The murmur of the other customers enhanced the awkwardness. Jack fiddled with his coffee mug while Mary stared at hers.

"Come home, Mary." He didn't realize he had voiced his thoughts until Mary's head popped up and she laughed. Jack winced at the bitterness emanating from his daughter.

"Home? Home to what, Dad? To make bread in the afternoons and knit countless baby hats for the hospital? To roam the streets of a small town where the only fun is getting dressed in pajamas and following some lame bagpipe band down Main Street on a Saturday night?" Mary leaned back in her chair and crossed her arms.

A twinge of pain plucked at his heart. He thought she liked doing that with him. It was their tradition, the Scottish Pipe Band Parade.

"I wanted a life, Dad." Mary spread her arms out. "It might not be the life you wanted for me, but it's my life. The one I chose." She hugged her body with her arms again. Jack wasn't sure if she was cold or defiant.

"It wasn't a bad life, princess. Was I really that bad? Did I make you run away?" Jack couldn't look in her eyes.

"It's Mom's life I ran away from, not yours." Jack lifted his head up, surprised at what she'd admitted.

"Then why won't you take my calls?"

Mary's head bowed and a tear trickled down her cheek. "Look at me, Dad. I'm not exactly that little girl you knew." Her fingers, nails bitten down except for her pinkie, drilled on the table.

"Come home." Jack knew she wouldn't, but he had to say it.

"No."

One small word—with the ability to shatter dreams.

Jack looked around the coffee shop. There was nothing unique about it. It looked like the same one in his town. Still, it felt colder, more hostile.

"Where are you staying?"

Mary shrugged. "Here and there. Mom calls the Martha House when she needs to get in touch. They'll give me the message when I'm around."

That night, when Jack sat with Dottie at their kitchen table, eating alone, he told her to include money in the monthly parcel she sent to Mary. Dottie refused. She wasn't going to supply Mary's drug habit. They agreed to send money to the halfway house instead.

When Dottie brought Emmie home, she said they didn't need to send any more money to Mary. He didn't ask any questions then, but he should have.

"Mr. Henry?" Jack dropped his pen. He looked about the kitchen. Still alone.

"Yes?"

"This is Dr. Shepherd. I'm sorry it took so long, but I was just going over your daughter's file. How can I help you, Mr. Henry?" The female doctor's voice sounded calm, soothing even. Too calm. Too smooth.

How can I help you? Didn't I make myself plain to the gal who answered the phone?

"I just want to speak with my daughter. Is she there?" Jack sat straight, determination filled his spirit.

Above him, a creak sounded. Footsteps pounded on the floor. Emmie was up. Jack glanced at the clock. He was out of time. The voice on the phone continued to speak but the words were mumbled. One word caught his attention, forced him to stand and stare at the stairway. He waited for Emmie to come down.

"I'm sorry? I don't think I heard you right."

"I'm sorry, Mr. Henry. But Mary . . ."

Emmie stood on the steps and rubbed her eyes with her fist. Her hair was all askew. Again. He listened to the woman on the phone, his shoulders tight as his world crashed around him. His vision blurred as dark circles swam before him. Jack grabbed hold of the chair, his knuckles white as he clenched it. Emmie stared at him, unaware of what was happening.

"Papa?"

"Mr. Henry? Sir, are you there?"

Jack pulled the phone away from his ear. His hand shook. He brought the phone back up to his ear.

"Um, thank you. Sorry to bother you. You have a good day now."

"Mr. Henry, did you hear me? Mr. Henry . . ." Jack placed the phone back on the receiver. His chest felt tight. He tried to take a deep breath, but a shallow one was all he could muster. He slowly sat back down in the chair. The sun still shone. The bees still buzzed around the flowers he'd placed in the window planter. All was right with his world, but him. Tiny footsteps echoed against the kitchen floor. Jack turned and stared at his precious granddaughter.

"Papa?"

Jack reached out his arms and waited for Emmie to throw herself into them. The split-second it took her to do so felt like years. Two years, to be exact. If Jack had known two years ago that bringing Emmie home would destroy his heart, he never would have let Dottie go and fetch her alone.

Never. He would forever regret that he did.

CHAPTER FIFTEEN

Megan blew a wisp of hair out of her face as she jogged home. Sweat dripped down her face with each jolt on the pavement. She preferred to run in the early morning, when the sun began its climb and it wasn't so hot out. But she'd slept in. When she called Laurie to join her, her best friend just laughed. By the time she managed to step out her door, it was after nine o'clock.

She jogged in place at a crosswalk while cars whizzed by. Her house was just down the street. Her side had begun to pinch about a mile back. She'd taken a long route this morning, headed down to the beach, along the boardwalk, and then ran down to the pier before she headed back.

A black Chrysler Sebring drove past, slowed, and pulled into her driveway. Her palms tingled when she recognized the car. She slowed her jog down to a walk and attempted to control her breathing as she neared her walkway. Why today, of all days, did he have to come?

Detective Riley leaned against his car, his white dress shirt a stark contrast to the sheen of his black car. Megan's breath caught in her throat. She wanted to look away, to not stare, but she couldn't.

She rubbed her sweaty palms on her jogging pants and placed a smile on her face.

"Detective Riley, this is a surprise."

"Megan." He took a step toward her and held the file folder up for her to see. "I have those sketches I mentioned on the phone yesterday."

Megan let out her breath. She fixed her eyes on the file, hungry for a look at her daughter. She held out her hand for the folder.

"Is this a bad time?"

"Not at all." Megan shook her head, unable to take her eyes off the file. Not until he placed the file in her hand did she raise her head. She met his green eyes; saw his understanding that she needed to hold the photo in her hands.

"May I come in? I won't take up much of your time. I'd like to go over the pictures with you, if that's okay."

Megan looked toward her house. If Peter found out . . . but she couldn't say no. She glanced down at her clothes, at the damp spots on her shirt from her run. *Why did I have to sleep in?*

"Of course. I just need to . . ."—she gestured with her free hand toward her clothing—"and then I'll put on a pot of coffee."

She walked past him, unlocked her front door, and waited for him to join her. Once he had entered the house, she ran upstairs and called down to him over her shoulder.

"Just give me a minute. Make yourself comfortable."

A nervous flutter took root in her stomach. She yanked her top off and then pulled off her running pants. She glanced at the clock. Her pulse raced. She tried to convince herself that it was the thought of seeing Emma's picture, of what she would look like now, that caused it.

Her new sundress, the one Peter had just bought her, hung on the back of the bedroom door. She pulled it on and ran her hands over the dress to smooth out the wrinkles. She yanked the elastic out of her ponytail and took a good look at herself in the mirror.

Her eyes sparkled. She looked at her dress, marveled at how well it fit over her hips. She shrugged her right shoulder. *I was going to wear it anyway. It's not as if I'm wearing it for Riley.* Megan shook her head. *Detective Riley, Megan. It's Detective Riley.*

The aroma of fresh-brewed coffee met Megan as she neared the bottom of the stairs. Detective Riley was bent over the table, his arm outstretched as he placed the sketches of Emma on the table for her to view. He looked up as she stood in the doorway.

"I went ahead and made coffee. I hope you don't mind."

Megan thought back to the days when Emma had first gone missing. Riley had become a fixture in their house. This wasn't the first pot of coffee he'd made here.

"Of course not . . ."

She headed to the table and stared at the images of her daughter. Her hands shook as she gripped the chair in front of her. Detective Riley walked toward her. She kept her gaze directed to the table, until his hand rested beside hers on the chair. She looked up at him, his gaze gentle.

Megan swallowed. She took a step backward, and lifted her hand off the chair.

"How is the walking program going?"

Megan knew his attempt at small talk was to put her at ease. She wasn't sure it worked.

"I have a meeting this week to finalize the program at a new school. That makes three in total. It's been slow, but the program is expanding." Megan bit her lip at the thought of the frustrating months of attending unending meetings with the school boards. You'd think they would jump at the opportunity to protect the children in their care.

"Good, good. What about those other meetings? The family support ones. Are you still going?"

Megan glanced up in surprise.

"I do. Not every week anymore, but I do go." It hurt to go.

Earlier on, when Emma had first gone missing, Megan couldn't attend enough of the small group meetings. To be in a place with other parents who understood what she was dealing with soothed her heart. There were no sympathy glances, no awkward silences. But as time passed and families she knew experienced reconciliation or closure, as tragic as that was, Megan felt alone. She knew that she needed to move on, to move forward and to do more than just attend meetings to talk about how to cope. Megan needed to do something. So, she started the Safe Walks program.

Detective Riley nodded and pointed.

"Why don't you sit down and I'll explain the process of these pictures to you."

Megan's face burned red as he pulled the chair out for her. She shook her head, sidestepped the table, and headed toward the coffeemaker instead. *Seriously, Megan, you need to calm down.* She grabbed the counter with both hands, closed her eyes, and counted to five. Slowly.

"Let me pour the coffee first. Still like yours black?" She pulled two mugs out of the cupboard and poured. Coffee splashed over the counter. She set the pot back in the machine, took another breath, and placed his mug on the island. She hated herself for remembering how he liked his.

"Here you go," she said as she faced the fridge and opened it. She grabbed her creamer, fixed her coffee, and headed back to the table. All the while refusing to look at the man who filled her kitchen with his presence.

Megan grabbed one of the pictures and studied it. *So, this is how Emma looks today.* Her curly hair in a cute, chin-length bob. A pink ribbon tied in a bow in her hair. Big blue eyes sparkling with life; dimples even more pronounced. She didn't look like the two-year-old Megan had known and loved. This was a little girl ready to enter kindergarten. A soft smile settled on her lips. *This is my baby.* She laid the picture back down on the table and reached for another one when a hand stopped her.

"Let me explain the pictures first. There is a forensic artist who works with police departments all across North America. What she does is provide sketches of suspects and missing persons. She's very talented and has been doing this for years. I heard she was in Seattle for a few weeks working on a case, so I contacted her and asked if she could create some age-progressed sketches of Emma for us."

"What's her name?"

Megan placed her fingers on the photo of Emma with the pink bow. With her index finger, she caressed the image.

"Elena Stokov."

"She's very good." Megan never altered her gaze. This was the only image she had of her daughter as she was now. Happy. Older. Alive.

Detective Riley pointed to the picture she held in her hand. "The picture you're holding is how Emma would look today if she were here at home or with someone who was taking good care of her."

Megan couldn't read the expression on his face. She placed the photo back down on the table and picked up another.

"And this?"

The picture in her hand didn't look like Emma. The face in the picture was narrow, her cheekbones protruded out, and her eyes were a dull blue. The stringy hair was past the child's shoulders, the curls nonexistent.

Tears welled up in Megan's eyes as she stared at this picture. She prayed to God that Emma didn't look like this. Not like this.

"If Emma were being held captive somewhere and being mistreated, this is how we believe she would look." He reached across the table and placed his hand on hers. "I'm sorry."

Megan forced herself to keep hold of the picture. It was a reality she never wanted to comprehend. Not with Emma. She would rather her daughter be dead than held captive by a monster who hurt her. She memorized the picture, took in every detail as a deep anger bubbled up inside of her.

"This isn't Emma." The harsh sound of her voice shocked her.

She placed the picture back on the table. Everything in her screamed to rip up the picture, to demand that it could never be real, that it wasn't Emma. But she knew better. Two years of silence, of imagining the worst and praying it would never come true.

She picked up the last image and gasped.

"Who is this?" Her voice choked on the words.

Detective Riley cleared his throat. He opened a file and sorted through the papers.

"Riley, who is this child?" Megan held the photo out in front of her.

"In some reported cases, a child's image is altered to avoid detection. If this happened in Emma's case, it's possible that she is being made to look like a boy. As in the photo, her hair would be cut short, she would wear boys' clothing and be treated like a boy. A form of disassociation for the captors. Making her look and act like a boy would deflect attention. I'm sorry to say that this happens quite a bit with kidnappings."

Megan stared in horror. Her daughter would look like a boy?

She picked up the photo again. Megan drew curls with her finger along the cropped hair line, imagined the dimples in the cheeks and the sparkle in the eye. She grabbed the first photo she had looked at and held them side by side. Her hands shook with rage as she compared them.

The front door opened. Heavy treads filled the entryway. Megan winced when the door slammed shut. Before she could say a word, Peter appeared. His eyes danced from Megan to Riley and back to Megan. She knew what he was thinking. She could read it in his eyes.

Megan closed her eyes. Peter. She could have kicked herself. After last night, she should have respected Peter more. She should have called him while she was upstairs getting dressed. Better yet, she should never have invited Riley in.

She turned her face and waited for him to enter the room. Her breath caught in her throat when he did. His eyes, cold with fury, met hers. The tic in his cheek stood out against the red flush on his face. His lips pursed together before he dropped his briefcase on the floor.

"What's going on here?"

Megan didn't say a word. She couldn't. She stared at the photos in her hands instead.

Out of the corner of her eye, she saw Detective Riley stand. *Fantastic.* Her husband stood at one end of the table while Riley stood at the other. And she sat in the middle. As usual.

"Mr. Taylor, I'm glad you're here. I wanted to show you some age-progressed sketches of Emma that a leading forensic artist created."

Megan looked from Peter to the detective. Peter's gaze had dropped to the table. She followed his gaze and noticed he was looking at the picture of Emma, the one that illustrated what she would like if she was being mistreated. She looked back to his face. Anguish filled his eyes.

She held out the photo of Emma with a smile on her face.

"Peter, this one."

Her voice was low, laden with the tears that continued to fall. She waited for him to look up. When he did, he reached across to where she sat and took hold of the paper, wrenching it from her grasp.

"Why are they so different?" Peter's eyes jumped from one picture to the other. Megan could almost read the thoughts tumbling through his mind. The same as hers.

As Riley explained the sketches to Peter, Megan took a sip of her coffee. She wished she could block out the words and the pictures. She wished she could press rewind and start the day over.

Better yet, rewind all the way back to the day Emma walked out the front door. She'd make sure the door was locked. She'd make the girls go around to the back of the house. Maybe she'd take them out for ice cream instead of having a picnic in the yard. She wished. . . . She wished wishes could come true, that the past could be erased. But wishes were only disillusions, places to wander in the mind when reality proved unfaithful.

"So, why the pictures? Why did you need to bring them over? Why couldn't this have waited until tonight when we were both home?"

Megan winced at the sharpness of Peter's voice. *Nice one.* Nothing like airing dirty laundry. She bit her lip to keep from saying anything.

"You're right. I should have waited until tonight." Detective Riley held his hands out before him, palms toward Peter.

"My mistake. I wanted to show you the pictures and explain them before they were distributed. The missing children's website has been updated with Emma's new sketches, and her image will appear in the flyers sent out in the next few days."

"Which picture will they use?" Megan glanced at the picture in Peter's hand before she looked back at the detective. When he nodded, she breathed a sigh of relief.

"So, why the need for the other pictures?" Peter cleared his throat as he pulled the chair out and sank down in it. His shoulders sank beneath the heavy weight they shouldered.

"Just in case," Megan said as she reached across and took hold of Peter's hand. She squeezed and waited for Peter to look at her before she voiced the question that hung in the air.

"Is my daughter still alive?" Megan turned her head to look at Riley. He shook his head.

"There have been no sightings in over a year. We haven't given up hope and we won't stop looking for her, but at this point, there's not much we can do. We'll continue to update her age-progressed sketches and make sure her picture is out there. But until someone comes forward with information, our hands are tied."

"So, you think she's dead then. Is that what you're saying? You've given up?"

Detective Riley tidied up some papers in the folder in front of him.

"I'm sorry. My hands are tied."

⚜

The front door closed with a thud. Peter rose from the table, stomped to his study, and slammed the door behind him.

Megan grabbed her coffee and rose from the table. The sketches of her daughter lay on the table. She wanted to hide two of the sketches. Wanted to ignore them, pretend they didn't exist, but she couldn't do that. What she could do, though, was put them away so the girls wouldn't find them.

She knocked on the study door and turned the knob. Peter stood at the window, staring out into the street. She crossed the room and opened a drawer in the filing cabinet that stood against the wall. She flipped through the files until she found the one she wanted. Pictures. She dropped the sketches of Emma in there. The drawer was full of folders, all regarding Emma's kidnapping. Articles in the paper, statistics about kidnapped children, letters from strangers who were praying. Until she found her daughter, she would keep these items.

Peter looked different to her. As if something was missing, but she couldn't put her finger on what it was. Maybe it was the grey in his hair, of the slant in his shoulders. Maybe it was the added lines on his face, or the frown that showed up more often than not. Whatever it was, she didn't like it.

She stood at the window beside him and looked out onto their street. Their neighbor was outside working in her garden. Her youngest, only three years old, chased after a butterfly. A soft smile settled on Peter's face as he watched the little boy toddle around the yard, arms waving in the air. Megan touched the sleeve of Peter's shirt, tentative, but he jerked his arm out of her reach.

"You promised me."

"I know." Megan bowed her head and studied the carpet at her feet.

"So, now what?"

Megan raised her head. She hadn't expected the harsh tone in his voice.

"What do you mean, so now what?"

Peter turned his head and stared at her. The cold fury in his eyes made her stomach flip until it was in knots.

"Did anything happen before I interrupted you?"

"Are you kidding me?" Megan gasped. She turned and looked out the window. Her jaw clenched while she dug her fingernails into the palms of her hands.

He grabbed her arm, his fingers dug into her skin. "You think I'm being unreasonable?" he spat into her face.

She wrenched her arm out of his grasp. "Yes!"

"So, explain this." Peter swept his hand up and down Megan's body.

She looked down. The dress. The damned dress. She closed her eyes, counted to five in her head, with slow precision before she was calm enough to speak to him. She rubbed her arm where he grabbed her. When she looked back at him, he'd taken a step back and crossed his arms.

"You think I dressed up for him? Seriously, Peter! Give me some credit. This"—Megan grabbed the hem of her dress and held it out—"was for you, you stupid fool. I thought I'd surprise you at your office again and see if you wanted to do lunch. Surprise!" Megan threw her hands in the air before she turned and paced across the room.

"I can't believe you would think otherwise." Megan shook her head, her body rigid with tension.

Peter shook his head and headed to his desk. He sat down in his chair with a loud sigh and leaned back.

"What else am I supposed to think, Meg? I come home to find that man in my house with you. Alone. In the dress I bought you. A dress you've never worn until today." He crossed his arms and his head fell back. "Why didn't you call me or tell him it wasn't a good time? How do you think I felt when I came home and saw his car in my driveway?"

Megan grabbed the back of the leather chair that sat in front of Peter's desk.

"Oh, I don't know, trust your wife maybe? That might be a good idea." Even when she knew he shouldn't.

Peter leaned forward in his chair and rested his elbows on his desk. "I never said I didn't trust you."

"Really? 'Cause it sure sounded like it." Her knuckles tightened on the chair.

Peter shook his head. "You're not listening to me, Meg."

Megan turned away from him. She'd listened to enough.

Once her hand gripped the door handle, she turned.

"No, I heard you. I broke another promise. One that you needed me to keep in order for your little world to remain on its axis. Sorry to burst your bubble, Peter, but life isn't fair. The sketches you saw of Emma today should prove that to you." Megan yanked the door open.

"I don't know how much more I can take, Megan."

Already in the hall, Megan half-turned back to the door. She heard the defeat in his voice. But there was nothing she could do about it. He expected more from her than she had to give.

"You don't know how much you can take? Get real, Peter. I'm not the only one here who's wrecked our marriage. It takes two, remember?"

CHAPTER SIXTEEN

A bowl of fish crackers spilled all over the floor. Sherri sighed. She had just finished vacuuming this morning. *Are you kidding me?* David, the culprit with the angel smile on his face, swung his scrawny little legs over the edge of the couch as he stared at her.

"Are you going to clean that up?"

David shrugged his shoulders. A mischievous glint appeared in his eyes. *Oh, no you don't.* Sherri tapped her foot and glared at him.

David a four-year-old angel, according to his mother, stuck his tongue out at her.

She closed her eyes, counted to ten, and crouched before him.

"You know, David, I had to have a talk with your mom about the fight between you and Travis, remember? Do you remember what we said would happen if you continue to ignore the house rules?"

He bit his lip. "Mommy won't take me to the baseball game."

Sherri picked up a fish off the floor. "Are you going to let a couple of spilled crackers take that away from you?"

He shook his head.

"So, how about you help me clean this up, okay?"

Sherri fought hard to keep a grin off her face. He'd been talking about this baseball game nonstop all week.

David jumped off the couch and crawled around on the floor picking up the loose fish crackers. Sherri grabbed a few and pretended they were going to nibble on his arm. Amid David's squeals, the doorbell rang.

Tonya and Sarah both rushed into the living room. Sarah's arms were flailing in the air at the noise while Tonya tried to grab hold of her. Tears streamed down Sarah's cheeks before she clamped her hands over both ears.

Sherri rushed over to the door and jerked it open. She'd forgotten to place the sign on the door to not ring the doorbell.

She expected to see the day-care procedure advisor on the other side of her screen. Not her elderly neighbors.

The screaming stopped. But a shouting melee occurred instead. Sherri wasn't sure which deafening noise she preferred. She turned her head and her jaw dropped. Travis, the little stinker, had decided to crush the fish crackers David was playing with on the carpet. Tonya, bless her heart, had her arms wrapped around Sarah who shouted, "My friend! My friend!"

Sherri knew her face was beaming bright red. "I'm so sorry about this. Please, come in."

Emmie tiptoed into the room, her eyes wide with wonder at the symphony of noise that filled the house. The grandparents were a bit more hesitant. Her grandfather placed his hand on his wife's back and murmured something she couldn't hear.

Sherri almost apologized again for the noise, but stopped as Dorothy took a step toward her.

"Is now a good time?" The older woman scanned the room. Her lips pursed when she noticed the fight happening between Travis and David.

Great. Just great.

"Absolutely," Sherri lied. "Don't worry about this." She motioned to the kids. "I was about to send them outside."

"Why don't we join you?"

Sherri twisted to look at Emma's grandfather. If there was ever a man who embodied the look of a grandpa, it was this man. She couldn't help but smile. A wide grin covered his wrinkled face, a pink glow reflected off of his bald head, and his coveralls conveyed a relaxed attitude.

She reached out and grabbed his extended hand. She laughed as her hand disappeared inside of his and he shook it. Her arm rattled with the up/down motion.

"I'm Jack, Emmie's Grandpa, and you've of course met my wife, Dottie."

"Nice to meet you, Jack. I'm Sherri. Welcome to my zoo."

She breathed a sigh of relief when she noticed a tease of a smile on Dottie's face. She wanted this woman to like her.

"My friend!" Sarah struggled to escape the confines of her sister's arms.

Emmie ran over to her. Sarah grabbed Emmie in a bear hug and squeezed until they were both red in the face. The girls laughed together. Sherri loved how quickly Sarah was able to make friends. The girls, hand in hand, skipped out of the living room. Tonya followed after them.

Sherri's attention turned toward David and Travis. By now, they were arm wrestling on the coffee table. Jack had moved from the doorway and stood in front of the boys. When the boys realized they were being watched, they looked up in unison. Their mouths gaped open as they took in the big bear of a man. Travis slowly rose and wiped the crumbs off his legs before he stuck his thumb in his mouth. Sherri shook her head. David stuck his hand out and waited for Jack to take it.

"Wanna arm wrestle?"

Sherri bit her lip but couldn't keep the smile off her face. Only David, with his scrawny arms, would suggest an arm wrestle with a man three times his size.

"Real men don't wrestle in garbage, son."

Sherri could have hugged him right then and there. Instead, she placed her hand on the side of Dottie's arm.

"It's a beautiful day. I made some fresh sun tea. Shall we take it outside?"

Dottie wouldn't budge. Her frozen face carried a lopsided smile while she would look only at her husband. Her arm moved under Sherri's until there was a space a hair's width between them.

"Well now, that sounds like an offer too good to refuse." A jovial smile settled across Jack's face as he took Dottie's hand in his.

Sherri led them out through the kitchen to the sliding doors that led to their patio. She made sure they were settled in the wicker chairs before she hurried back indoors to fetch the iced tea and glasses. She felt the glass container. It was cold. *Thank you, Jesus.*

She poured them all a glass while an awkward silence settled between them. Dottie kept her gaze focused on Emmie, who pumped her legs with vigor beside Sarah, whose legs dangled on the swings. Coordination never came easy to Sarah on the swing.

A little girl ran up to Sherri with a bouquet of weeds in one fist.

"Is that your daughter?" Dottie's attention finally left Emmie.

Sherri smiled as she took the flowers from her daughter's hand. Her long, golden straight hair hung down to her waist, while her baby-blue eyes sparkled.

"Yes, it is." She touched her daughter's jaw with one finger and tilted it up so she looked into her eyes.

"Marie, these are Emmie's grandparents. Can you say hi, please?"

Marie's tiny fingers moved in a quick motion before she grabbed hold of the bottom of her summer dress and curtsied. Her eyes twinkled with merriment before she skipped away to join the girls at the swings. First Sarah jumped off her swing, followed by Emmie. Sherri held her breath, but soon realized it was a silly thing to do. Both Emmie and Sarah grabbed onto Marie's outstretched hands. Not until she watched the three girls skip together toward a hill covered in dandelions did she look at her guests.

Dottie's brow furrowed as she frowned, but Jack's face looked like it had melted.

"Your daughter is deaf?"

She smiled. Out of the two, she figured he would be the one to ask.

"Partially. She was born premature and has a 70 percent hearing loss. She can read lips and hear certain sounds, but for the most part, unless she's really comfortable with people, she'll use sign language."

"She seems happy." Dottie's face gentled at Sherri's words.

"She is. She's my little bundle of joy. I think she and Emmie could be good friends."

Dottie's lips pursed. Jack placed his hand on Dottie's arm before he turned toward Sherri.

"Having a playmate will be good for Emmie. Thanks." Dottie's hands fisted together at his words.

For the next fifteen minutes or so, Sherri struggled to make small talk with her neighbors. She knew Dottie felt uncomfortable. The way her back remained straight as a rod in the chair, the way she took tiny sips from the glass and rarely looked Sherri in the eye despite the younger woman's repeated attempts to draw her into the conversation. Dottie's focus was on her granddaughter.

In contrast to his standoffish wife, Jack was a pure gentleman. He asked about the day care and the children. He even asked after her husband. His eyes brightened when she mentioned where Matt worked. Men and their toys, or trucks, for that matter.

"I think we need to leave now." Dottie bolted out of her chair.

"Emmie," she called out, her voice tight.

"Now, Dottie." Jack pushed himself up out of the chair. "We just . . ."

"No, Jack, I want to go. Thank you for the iced tea, Sherri. Sorry we popped over uninvited."

Dottie marched across the lawn toward the girls. Emmie ran to Dottie, who then grabbed her hand and pulled her back toward the house. Sherri wanted to say something, but the look on Jack's face stopped her.

"Thanks for the iced tea. We'll have you over next time to taste some of Dottie's home-baked cookies." Jack shrugged his shoulders as he watched his wife storm back to him. She didn't even look at Sherri as she headed to the walkway at the side of Sherri's house. Jack nodded at her but then followed his wife.

Sherri sank down in her chair, befuddled at what just happened. So much for the woman liking her.

CHAPTER SEVENTEEN

And we picked pretty flowers and made chains from them. Just like Daisy and I do. It was so much fun!" Emmie chattered away at the kitchen table while she played with the peas on her plate.

Jack chuckled. His granddaughter's enthusiasm was contagious. For him at least. Dottie, on the other hand, just glowered at the opposite end of the table. Jack ignored her. She was in a mood. Had been since they left their neighbors' house so rudely. It was so unlike Dottie that Jack questioned her once they arrived at the house, but Dottie would only slam her pots around in the cupboards until he escaped outside.

"And she looks like my sister too. Isn't that funny, Papa?" Emmie continued to push her peas around her plate. "I think it's funny."

"Is that right?" Jack continued to stare at Dottie, and merely placated Emmie, until he noticed the look in Dottie's eyes. They were wide. With fear.

"Yep. And Papa, you know what?"

"No, Emmie. What?" He glanced at Emmie. Her eyes were wide too. With joy.

A fork rattled against a plate. Dottie placed her fork down, picked up her napkin, dabbed her mouth with the linen, and placed it down on the plate. A plate full of uneaten food. *What is going on? Did Dottie forget to take her medication today?*

"She's just as nice as my sister too! Isn't that great? I wish my sister could meet her. Then we'd all be friends!" Emmie flung her arms up in exuberance.

"Sister? What sister?" Jack shook his head. He must have missed something.

"My friend's sister. She's so nice!" Emmie forked a helping of shepherd's pie into her mouth.

"Well, that's nice now, isn't it?"

Jack had no idea what she was talking about, but figured that she'd chatter away enough for him to figure it out. At least Emmie had friends now. At least something good had come out of the awkward visit.

"Well, wife, you made another fine meal." Jack patted his stomach and winked. Dottie glared back at him. She grabbed her plate, pushed her chair back, and stood. *Now what?*

He followed Dottie to the sink. He laid his plate on the counter and placed his hand over hers as she reached to turn on the sink taps. She shrugged his hand off.

"Don't you think that would be cool, Papa?"

Jack stared at Dottie and struggled to read her eyes, but they remained shuttered, closed to him. He sighed, his shoulders deflated as he accepted defeat and turned back to Emmie.

"What's that, princess?"

"If they could meet?"

Emmie's voice sang with happiness. Jack closed his eyes. In all his years, he'd never mastered the language of women. Never would either.

"If who could meet?" Jack started to worry. Dottie's lips were pursed so tight he could see the individual white lines and her chin wavered.

Emmie turned in her chair and sat on her knees. Her hands gripped the top of the wood. She shrugged her shoulders and sighed.

"Papa, you weren't listening! My sister and . . ."

Dottie whirled around, her body quivered as she pointed a finger at Emmie.

"That's enough! I knew letting you play with those strange children was wrong. I knew it."

She turned to face Jack and jabbed her finger into his chest.

"I told you it was wrong, but you insisted. Now look. She's lying. She never used to lie to us. Our Mary never lied!"

Tears welled up in Emmie's eyes before they streamed down her cheeks.

"But, but, Grandma, I'm not lying! I promise!"

"Now, Dottie . . ." Jack knew if he didn't intervene now, things would get nasty.

Dottie jabbed him again. This time he winced.

"Don't. Don't, Jack. I won't put up with these lies." She turned her back to him. "Go. Up those stairs, little girl. I don't put up with liars. You can spend the rest of the night in your room." She pointed toward the stairs. "Go!"

Jack's heart almost broke when Emmie's gaze turned to him. She pleaded with him, but he only shook his head. Tonight was not the night to fight Dottie. He jerked his head toward the stairs.

With her head tucked almost to her chin, Emmie climbed down from her chair. Her body folded into itself and her arms dangled at her sides as she trudged to the stairway. She stopped, lifted her head, and looked at Jack. He smiled at her. Her lips protruded into the largest pout he'd ever seen on her. She lowered her head and lifted one foot to rest on the first step.

Jack glanced out of the corner of his eye to make sure Dottie wasn't looking. He took a small step toward Emmie, but Dottie's voice stopped him cold.

"Don't. She needs to learn, Jack."

Emmie climbed the stairs. She sniffled with each step. Jack turned away from Dottie. He waited until he heard Emmie's bedroom door close before he turned to his wife. As he was about to barrage her with questions, the tears in her eyes silenced any words he wanted to say.

"Sisters," Dottie muttered under her breath. "Why would she think about sisters now?"

Jack's body stilled, frozen in silent horror. Dottie never looked at him. It was as if she forgot he stood right beside her, close enough to hear her thoughts. He wanted to beg her to look at him, to stop thinking out loud, but he couldn't. The next words out of Dottie's mouth robbed Jack blind.

"I never thought she had sisters."

⚜

Dottie's body quivered. Her hands gripped the bottom edge of the kitchen counter until they were white. It had been over two years, why would she talk about sisters now?

With slow precision, Dottie released one hand at a time from the counter and turned on the taps to the sink. She grabbed each plate, fork, and cup, one at a time, until the sudsy water covered the dishes.

She tried to remember the day she brought Emmie home with her. It was all a blank. She couldn't remember the drive into the city. She couldn't even recall seeing her daughter. When was the last time she remembered seeing her daughter? Why couldn't she remember?

The only memory she had of that day was the feel of her grand-daughter's hand inside her own, the tight grip as they walked into the house together.

A sob welled up within Dottie's body. She sucked in her breath and held it. It didn't matter, though, the sob tore through her body until it caved in upon itself. Did Mary have other children she never knew about?

Dottie collapsed—any strength her body held was gone with that thought. Jack's strong arms caught her before she hit the ground. She rested her head against his chest as she gave in to the pain that flowed through her body.

Why couldn't she remember? Why did the memory of seeing her daughter for the last time escape her? Her head pounded as the questions swirled through her mind.

"Dottie?"

Jack's eyes stared down at her. She struggled to stand. Jack's arms tightened around her before he pulled her up. She leaned against the counter and closed her eyes. A pounding pain settled right behind her left eye.

"Dottie? Are there sisters?" There was hesitation in Jack's voice.

She shook her head. She didn't want to talk about it. Not with him. Not now.

"She shouldn't be lying, Jack. Mary would never lie to us. Why is she now?" She couldn't look him in the eye. She concentrated on the dishes instead.

"She's not Mary. She's a little girl with an active imagination. Sending her to her room was wrong." Dottie's body sagged when Jack walked away from her.

"I know who she is." A dish clattered in the sink as it slipped between her fingers.

"I think you should let her come out of her room."

Dottie whirled around; the dishcloth dripped water onto the floor. "Don't you dare tell me how to raise that little girl."

She bent down and wiped up the water that pooled by her feet. She didn't understand her anger. Jack was right. She'd overreacted and she knew it.

"I just think you're being too harsh with her, that's all." Jack shrugged his shoulders. He gathered the plates and cutlery off the table and brought them over to her.

Dottie sighed. "That's because she's your princess. I know what I'm doing, Jack. We can't have Mary lying to us. If we stop her now, then the past won't be repeated."

"Emmie."

The pounding in Dottie's head intensified. Her eyes hurt. Jack's hands rested on Dottie's shoulders. She groaned and dropped her head forward as his fingers massaged the knots.

"Who?" The pounding increased, until a dull roar filled her ears.

"Our granddaughter."

Dottie rolled her head as the pressure of Jack's fingers did wonders. She didn't feel as tight in the neck as she did earlier. Now only if this headache would go away.

"I don't understand, Jack. Mary never had a daughter."

An intense, shooting pain exploded behind Dottie's eyes. She cried out as her body bent forward. Jack's arms encircled her. He took her hand and led her out of the kitchen. He muttered something under his breath, but she couldn't make it out.

With his hand on her back, he helped her walk up the stairs and into their bedroom. She sank on their bed. Her feet lifted and she rested her head on her pillow. It felt good, so good to lay her head down. A thought nagged at her; she was missing something, but she couldn't remember what.

But she knew it had to do with Mary.

CHAPTER EIGHTEEN

A small box lay on the mat at Megan's front door. A brown box with a chocolate satin bow. She picked it up. It was light. The delicate scent drifted from the box. She brought it closer to her nose. *Hmmm, chocolate.*

Inside the house, she kicked off her shoes and headed to the kitchen. She had an hour before she had to pick up the girls. After their argument this morning, Peter had rushed out. She tried calling him all afternoon but he never answered. When he didn't bother to show up for dinner, Megan knew he wouldn't be coming home.

She seethed the more she thought about it. He knew tonight was a busy night. They both needed to be on duty. Alexis had soccer practice at the same time Hannah needed to be at the pool for her swimming lessons. So, she dropped Hannah off early at the arena before she took Alexis to the soccer field. Alexis didn't want her to stay and watch, so instead of heading to the pool, she had come home to see if Peter had shown up at the house while they were gone.

He hadn't.

But there was this small package for her at the door. A tiny sliver of hope settled in her heart. Maybe Peter wanted to surprise her. Maybe this was his way of saying sorry.

She positioned the box on the counter and opened the envelope attached to the front. She smiled as she pulled the card out. It was a picture of a girl diving into a box of chocolates. It wasn't from Peter. But she had an idea who it was from. The handwriting in the card proved it.

When life hands you a box of chocolates, I say we just dive right in! xoxo Laurie.

She smiled and reached for the phone. It was answered after the first ring.

"Did you open it yet?" Laurie asked.

"No, but I love the card. You're a sweetie." Megan tucked the phone between her shoulder and ear. She untied the ribbon and lifted the lid.

"So, open it, will you?" Excitement laced Laurie's voice.

With the box open, Megan laughed. Laurie had given her a box of chocolates to go with the card. Except half of the chocolates were gone.

"So, that's where the 'we just dive in' part takes place, huh?" Megan couldn't stop smiling.

"Well, you weren't home when I dropped it off. Plus, I know you; if I didn't take some now, there'd be none left for later, so . . ."

"So, you helped yourself." Megan picked up a delectable square piece and bit into it. *Mmm, caramel.* Her eyes closed as she savored the creamy flavor.

"Oh. My . . ." She sighed into the phone.

"Good, huh?"

"Mmmm. . ." Megan shoved the rest of the chocolate piece into her mouth.

"Like I'd buy you, the ultimate chocoholic, anything less than the best."

Megan looked through the rest of the chocolates. "You have no idea how much I needed this."

"Bad day?"

"You could say that. Peter came home to find Detective Riley here." Megan grabbed another chocolate and headed out to the back porch.

"Uh-oh."

Megan sat down in one of the deck chairs. She leaned her head back and closed her eyes.

"He accused me of having an affair." Her shoulders slumped.

"Talk about the pot calling the kettle black. You're kidding me, right? Did he actually say that?" The shock in Laurie's voice was quite evident.

"No." Megan shook her head. She thought back over the words flung between them this morning. She wasn't sure if she'd ever be able to forget.

"I'm not sure where we'll go from here. We're at rock bottom. I think instead of heading up, we're just running parallel. Opposite ways. Alone."

She knew she should probably be upset, distressed or even a bit sad about this. But she wasn't. She was just . . . flat. Empty. She shrugged her shoulder at the thought. Indifferent.

"Is it that bad?"

"I don't know. Maybe? I guess we'll see. We're both on edge right now. Riley came by to show us the updated sketches of Emma. I think we both just reacted badly and took it out on each other."

The image of Emma as a boy haunted her. It had invaded her thoughts all day. She'd tried to drown it out by watching old movies in bed, but she couldn't stop thinking about it. It was all she could do to not go down to Peter's study and pull out the pictures again.

"Is there anything I can do?"

Megan bit her lip. She didn't know where she'd be without Laurie. She'd done so much for her, been there for her through everything.

"No, just keep the chocolate coming. I'll meet you at the corner for our run tomorrow."

Megan hung up the phone. It was so quiet outside. Maybe instead of waiting to see if Peter came home, she'd just head down to the beach and walk along the boardwalk until the girls were done.

She picked up the phone. She should call Peter. She placed the phone back on the table. She didn't want to. She didn't know what to say.

She headed back into the house. Laurie's question wouldn't leave her thoughts. Was Peter having an affair? Despite having accused him of it in the past, she didn't think he was. Or had. Yet. It was a nagging fear in the back of her mind, though. And the wife is always the last one to know, isn't she? Sure, he'd been working a lot of late nights recently, but . . .

Megan grabbed her purse and another piece of chocolate and headed to the front door. There was only one way to find out. She only hoped she was ready for the answer.

❧

"Can someone open the door for me?" Megan juggled the containers of ice cream in her hands as she stood at the front door.

"My hands are full," said Alexis as she kicked her soccer ball with her feet while carrying her shin guards.

"I got it." Hannah came along beside Megan, dropped the bag containing her wet bathing suit and towel, grabbed hold of the keys, and opened door.

"Where is Dad?" she asked.

Megan shrugged. Ice cream dribbled down the side of a cup onto her hand. She rushed into the kitchen, placed the containers of ice cream down on the counter, and washed her hands as the girls paraded into the kitchen.

"Well, should I put his ice cream in the freezer if he's not home?" Hannah asked.

Megan bit back a reply. He didn't deserve the treat they bought. But she needed to keep a united front. That's what all the parenting books say when it comes to raising your teens.

Instead, she grabbed his sundae from the counter and placed it in the freezer herself. There. Now he can't say she didn't think of him.

"How about we take our ice cream outside? It's a beautiful night and it's too stuffy in the house."

Alexis stood at the kitchen table where she'd dumped out the contents of her school bag and sorted through it.

"What are you looking for?" Megan brought a sundae to her daughter and set it beside her. A scowl filled Alexis's face as she tore through all the papers.

"Mr. Morley sent a note home for you. It's the last week of school. You'd think he'd let up a bit," she grumbled.

She held a white envelope with *Mr. & Mrs. Taylor* scrawled across the front. As soon as Megan took hold of the envelope, Alexis dug into her ice cream.

"Why don't you eat that outside with us?" Megan headed outside with her own sundae in one hand and the envelope in the other. She wasn't too concerned about the letter. There were only a few more days of school left. What could possibly be wrong?

The silence between the three at the patio table spoke volumes. Megan enjoyed her hot fudge sundae. She loved the taste of the chocolate on her tongue and made sure she savored each spoonful. Alexis inhaled her butterscotch sundae, while Hannah dipped her spoon into the ice cream with delicate precision. She was usually the last to finish.

The white envelope, discarded on the table, caught Megan's attention. Alexis hadn't brought home a letter from her teacher in quite a long time.

"You're not going to read that in front of her, are you?" Alexis pointed toward Hannah with her spoon.

"Alex!"

"What? It's personal. I don't want her to hear." Alexis shrugged her shoulders. Hannah stuck her tongue out.

"Hannah."

"All right, all right. I'll go inside." Hannah stood and gathered the trash.

Megan waited for a nod from Alexis before she opened the envelope. Since it was the last week of school, she doubted Mr. Morley would have anything negative to say.

She should have known better.

"Alex, what is this?" She waved it in front of Alexis, who now slouched in her chair, her arms folded and her head down.

"Is it about today?"

"Of course it is, you know that." Megan's blood pressure rose as she looked at the letter in her hands. She had to remember to breathe, in and out, in and out.

"I didn't mean it." Alex peeked up at Megan.

"But you said it." Oh God, how would she deal with this now?

Dear Mr & Mrs. Taylor,

An incident occurred today after school that I wanted to bring to your attention.

Words were said between Alexis and a fellow classmate. Alexis brought the incident to my attention, but also said something to me that raises my concern.

Has she ever said to you that she wished it were her that was taken instead your other daughter?

Alexis has made a tremendous effort this year and her attitude has improved, but I wonder if seeing a child psychologist would benefit her in dealing with her emotions. There is one that I can recommend if you would like to pursue this.

I know this has been a difficult time for you, but I am concerned for your daughter.

She placed the letter back in the envelope and laid it down on the table. Her heart fluttered with unease.

"Alex, honey, why . . . how could you even wish this? Do you think . . . you don't think . . . that I love you less than Emma, do you?"

She reached across the table and laid her hand on her daughter's arm. It was cold to the touch. Alexis unfolded her arms and grabbed onto Megan's hand for a moment before she let it go.

"But you do love her more."

Megan's heart twisted. She didn't know how to answer without hurting her daughter even more.

Alexis's chair scraped along the wood deck as she pushed it back and stood.

"Seriously, it's fine, Mom, you don't have to explain. You love us all the same, yada yada." She stomped away in a huff, wrenched open the patio door, and turned.

"Sometimes I just wish you could love me more. That's all. Not all the time. Just sometimes. More than Emma."

Megan reached her hand out and caught her daughter's arm before she entered the house.

"I do love you, Alexis. I love you more than life. If it were you that were missing, I would be doing every single thing that I could to find you. Everything. Just like I am for Emma."

Alexis's back straightened and a light shone in her eye. Megan knew that light. Alexis was ready for a fight.

"Yeah, but would you forget about Emma if she were here and I wasn't?"

Megan's stomach clenched as if she'd been sucker punched in the gut.

"What? Why you would you say that?" She gasped, fought for her breath as her daughter stood there. The light in her eyes shone brighter.

"'Cause it's the truth. Isn't it? Ever since Emma disappeared, it's like you forgot that I was here still." Alexis shrugged her shoulder. "It's okay, Mom. You don't have to worry about me. I've got Dad. At least he loves me." Megan flinched at Alex's scathing look.

Megan stood helpless as her daughter walked away. The patio door stood open. She cringed with each stomp up the stairs Alexis made. When her music blared through the open windows, Megan covered her ears. She wanted to block out the sound.

Hannah stood by the kitchen table. Megan reached for her, wanted to hold her close. She prayed Hannah didn't feel the same way. Her daughter didn't move. She just stood there, sorrow etched in her eyes. Megan took a step toward her, but Hannah shook her head.

"You can't ignore everything, Mom. I try to fill in the gap, but I'm just a kid." She turned and walked away.

Megan stood there, with her hand stretched out. She'd been left alone.

Where was Peter? How dare he leave her alone to deal with this? It was after nine o'clock at night. Why wasn't he home yet? He hadn't called, hadn't emailed or answered any of the texts she sent him on her walk along the beach that evening. On their way home, the girls wanted to stop at the office to give him his ice cream, but his truck wasn't there.

Only one thought came to mind. There was only one place he could be. One place he would go to if he thought our marriage was over. HER house.

Megan's heart broke. If he was there, it was all her fault.

❧

The porch swing creaked as Megan stared into the night sky. It was almost midnight and she was still alone. The night breeze kissed the skin at the back of her neck. She tugged the blanket wrapped around her body tighter with one hand. The other held a cup of lukewarm mint tea.

She knew she should head to bed. If Peter hadn't come home by now, he probably wouldn't. Yet her lethargic body wouldn't move. Her legs were tucked under her, covered by the blanket, and the cushion behind her head was soft enough that she could pretend it was a pillow.

With her head leaned back, her eyes closed, Megan began to hum. It was a soft song, barely distinguishable. A lullaby she would sing to the girls when they were little. The distant sound of a car door as it closed reached her ears. Part of her hoped it was her husband, but it could have been their neighbor arriving home from the late shift.

It wasn't until the patio door opened that she knew her husband had come home.

Her eyes remained closed even as the swing shifted under his weight when he sat down. An uncomfortable silence stretched between them.

"There's a chocolate caramel sundae in the freezer for you." Megan's mouth barely opened when she spoke.

"Thank you."

"Thank the girls. They wanted to surprise you after their lessons, so we stopped by the office."

She opened her eyes then. She wanted to see the expression on his face as he thought of an answer. He wouldn't look at her. His face was turned so she only saw the outline of his face. She shook her head.

"You weren't there," she said when he didn't say anything.

"Sorry. I needed time to think."

She lifted her head off the cushion. "I'm sorry. Did you say you needed time to think? About what, if I'm allowed to ask?" If he didn't grasp the sarcasm in her voice, she'd be shocked.

"Yesterday and today kind of threw me for a loop. I thought after last night . . . I overreacted today and that's not me." He still wouldn't look at her.

Overreacted? You think? A torrent of accusations pooled on Megan's tongue, but she kept her mouth shut. What else needed to be said that hadn't been already?

"Where were you?" She whispered instead.

A picture of Peter and HER filled Megan's mind. HER—with her long legs and short skirts. HER—with her long hair and Angelina Jolie lips. HER—the woman she despised.

She suppressed the picture in her mind. A cold fury settled deep within her.

Peter bowed his head. "At the office."

Megan snorted in disbelief. "Really?"

This time he looked at her. There were bags under his eyes and new frown lines around his lips.

"At the office. I swear."

She wanted to believe him. She needed to believe him. Every marriage has its ups and downs. Theirs was no different. But there was something in the back of her mind that wouldn't let her believe him. Not yet.

"You don't need to lie to me, Peter. I already told you I stopped at the office with the ice cream. Where were you?" She gripped the blanket tighter around her body.

"I went for a drive. I must have just missed you. Honest."

Megan pursed her lips. A drive. Uh-huh.

"So, that's where you've been. All night? You couldn't call or answer any of my texts?" Her fists gripped the blanket so tight, her knuckles turned white from the pressure.

Peter rubbed his face. "I don't want to fight anymore, Meg. I just went for a drive. I stopped somewhere and walked along the beach. I just needed to think."

She wanted to believe him. If their marriage was going to work, she needed to believe him. But she also needed to know.

"Were you alone?"

Peter straightened and shot her a look of horror. "Yes, of course I was. You didn't think . . ."

She refused to blink as he stared at her. He had the gall to accuse her this morning of having an affair. But what about him? Did he accuse her of something he himself was guilty of?

She wasn't going to let him off that easily. He grabbed her hand and squeezed it. She didn't squeeze back.

"I was alone, Meg. I swear. I was thinking, that's it." He rubbed his face again. "I can't believe you would think that . . . what have I done?"

Megan shrugged her shoulder. She had no answer for him. Not one he wanted to hear anyway.

"I miss her. Emma. I miss her. Seeing those pictures today, it opened my eyes. To us. You and I, we've held different roles. You've dedicated everything you have into finding her, while I"—he shrugged his shoulders—"I focused on our family. Trying to keep it together, be there for the girls."

The swing rocked as he shifted his position and faced her. His thumb rubbed her hand.

"I realized today that we forgot to focus on us throughout all of this. And I think we lost each other. Not only have we lost Emma, but we lost each other. I was trying to figure out if there was anything left between us, if there was still hope in finding what we once had. That's why I went for that walk. Why I didn't call you."

Megan bowed her head. The pain that crept into Peter's eyes as he spoke hurt too much to watch. They were lost. They'd been lost for a while.

"I realized that most of all, Megan, I miss you. I miss the woman you were before this nightmare entered our lives. I miss my wife. And the girls, they miss their mother. We've all become a shell. No matter where Emma is,"—Peter's voice caught—"she would never have wanted us to be like this."

Megan wiped away the tears that poured down her cheeks. She raised her head and looked her husband in the eyes. She saw heartbreak, loneliness, and fear. But most of all, she saw a small glimmer of hope there. She believed him. She didn't want to squash it, but she needed to tell him the truth.

"I don't know how to live life without Emma. It's like my life is on pause. If there were a rewind button, I'd push it. I'd wish it all away. But God's not that nice. He doesn't give us those options. Instead, He toys with us, sees how much we can handle. Why else would He tear our child from her home? Why else would He destroy the life that we lived and loved? You ask too much of me, Peter. I'm sorry." Her head shook as tremors flowed through her body until she couldn't determine where they stopped or began.

"Have you talked to the girls about Emma? I mean really *talked* to them? Did you know that Alexis keeps a journal like me? That she writes to her sister every day? We do this together, she and I. And did you know that Hannah writes stories for Emma? She draws pictures and everything, so that when she comes back, Hannah can read them to her."

Megan shook her head. She had no idea. She was clueless to their daughters' pain. What kind of mother doesn't know these things? She covered her mouth as a sob ripped through her throat.

"I had no idea. None. What have I done?"

Peter wrapped his arms around her and pulled her close. Megan sobbed on his shoulder.

"I don't want to lose you, Meg. I don't want our children to lose their mother." He stroked her hair as he spoke.

Megan wiped the tears from her eyes.

"You're asking me to give up on Emma, though."

"I'm asking you to not give up on us. Emma is included in that." The gentle pressure of a kiss on the top of her head spread heat throughout her body. The swing rocked back and forth as they listened to the night sounds in their yard.

"I was thinking that maybe you should see someone. Someone to talk to. We could go together, if you want."

Megan struggled to sit up. She pushed Peter's arms away.

"Like a counselor?"

She wasn't sure how to respond. Shortly after Emma's disappearance, they'd all gone to psychiatrist as a family. But that was well over a year ago.

"I was thinking more along the lines of the pastor at the church, or even the pastor's wife? Maybe we could even try going back to church?"

Megan shook her head. No way. No way was she stepping back through the doors of their old church. Nor would she talk to the pastor or his wife. No.

"Peter, where was God when Emma was taken? Why hasn't He answered any of our prayers for her return?" She shook her head again. No way.

"Maybe it's not God's fault . . ."

"NO. Don't you dare. I don't want to hear any platitudes from you or anyone else about how God doesn't take small little girls from their families. If you want to go see a marriage counselor, fine. Let's go. Let's see if we can salvage our marriage. A counselor. Not a pastor."

She stood up from the swing and faced Peter as he sat there with a shocked look on his face.

"I'm going to bed. It's late and I'm exhausted. Don't forget the ice cream in the freezer." She gathered the blanket around her and walked into the house.

The trail ends of the fabric caught in the door as it closed behind her. She tried to yank it out, but it wouldn't budge. She cried out in frustration. How dare he suggest they needed to bring God back into their life?

They weren't the ones who abandoned God. He abandoned them first.

CHAPTER NINETEEN

The light filtered through the white curtains and showered Emmie's room with its golden presence. Her eyes fluttered open. With a yawn, she stretched out her arms and rolled over. She grabbed onto her pink lion and cuddled it close. She loved her lion. Grandma said that she came to their house with Pink, so she must be a special lion. Maybe Mommy gave her Pink before she went away?

At the thought of Mommy, Emmie sat up in bed, threw the covers off, and scrambled to the floor. Her toes flexed when they met the carpet. She slid her feet into her slippers and wiggled her toes; they didn't like being cold.

She headed to her bookshelf, grabbed some white paper and her basket of crayons and carried them to the table. Something was missing. Emmie glanced around her room and spotted Pink alone on her bed. She tiptoed across her floor, careful not to make any noise, and grabbed her lion.

She had a dream last night that she wanted to draw. Papa said that she was good at drawing.

Emmie was hunched over her table when the door opened. It used to creak but Papa had fixed it with some oil. This way she wouldn't wake up Grandma in the mornings when she went down to color with him. She peeked up and smiled. She knew it would be him. Papa looked happy this morning. She liked it when he was happy. Maybe he would have another surprise for her today.

"So, there you are, sleepyhead." He patted her hair and pulled out a chair. Emmie giggled. He always looked funny when he sat in her chairs. They were too small for him. But he never broke them, not like Goldilocks did to Baby Bear's chair.

Emmie reached into her basket for the pink crayon. "What does heaven look like?" She loved to draw fluffy clouds. Would they feel like the cotton balls Grandma let her use to make snowmen?

Papa leaned forward until his elbows rested on the table. He looked like a bear all bunched up. He was looking at her picture. Did he like it?

"Well now, princess, I think . . ." He rubbed his bald head. "Well, why do you want to know?"

Emmie shrugged her shoulder. She finished her pink clouds and tapped the crayon against her cheek. *What else is in heaven?* She sat up, dragged the basket of crayons from the middle of the table to beside her, and looked for the grey one. She held it up for Papa to see, then began to outline her castle. There's always a big castle in heaven. Just like at Disneyland.

"'Cause," Emmie said. She didn't look up. "Mommy must be in heaven."

Once the castle was done, Emmie reached into her basket again for another crayon. Purple. She drew flowers all around her castle.

"Well now,"—Papa cleared his throat—"why would you be thinkin' that? Heaven is too heavy of a topic to clutter your pretty little brain so early in the morning."

Emmie shook her head. She didn't want to tell Papa about her dream. It would make him sad. She saw Mommy in heaven. Mommy was holding Pink in her hands and calling out to Emmie.

"Mommy has to be in heaven, Papa. She has to. She never calls me or comes to see me, and I know she loves me. So, she must be in heaven."

⚜

Jack leaned back in his chair. He didn't know what to say.

Why would Emmie believe such a thing? He shook his head. He was glad she believed in heaven, but why did she think Mary was there? Neither Dottie nor himself had ever said anything to make her think that.

He coughed, pushed his chair back, and stood up. He looked around her room and found the children's Bible Dottie had given her at Christmas on the nightstand. Emmie's tongue was caught between her teeth as she concentrated on her drawing.

He grabbed the book and sat on her bed. He wished Dottie were here. She'd know how to deal with this . . . girl stuff. He opened the book and flipped through the pages until he found the picture he needed.

"Emmie, come over here, will ya?"

After she'd climbed onto the bed and settled herself, Jack showed her the picture. "Is this what you're drawing?"

"Yep, heaven."

Jack took in a deep breath. He was out of his league here. Grandpas were for building swing sets and picnic tables, for sneaking cookies behind Grandma's back and giving good whisker rubs. Not for all this foolish talk about heaven. Next she'd be asking about angels. He shook his head. He would not talk about angels.

"Emmie, heaven is for those who are ready to see God. For old people. Like me."

Emmie looked up in horror. He could see the questions in her eyes.

"No, no . . . I'm not going to heaven, well, not right now. But when I die." He grunted. "Thinking about heaven is not for little girls, though, okay? And If I'm not ready to go there yet, I'm sure as . . . well, I'm not ready for you either. Okay?"

"Okay, Papa." Emmie shrank back. He'd been too gruff with her. He put his arm around her and squeezed.

"Oh, Emmie. Heaven is where you go when you die. But you've got a long time before you'll even need to think about going there, okay?" He smiled.

A tentative smile lit her face as she gazed up at him.

"I know, Papa. But maybe, when we go there, we can look for Mommy?"

CHAPTER TWENTY

A lexis called me this morning," Megan's mother said to her on the phone.

Megan tucked her legs under her body as she relaxed on the couch.

"Why did she call?" It wasn't unusual for her children to call their grandmother, but it was odd that Sheila would call to tell her.

"She wanted to come for a sleepover."

"For when?" Megan picked up her glass of water and took a sip.

"Tonight."

Megan snorted. Like that was going to happen. "You told her no, right?"

"Of course I did. It's a school night. But, she told me about the teacher's note . . ."

Megan winced at the thought of that note. She'd shown it to Peter this morning before he left for work.

"She feels bad, Megan, for what she said to you."

That shocked Megan. Alexis hadn't said anything to her this morning. She was late for breakfast, grabbed an apple, and waited outside in the Jeep for Megan. She must have been on the phone.

"Megan, did you hear what I said?"

"I heard. Thanks for letting me know."

"Well, just don't be too hard on her, okay?" Sheila said. Megan heard the judgment in her voice. She bristled.

"Thank you for telling me how to raise my daughter." Sarcasm laced her response.

An audible sigh came through.

"Megan, for pity's sake. I shouldn't even have to call to tell you that Alexis called me. But you've got blinders on . . ."

"Blinders, Mom? I've got blinders on? Wow. That's a good one, coming from you." Her blood began to boil. Of all people . . .

"Now that was uncalled for." Megan knew what was about to come. The sympathy card.

"I did the best I could for you, Megan, and you know it. Honestly, I'm tired of you holding my parenting skills, or lack thereof as you often remind me, over my head. You're an adult now. Time to grow up and deal with life."

Megan jumped up from the couch.

"I *am* dealing with life. The best way I can." Her eyes started to fill up with tears.

"No, Megan. I don't think you are." Her mother's voice was quiet but firm. To the point. She'd expect nothing else from her. Sheila wasn't known for her tact.

"Mom . . ."

"No, you need to listen to me. You have one daughter crying out for attention and another carrying such a huge load that she's forgotten how to be a child. I know you are desperate to find Emma. We all are. But in your quest to find your missing daughter, you've forgotten the two that are still by your side waiting for you to look at them."

Megan gulped back a reply. She was looking.

"Doesn't your Bible say something about how Jesus left the ninety-nine to go find the one lost sheep?"

"Megan, you're not Jesus. You're just a mother with a heavy heart."

Megan sank back down on the couch. Tears flowed down her cheeks. She wiped them away with the palm of her hand, but it did little to dry her face.

"I don't know what to do, Mom. I feel lost. I don't want to give up on Emma, but I can feel the other girls slipping away from me."

"Oh, Meg. You'll never give up on Emma. You know that. And you know what to do, don't fool yourself. You are a mother first and foremost. Deep inside you know what it will take to draw your girls back into the shelter of your arms. That's how God made us." A surprising gentleness emanated from Sheila's voice.

Sobs ripped through Megan's body at Sheila's words. She wished her mother were there now, so she could curl up in her arms like she used to do as a child.

With a tearful good-bye, Megan hung up the phone. Her body was depleted. The past few days had been nothing but emotional for her. When would this nightmare end? She only had a few hours before she needed to pick up the girls. She dried her eyes, grabbed the last pieces of chocolate from the box Laurie had dropped off, and headed upstairs.

She used to believe there was nothing in the world chocolate and a hot bubble bath couldn't cure. At this point, though, she was willing to try anything.

❧

The long line of vehicles waiting at the curb amazed Megan as she sat in her Jeep. Yes, they were all there to pick up their children, but the majority of mothers in the lineup had driven from their house to the school and back again. What happened to the days of walk-ing to school to pick up the kids?

When the girls all started kindergarten, a bunch of mothers from the neighborhood would all walk together and stand around the school grounds, coffee in their hands as they talked and got to know one another. Some long-lasting friendships had been made during those years.

That's how Megan had met Laurie. After dropping off Hannah, Megan often would sit alone with her coffee on a bench at the little playground and let Alexis burn off some energy. One day, Laurie walked by and her son begged to play too. Megan smiled at the memory. She'd be lost without Laurie now. Who knew back then how much this friendship would mean?

Megan inched her vehicle ahead as a couple of cars left. She scanned the crowd for her daughters. They weren't expecting her. Unless the weather was horrible, they walked home with one of the program volunteers.

A group of girls headed toward her. Hannah and Alexis were part of the group. Alexis lagged behind with Laurie, while Hannah led the crowd as she walked backward. Megan honked the horn and waved. Alexis saw her first. With a sprint, she ran toward the Jeep and swung into the front seat, all before Hannah had even made it halfway.

"Hey, Mom, what's up?" A wide grin spread across her face as Hannah approached the Jeep, a pout on her face. Laurie walked past, smiled, and waved. Megan waved back.

"No fair. You sat in the front last time too!" Hannah flopped in the backseat, her arms crossed as she glared at her sister.

"Guess you should have been paying attention." Alexis pulled down the visor and patted her hair into place. When she spotted the glare from Hannah, she stuck her tongue out and slammed the visor back into place.

"Mom, did you see that?"

Megan tapped her fingers on the steering wheel and counted to five. *Today is going to be a good day. Today will be a good day. Today is a good day.* She repeated the phrase three times before she faced her daughters, making sure she had a smile firmly placed on her face.

"All right, you two, settle down. I have a surprise for you, but if you keep it up, we can go home instead. Your choice."

Hannah was the first to pop up, as Megan knew she would. "A surprise, really? Like what? Ice cream? Shopping?"

"Yeah, Mom, what are we doing?"

Megan pretended to hem and haw. "Oh, I don't know. I figured we would just drive around and see where we ended up."

"Does Dad know we're going out?" Alexis asked. She grabbed the phone from the holder on the dashboard.

"Yes, he knows, so you can put my phone down, thank you."

"So, where are we going?" Hannah blew a bubble that popped. Megan peeked in the rearview mirror and laughed.

"I thought it was time for a girl day. Just us."

Megan let her words sink in. She used to do this with the girls. Before, when life was normal. Before, when Emma was around. Before . . . Megan shook her head. She had made a promise to herself and to Peter that she would not reflect on anything but Hannah and Alexis. Today. On the here and now.

"Dad was okay with this?" Alexis stared out the passenger window, but Megan felt her gaze.

She reached over and touched her daughter's hand. "Yes, Alex. Dad was okay with this. He is expecting us to bring him home something, though."

"Did he eat the ice cream we brought home last night?"

"He sure did. He came home at lunch today just for that." Megan smiled at the memory.

Peter had called from the front door and told her he had a bag of fries and hamburgers in his hands from the Double Decker bus parked at the beach. She loved their french fries. He had wolfed down the ice cream in the freezer after he inhaled his lunch and agreed with her suggestion that she take the girls out after school. He'd even seemed kind of shocked.

The moment Megan pulled into the small shopping complex, Alexis groaned while Hannah whispered "yes, yes" under her breath. Megan knew this would happen. She just hoped Alexis would enjoy herself today. Despite her pleas, Megan knew Alexis loved to shop.

After the Jeep was turned off, she twisted in her seat and faced her children.

"So, here's the plan. I made an appointment at the nail salon to get a manicure. For all of us. Then we'll stop for some chocolate and then I figured we could walk around and see what grabs our attention. Shoes, earrings, or something. When we're done, we'll stop and pick up something for dinner. Chicken or burgers, your choice. How does that sound?"

"Fantastic!" Hannah cried out from the backseat. Her hand was on the door, ready for Megan to release the lock button. Hannah was a born shopper.

"Can I get a book?" Alexis asked. She too had her hand on the door. Megan turned her head so Alex wouldn't see the smile. She tried so hard to not like anything her sister enjoyed.

The moment she unlocked the car, both girls jumped out. When Megan reached the back of her Jeep, the girls stood there tapping their feet against the hot pavement. Alexis pointed to her wrist—the one that didn't have a watch on. Megan rolled her eyes, grabbed each girl by the arm, and together they walked into the mall.

❧

Three hours later, Megan's feet ached to sit down on one of the benches in the middle of the mall. Hannah had talked Megan into getting pedicures as well, so not only were their fingernails all decked out with the latest bling but their toenails sparkled against the bright flip-flops Megan ended up buying. Hannah chose baby blue to complement her light pink nails, and Alexis went with a bright orange that contrasted with her neon-green toes. Megan opted for white. She stuck her feet out in front of her, twisted them side to side. The ruby red did look nice. Now if she could just click her heels twice, she could be home with her aching feet up, and life would be perfect.

It wasn't just her feet that hurt. It was her heart. She tried to keep her gaze averted whenever she saw a young child. She'd made a promise. Another one. She couldn't break it this time.

"Mom, can we get ice cream now? My arms are hurting from carrying the bags on my wrists." Hannah stood with a pout on her face as she held out her arms. She didn't want to ruin her manicure, so she refused to hold on to the bags.

Megan groaned. "Weren't the chocolate croissants enough?"

"Can we go home now?" Alexis flopped on the bench beside her and dropped the one bag.

"There's one more store I want to check out." Hannah kicked at her sister's feet.

"Sorry, sweetie, but I think I'm done. Next time, okay?"

"Fine." Hannah sat on the bench with her shoulders slouched. "It was fun, though; thanks, Mom."

"Yeah, thanks," Alexis muttered.

"It was fun, wasn't it? I'm sorry we haven't had a girls' day in a long time." Megan reached her hand over and touched Hannah's shoulder.

"More like two years," said Alexis.

Ouch. Megan blinked her eyes. Two years. Her shoulders deflated at the thought. She remembered the words spoken last night. She would not lose her daughters. Not if she could help it.

"You're right, Alex. It's been way too long. That's my fault. I'm sorry."

"Can we do it again?" A smile flitted across Hannah's face. Forgiveness shone through her eyes. Megan's heart lifted.

"Can we do something else next time, though?" Alexis peeked from under the bangs that covered her eyes. Forgiven. Again.

Free from a load she didn't want to carry, Megan's back straightened. "Tell you what: Let's make it a date. Once a month. Just us."

The mall crowd swelled around them. Megan's feet stopped throbbing. She glanced at her fingernails. It had been a long since she'd last had a French manicure. Actually, it had been a long time since she'd had nails.

"If Emma were here, she'd be old enough to come on our girls' date, wouldn't she?" Despite the crowd noise, Megan heard Hannah clear as day. Yes, Emma would be old enough.

Alexis jumped up. "Come on. Let's go. Can we grab some burgers and fries to take home?" She reached for Megan's hands and pulled her up. Megan then reached for Hannah's hands, and did the same.

"Make mine a poutine, and we're set," Megan agreed. After today, she deserved it, calories and all. Fries, smothered in cheese curds and gravy. Megan's stomach grumbled. Yep, today was a poutine type of day. There were only two places in town that made the dish. Both had thought Megan nuts when she first asked for the dish. It was Canadian, after all. Now they carried it on their menus.

Peter had made a comment just before she left that afternoon that was nagging at the back of her mind.

"I should be home," he'd said. *Should.* She didn't like that word. Not after last night.

Megan looked at her watch. By the time they made it home, it would be close to eight o'clock. No reason why he shouldn't be home. Yet, what if . . . Megan gave her head a tiny shake. No. He told her last night he'd been alone. She believed him, or tried to at least. He even came home at lunch today. He'd be home.

CHAPTER TWENTY-ONE

Finally! I thought you'd forgotten all about me."

Peter grabbed the bag out of Megan's hands and opened it up. His hand dove in and came out with a fistful of french fries.

"Mom had to get her poutine." Alexis meandered into the house, her hands full with a bottle of pop and a bag.

Megan followed Peter. Together they unpacked the bags of food and laid everything out on the table.

"Sorry, it's fries again. I tried to opt for something a tad bit healthier, but the girls chose this," she said as she popped a french fry into her mouth.

Peter grinned. She knew he didn't care.

"I wasn't sure if you would be here," Megan said. She didn't want the girls to overhear, so she kept her voice low.

Peter's eyebrow rose. "Why wouldn't I be?" He found her poutine and placed it on her plate.

Megan lowered her head. Her cheeks heated. "You told me you might not be. I figured you had plans." She didn't look at him.

Peter's fingers touched her chin and with a gentle tug, she lifted her face. There was a gentleness to his gaze she didn't expect to see.

"The only plans I have are spending the night with my family."

Megan searched his eyes. She believed him. Why this sudden case of doubt?

"Can we eat?" Alexis flopped down in her chair and unwrapped her burger. Hannah joined her and dug into her french fries.

Megan exchanged a look with Peter. A wave of happiness flooded her body. This was her family. She'd taken steps today to become a part of them again.

"So, how was shopping?" Peter addressed the girls, but Megan knew the question was directed toward her. She concentrated on her dinner, giving the girls time to tell him first.

His eyes met hers. "Did you survive?" A hint of a smile appeared.

"She bought just as much as we did, Dad." Hannah answered for her.

"Did she now?"

Megan nodded her head. She survived.

Peter clapped his hands together. "Well, I don't want to be left out, so I have a surprise of my own." Peter's face became animated. The dimples in his cheeks appeared beside the huge smile; his eyes danced at the announcement.

"We're getting a puppy?" Alexis asked.

Peter shook his head.

"We're going to Disneyland?" Hannah piped up.

Peter shook his head again. He fidgeted with excitement, like a little kid in a candy store. Alexis looked to Megan, but she only shook her head. This was a surprise to her as well. She pushed her fork into her poutine dish, and swirled it around.

"The Hanton Fair is this weekend," Peter said. No one responded. "I think we should go."

Megan was taken aback. The Hanton Fair? Megan bent her head and gulped back her hesitation. Too many ugly memories surrounded the fair for Megan.

The last time they'd planned to go, Emma had been kidnapped hours before they were to leave. Megan thought Emma might have been tempted by all the balloons she saw at the Kinrich town parade they'd just attended that day. Emma had fallen in love with the clowns walking by and begged to have a red balloon.

"Megan?" Peter placed his hand onto hers and squeezed.

She took a deep breath. "The Hanton Fair, huh? Wow. It's been a while since we've gone to that. Talk about a surprise." She tried to infuse excitement in her voice, but it fell flat.

"Can we go? Please?" Alexis begged.

"I think it would be good for us. A step forward." Peter squeezed her hand again. Megan's fingers tightened around the fork in her hand.

She nodded her head. She'd go to the fair. It might kill her to do so, but at least her family would be happy.

⚜

"Higher, Papa. Higher."

Jack pushed the swing harder. Emmie laughed as she pumped her legs. Her shoe flew off. Daisy chased after it, picked it up, and brought it back, only to have Emmie swing above her.

"Last push," Jack said. His arms ached from the constant motion. Ever since he'd hung the old swing, all she'd wanted to do was swing higher. Next, he'd have to build her a stool so she could climb on the tire herself.

Dottie sat under the large maple tree. With her eyes closed and her head resting against the back of the chair, a smile graced her face. Still as beautiful as the day they met. She loved the warmth. He remembered when they were first married, how she used to lay on a blanket on the lawn for hours. Now, she hid in the shade. A light breeze played with the strands of hair that had escaped the bobby pins.

"Are you sleeping, love?"

"Hmm, not quite. Just enjoying the breeze." She slid one eye open and looked at him. The corner of her mouth lifted before her eye drifted shut again.

Daisy ran over, jumped up, and placed both paws on Dottie's knees. She dropped Emmie's shoe in her lap.

She glanced down her nose at the shoe in her lap and grimaced. "Emmie, if you continue to play fetch with your shoe, it's going to get wrecked." Dottie dropped her hand and wiped her fingers on the grass.

"Sorry." Emmie continued to pump her legs on the tree swing.

Jack stepped to the side as Emmie swung back and forth without his help. "You don't want to do that. If you don't have your shoes, you can't come on the surprise."

She twisted her head around. "A surprise? For me?"

"Yeppers. But you need shoes." Jack looked down at Daisy who sat in the middle of the swing path.

Emmie tucked her foot inside the tire swing. "No more shoes, Daisy."

Jack crossed his arms and waited. He turned his head slightly to the side and winked. Dottie smiled back.

"Papa? What's the surprise?"

The tire swing began to slow as Emmie stopped pumping her legs. She turned to look at him and the swing twisted. A frantic look swept across Emmie's face as she swung wildly about. Her arms flailed as she panicked. Jack grabbed onto the rope and steadied her.

She reached her hands out and grabbed hold of him. Despite the shakiness in his arms, he lifted her out of the swing and pulled her close. Emmie wrapped her legs around his waist and dug her face into his neck.

"Shh, now. You're all right," Jack crooned as he walked over to the chair and sank down with Emmie.

When Dottie reached across, Emmie scooted out of Jack's lap and crawled into Dottie's. Jack rubbed the scratches on his neck. The girl needed to cut her fingernails.

"Now, Papa was about to tell you about the fair. Don't you want to listen?" Dottie rubbed Emmie's back.

Jack groaned as Emmie's head popped up. "What part of the word *surprise* didn't you hear, woman?" He shook his head and crossed his arms.

Dottie's eyes widened. "Oops." She covered her mouth with her hand.

Emmie giggled. A wide smile appeared on her face.

"The fair? Really? Oh, I love the fair," Emmie said. She jumped out of Dottie's arms and danced around in a circle. Daisy sprang up from her crouched position and followed.

"Whoa, there, princess. You don't want to get all dizzy now."

Emmie dropped to the grass in a heap and clapped her hands together. "Can we go now?" She scooped Daisy up in her lap and cuddled her close. "I want to go to a fair, Papa. Will there be clowns and balloons?"

Jack scratched his chin. How did Emmie know about the clowns and balloons? He looked to Dottie, but she shook her head at him. A frown appeared on her face.

"Did you see a commercial on the television about the fair?" That was the only way she could know about the balloons and clowns. They'd never taken her before. Dottie always said no.

Emmie shook her head. "Nope. With Mommy." She picked at a dandelion at her feet and rubbed it underneath Daisy's chin.

"Not this fair, dear." Dottie's face scrunched up and her lips puckered as she watched Emmie. Jack didn't like what he saw.

"Can we get the pink fluffy stuff? I like that kind. Can we, Papa?"

Jack leaned forward. "Cotton candy? Oh, I think we can. Grandma likes the pink one best too."

Emmie sprang up from the grass, grabbed onto Jack's outstretched hands, and jumped into his lap. "Can we go on rides too, Papa? Please?" Emmie reached across and grabbed Dottie's hand. "Grandma, you too?"

"Oh, I don't think so, Emmie." Dottie shook her head while she patted her stomach. "Grandma doesn't do rides very well."

Jack laughed. The last time he'd managed to cajole Dottie to go on a ride with him, she ended up sicker than a dog. They stayed at the fair for only an hour before they had to leave.

That had been five years ago. He thought about the Ferris wheel. Going up so high you could see straight across town and halfway across the lake. His stomach turned at the thought of going up so high. Seems the older he got, the more he liked his feet on the ground.

Emmie pouted. Jack tickled her until a smile appeared. "Just 'cause Grandma won't go on rides doesn't mean Papa won't. Silly girl."

"I'm not silly!"

Jack worked hard to place a stern look on his face. "Of course you are. Only silly girls pout when they don't get their way."

Emmie dropped her chin to her chest. She fiddled with her fingers for a few moments.

"Okay."

Daisy jumped up and chased after a bee. Emmie laughed and chased after Daisy. Jack shook his head. He was about to chase after her when her words stopped him short.

"I want a red balloon, Papa!"

CHAPTER TWENTY-TWO

Hundreds of feet had trampled grass at the fair into matted clumps. Megan was careful where she stepped. Her flip-flop had already come off once when her foot had landed on a wad of sticky gum. She knew she should have worn her running shoes. But on this hot summer night, the last thing she wanted was sweaty feet. Something crackled under her foot. With a grimace, Megan hopped on one foot as she took off the flip-flop and shook it. She'd stepped on a cup that obviously wasn't empty. She took a deep breath and let it out.

Peter, who walked ahead of her, glanced back with a questioning look on his face. She forced her lips to resemble something that should look like a smile. It worked. Peter gave her the thumbs-up gesture. With a nod, she looked down at her shoe as droplets of pop formed a puddle on the ground.

She hated the fair. With a passion. A wave of anger flooded through her. She wished she had never agreed to come.

Hannah walked beside her. She hummed quietly under her breath, keeping her gaze down on the ground. Megan had snapped at her back in the car as they drove up and down the crowded parking lot trying to find a space wide enough for the Jeep. Full of excitement and energy, Hannah had jabbered on about the rides she wanted to go on and if she could get cotton candy and maybe even win a prize. With a bout of impatience, Megan turned her head to look back and a sharp stab of pain sliced through her right eye. She should have just kept her mouth shut, but instead she told her daughter to shut her mouth before she did it for her. Megan pursed her lips. She wished she could rewind her life. Again.

She reached for Hannah's hand that swung by her side and held on to it.

"I'm sorry, Hannah. I should never have said that." She wound her fingers with her daughter's and waited for a response. It didn't take long.

Hannah beamed a smile at her. "It's okay. I know this is tough for you. Do you still have a headache?"

Megan wanted to hug her. Instead, she swung her hand and kept an eye on the ground for other messes to avoid.

Peter and Alexis waited at the opening gate. Alexis kept looking through the crowd at the different rides. Scouting it out, just like she said she would. She held something that looked like a map in her hand. Peter held tickets in his. Megan closed her eyes for a brief second and repeated the mantra she made herself memorize.

I will enjoy tonight. I will laugh and smile and have fun. I will focus on my family. I will not . . . no, don't think about Emma. She promised Peter she wouldn't. A bit of self-loathing filled her heart. Disgust at herself for giving in so easily.

Alexis grabbed onto her arm. "Mom, can we go to the games first? I want to win a frog. Please?"

Megan looked through the crowds to the midway. Lights blinked on and off along the top of the booths. A roving pack of teenagers, their eyes bright with excitement and their hands full of popcorn bags and large cups of pop, mingled. The obnoxious calls of the carnival game barkers filled the air. Megan's head pounded with each *ting! ting!* of the plastic rings being thrown against the glass bottles and the *bam! bam!* of the popped balloons as they popped from the darts thrown at them.

"Please, Mom, please?"

Megan threw Peter a look. She hoped he saw the daggers she mentally flung at him. He only shrugged his shoulders and smiled. The dimples in his chin appeared. She couldn't stay mad at him. Not tonight. A whiff of fried grease caught her attention. Hmmm, mini-donuts. Okay, she could be happy if mini-donuts were thrown into the mix.

Peter placed his arm around Alexis and squeezed. "Let's go, sweetie. Your mom has the camera; we'll make sure she takes pictures of us winning armloads of prizes, okay?" He winked at Megan.

Megan brought her hand up to the camera that hung from her neck. She'd forgotten all about it. When Peter had looped it around her head earlier, it had felt so foreign to her. The heaviness pulled at her neck. Like heavy chains with a padlock. Once upon a time, she would have never left home without it. Peter used to joke that it would become an appendage if she wasn't careful. Now, effort was required to take a picture. A moment captured forever. Pictures signified the continuation of life.

She held the camera up, forced a grin to overtake her lips. "Let's get started then, shall we?"

She followed behind Peter and Alexis, careful of the black cables wrapped together in duct tape. Just her luck, she tripped over one and landed in a pool of gooey mud. Hannah held her hand out. Megan grabbed it and was amazed at her daughter's strength as she helped to pull her out of the mud. A sense of pride filled Megan. Her daughter was trying so hard to be aware of Megan's feelings.

"Go on, Hannah. Go win a prize with your sister." Megan motioned ahead. Hannah's face lit up. She ran ahead and grabbed Peter's other hand. He glanced over his shoulder at Megan, his eyes bright with life. He always loved going to the fair.

Megan thought back to the night they first met. At this fair, many years ago. She'd gone with a group of friends, their first time out at the fairgrounds alone, at night. Megan smiled as she remembered the freedom of that night. Her girlfriends had each won their own share of stuffed animals, but Megan was a lousy shot. Her darts missed every balloon, the rings never made it over the coke bottles, and she was incapable of using a water gun to shoot ducks.

Peter, a senior to her junior, waited in line behind her. He paid for her to try her luck again, but this time, he helped her aim. Along with her very first stuffed duck, she was also asked out on her first date. A perfect night for firsts.

At the weathered duck-shooting booth, where Alexis stood with her feet wide, Megan picked up the camera, turned it on, and waited. Peter stood behind their daughter and steadied her arm. She threw him a smile. That's when Megan clicked the camera. A moment stolen between a father and daughter. It felt right, taking that picture. The camera wasn't as heavy as before. It was as if the flash turned a light on within Megan's heart.

Alexis hit every shot and won a duck. Megan snapped her picture as she flung her arms around Peter and squeezed tight.

"Can you help me too?" Hannah held the water gun in her hands as she looked at Peter. Her eyes begged him to help.

Peter stood behind Hannah, had her rest her arm over top of his, and helped her aim. "You know, your mom couldn't play this game either without my help."

Megan stuck her tongue out at him as he winked at her.

"Really?" Alexis's mouth hung open.

"Close your mouth, honey," Megan said. She glared at Peter. "Your father only thought I couldn't shoot the ducks. What he didn't know is that it was my plan all along for him to help me."

"Oh, really?" Peter's eyebrow lifted.

Hannah took another shot, this time on her own. And missed. Peter held her arm straight; she aimed for a duck. Megan lifted the camera once again, focused the lens, and took the picture of Hannah hitting the duck, throwing her arms up in the air, and smiling big.

Peter smirked at Megan while he gave Hannah a high five. "Prove it."

Megan tossed her hair over her shoulder. "I don't need to prove anything." She winked at Alexis.

"Do it, Mom, do it," said Alexis.

Megan unhooked her camera from around her neck and handed it to her daughter. "We'll need evidence of this. Take a good shot, okay?"

Megan moved up to the booth. The ducks moved along in lines, large circles on their bodies. Peter handed her the water gun. "Good luck," he said. When he didn't move, she elbowed him in the side. She knew if she tried to follow the ducks, she'd never hit one. But if she aimed in one spot and waited for a duck to come toward it, she'd be fine. All she needed was one shot. Megan swallowed, took aim, and pulled the trigger. When she realized the spray of water actually hit the duck, she turned and held her arms up high.

"Two more shots." A smirk covered Peter's face. Almost as if he knew it was a lucky shot.

"You can do it, Mom." Hannah's eyes lit up like a Christmas tree. Alexis held the camera up to her face, waiting to take another picture.

Megan stuck her tongue out at Peter, who only smiled back. She turned to watch the ducks, their yellow plastic bodies bobbed along the conveyor line. No sweat. She brought her arm back up, cupped her hand to steady it, and waited for another duck to drench. She pulled the trigger. And missed.

"That's okay, Mom. One more shot. You can do it," Hannah encouraged her.

"Do you need my help this time?" Peter smiled.

Megan shook her head. She could do this. She repeated the process, but this time waited for a few ducks to pass before she pulled the trigger.

"Argh," Alexis groaned. "So close." She had just missed the tail.

"Maybe next time, eh?" Peter gave her a side hug. "Guess you still need me around."

Megan motioned for Alexis to take another picture. She wrapped her arms around Peter and looked up. "Well, you're good for some things, I guess." She smiled.

He leaned down to give her a kiss as the flash went off.

"Can we try the fishing one now?" Hannah pulled on Megan's arm.

With the camera back around her neck, Megan trailed behind her family as they jostled through the crowds. Megan snapped pictures of the girls as they enjoyed the fair. She kept her focus on her daughters. She'd made a promise.

After Hannah won a fish at the fishing pond, Megan had the girls stop so she could take the picture. She wanted to ensure the atmosphere of the grounds filled the room, the bright lights, the clowns, and the booths.

As she focused the lens, an outline of someone in the background caught her attention. A little girl with pigtails filled the background of the frame. Megan's heart skipped a beat. Everything else around her muted, the sounds, the smells, the sights—everything but the sight of the little girl. She took a step forward.

It was her blonde hair and white dress that stood out to Megan. From the distance, it looked like Emma. From a distance. Megan took in a deep breath and exhaled. She'd made a promise. She would not, could not, see Emma in every little girl with pigtails.

Peter stood beside her, and despite how hard her hand shook, she didn't lower the camera for a better look. It must be her imagination, wanting to see something that wasn't there. It always was. How many times had she thought it was Emma only to realize too late it wasn't? How many children had she scared?

How many times would she continue to break her own heart? With the little girl still in the background, Megan snapped the shot. She lowered the camera with slow precision and smiled at her daughters. Tonight was for her family. Tonight she would ignore her own pain and step out of the past. Peter grabbed her hand, entwined his fingers with hers. She tried to find the little girl, but a crowd of teenagers swelled behind Alexis and Hannah, jostling them from their spot.

"You okay?" Peter asked. He squeezed her hand.

Megan looked at him, and then back into the crowd. She saw the concern in his eyes. "I'm fine," she said. She planted a smile on her face and squeezed his hand.

She wanted to tell him that she'd just seen Emma. She needed to tell him. But he wouldn't believe her. She wasn't even sure she believed herself anymore.

❧

The heavy weight on his shoulder wiggled with each step he took. His shoulders ached. Dottie warned him not to carry Emmie on his shoulders, that it would hurt his back too much, but how could he deny his little girl?

"I see it, I see it! Over there, Papa, do you see the lights?"

Jack held tight to her legs as she pointed out ahead of her. They skirted the cars that waited for a parking spot to open and headed closer to the fairgrounds.

"What people have against walking a few extra steps instead of parking close is beyond me," Dottie said as she glared at the passengers in the vehicle that waited for them to pass before cruising down the rest of the pathways to find an open spot.

"Good exercise never hurt a person. I'm telling you, kids these days are growing up lazy."

Jack shook his head. "Stop your mumbling, woman."

"Why don't you put her down? She can walk the rest of the way." Dottie reached up to grab Emmie's waist.

Jack shooed her hand away. "Leave her be. She's fine up here. The girl wants to see the lights, and see the lights she will."

Jack shrugged his shoulders in an effort to distribute his granddaughter's weight. She barely weighed anything, but at the moment, a feather would have felt like a ton of bricks.

"Do you want me down, Papa?" Emmie leaned down until her cheek pressed up against his.

"No, kiddo, you're fine. Once we get inside the grounds, then you can get down. Deal?" He readjusted his arms around her legs. He should have taken her shoes off earlier. Her heels kept digging into his chest.

A cluster of balloons flew up into the sky. Emmie giggled as she watched them.

"Can I get a balloon when we get there?"

"As long as there are some left," Jack said. He groaned as he stepped in a pile of spilled fries.

"Put her down, Jack," Dottie said.

She grabbed Emmie's hand and began to pull. Jack reached up for her other hand and after a bit of maneuvering, Emmie climbed down and off his back. Jack straightened and stretched. A loud pop sounded, pressure relieved. Ahhh, now that felt better.

"I wish Daisy could have come," Emmie said as she reached for both Jack and Dottie's hands and began to swing them back and forth. "She'd have so much fun."

"Emmie, we already talked about this. A fair is no place for a puppy." Dottie sidestepped some soggy napkins on the ground.

A clown stood at the entrance to the fairgrounds. In his hands were bunches of balloons. As they approached the clown, Emmie dragged her feet. Jack glanced down, unsure why, and saw that Emmie's eyes were wide open. Jack stopped and crouched down.

"Emmie, have you ever seen a clown before?" He stroked her hair and made sure a smile was on his face.

Emmie nodded her head.

"Are you afraid of clowns?"

She shook her head.

Jack glanced up to Dottie. She shook her head and shrugged her shoulders.

"So, what's wrong, princess?"

Emmie leaned forward until her lips touched his ear. "Can I have a balloon?"

Jack smiled. Sometimes she amazed him. Shy because of a clown. Go figure.

"Well, let's go ask him, shall we?" Jack grunted as he stood back up. His knees weren't made for kneeling anymore. Hand in hand, Jack led Emmie to the clown. The look on his granddaughter's face was priceless.

Jack studied the clown. It didn't look scary. A huge floppy hat with a large daisy rested on a red curly wig. A wide red smile was painted on the face, along with bright yellow stars around the eyes. Emmie's eyes widened as she took in the outfit, the multicolored patches with flowers attached to the pants. When the clown bent down and looked Emmie in the eyes, Jack had to bite back a chuckle. She stepped back and hid behind Jack's legs.

The clown held out a bright-red balloon and waited for Emmie to take it. She glanced up at Jack as if asking permission before she inched her hand out and grabbed the string. The clown moved on to surprise another child with a balloon, but Emmie never noticed. She'd caught sight of the bright flashing lights, the rides, and the popcorn booth located directly inside the grounds.

Jack grabbed Emmie's hand while he turned to face Dottie. "Where should we go first?"

His hand jerked. "Can we go on a ride, Papa?" Emmie pulled at his hand again. There were so many things he wanted to do with her. Go on rides, find the mirror house, eat some cotton candy and candied apples, win her a prize. Especially win her a prize. The game booths were off to the side and he saw some stuffed ponies. Maybe one of those.

"I think we should do those last, Jack. Do you want to be lugging around a large stuffed animal all night?" Dottie grabbed Emmie's other hand and motioned in the opposite direction of the game booths.

Jack looked around. The fair never changed. Year after year it looked the same. The bright lights, the loud carnival music, and the crowds. Especially the crowds. As they walked around the grounds trying to locate some rides Emmie was big enough to go on, Jack watched the crowds. Groups of teenagers flocked together, moving from game to game in swells. Families meandered along, little children skipping in the dirt as their parents followed them with tired eyes and arms full of stuffed animals, popcorn, and half-eaten bags of cotton candy.

Jack bumped into a woman who stood in the middle of the midway. The camera in her hand tumbled. Jack bent down to catch it, horrified that it might break, but it only swung on her neck. Shamefaced, Jack mumbled an apology for bumping into her and backed up.

Emmie tugged on his arm. The woman gave Jack a brief smile as he nodded his head before he followed Emmie. She'd found a ride. Teacups. Mary used to love this ride. She loved to spin the wheel as fast as she could, so that the teacup spun even faster.

"So, you want to go on this one, do you?"

"Can we, Papa?" Emmie looked up at him, her eyes big and round with delight.

"Hand me your balloon, Emmie. I'll stay here and watch, okay?" Dottie bent to untie the balloon from her wrist.

Jack took her hand and they got in line for the ride. He glanced behind him. The woman still stood there, camera in hand. He scanned the crowd and noticed that she was taking a picture of a man with two kids. Must be her family. Jack placed his arm around Emmie. Back when Mary was a child, they would do the same thing. Dottie was in charge of taking all the pictures, but with a Polaroid, not those new digital toys everyone had nowadays.

Emmie jumped up and down as they inched closer to the front of the line. It was their turn to ride the teacups. Emmie's first real ride. Mary used to do the same thing at this age, jump up and down as she clapped her hands in excitement. The teacups were the first one she would beg to go on every time.

Like mother, like daughter.

CHAPTER TWENTY-THREE

Megan's eyes swam as she watched the girls on their latest ride. She didn't handle rides well. She'd like to blame it on old age, except then she'd have to admit she was getting older. Peter stood beside her. He leaned his arms on the wood fence as he watched their girls scream as they rode the Tilt-A-Whirl.

"Bet you wish you were on there with them," Megan said. The longing in Peter's eyes as he watched the ride go round and round and round was unmistakable. Just like a little kid.

"Nah, they don't want their old man going on all the rides with them," Peter said as he shrugged his shoulders. Megan had to look away—she was getting dizzy just watching them.

"You should have gone, Peter," Megan said.

Alexis wanted to go on one ride by herself, but at the last minute she freaked out and begged Hannah to go with her. Peter offered, but the line was full of kids and teens, no parents. The last thing Alexis wanted was to be embarrassed. Megan remembered when she went through that stage. *God help me, please.*

"Wonder if they'll be able to handle any more rides? I promised Hannah we'd go on the Ferris wheel right before we left." Peter pointed to the ride.

Megan glanced up to the Ferris wheel and shuddered at the swinging seats on the ride that paused to let others off. The thought of sitting in that seat, staring out on the grounds as it swung back and forth, caused Megan's stomach to flop. A shiver ran down her spine. Nope.

"I think I'll sit out on that one, too."

Peter placed his arm around Megan's back and squeezed. "Won't you come on at least one ride with me?"

Megan turned, so that her back rested against the wooden fence. She looked at Peter out of the corner of her eye. He laughed.

"You're kidding me, right?" She turned back around. The Tilt-A-Whirl slowed. Thank goodness.

As the girls exited the ride, she noticed Hannah wobble. Megan rushed over and helped her off the stairs. Hannah's face was white, her lips pale, and her body swayed in half circles. Megan led her over to a ledge where she sat her daughter down and rubbed her back. Alexis jumped down the stairs, rushed over to Peter, and gave him a high five.

"That was awesome!" She grabbed the large pop out of Peter's hands and guzzled it down. She then took her half-eaten candy apple from his hand and licked it. Megan shook her head. That girl loved rides. She went for the thrill every time.

"I never want to go on that ride again," Hannah said. Megan continued to rub her back. A pale pink glow was returning to her cheeks. Megan handed her a bag of popcorn. Hannah plunged her hand inside the bag and filled her mouth with the kernels.

"You're just a big chicken. That was totally fun." Alexis grabbed Peter's hand as she taunted Hannah.

"Wanna come with me this time, Dad?"

Megan shook her head at Peter. The yearning on his face made her smile. This was the man she had fallen in love with. The man who made life fun for her. Or at least used to. He wanted to do that for her again. Tonight was a step in that direction. To keep life fun. Somehow, he managed to overlook the horror in their life. She didn't know how he did that. Lately, it seemed like that's all she could see.

Until she looked at Alexis. The excitement in her face, the way her eyes twinkled, it helped. It helped her see that there was another way of looking at life. She held up her camera and waited for the lens to autofocus. The way Alexis pulled at Peter's arm, it would make a great photo.

"Tell you what," Peter said as he walked Alexis over to where Megan and Hannah sat. "It's getting late and I promised Hannah we'd go on the Ferris wheel before we left. The line is pretty long, so I figure by the time we get to the front, Hannah's stomach should be settled and we might even be able to convince your mom to go on. What do you say?"

Megan glanced at the line that snaked around a cotton candy booth. Maybe by the time they reached the front of the line, she'd be able to convince them she was better off watching them.

Alexis rushed to the end of the line. "Hurry up, you guys, before someone else comes along."

Peter grabbed Megan's hand as they joined Alexis. He gave it a squeeze. She leaned over and kissed him on the cheek.

"Gross! Do you have to do that here?" Alexis shielded her eyes with her hand and groaned.

Hannah beamed a smile their way. She snuggled into Peter, placed her arms around his waist, and leaned her head against him. The color had come back to her face.

As they stood in line, Megan idly listened to the girls talk about the rides they had gone on and found herself looking out into the crowds of people who walked by. Families, faces wreathed in smiles, as they walked through the fairgrounds, wowed by the sights and smells. Older couples reminiscing as they sauntered along, hand in hand. Children who escaped the confines of their parents' attention and played tag in the matted grass. The squeals of laughter, the loud music from the game booths, and the cries of a tired child all mixed together. A smile settled on Megan's face as she took it all in.

Peter tapped her on the shoulder. "You okay?" His words may have asked a general question, but she knew the look in his eyes. They asked for more. *Are you staying here with us? Are you keeping your promise?*

She nodded her head. She was fine. Not okay in the sense that she felt complete, whole. But fine. Fine—as in, *I'm here, I'm learning to enjoy the moment.*

"Just a few more stops of the Ferris wheel and then it's our turn." Alexis bumped into Megan. She tore her eyes from Peter's gaze and ruffled her daughter's already messy hair. Beyond Alexis was a bench.

"You know what? I think I'm going to go sit over at the bench over there and just watch you guys. There's only room for three in a seat, so I'll take pictures. Deal? Plus, then I can hold onto all these prizes and eat your popcorn." Megan gestured to the bench that remained empty. A miracle on a night like this. One Megan was determined to take advantage of.

"You just don't want to go on the ride. Admit it." Alexis crossed her arms as she pouted.

Hannah glared at her sister.

Megan stepped out of line and held her arms out. Alexis threw her items at her, the stuffed animals and the bag of cotton candy. Hannah laid her items on top and gave her mom a smile. Peter just laughed. Megan shot him a dirty look. The least he could have done was help her get out of the ride without Alexis being upset. She picked her way through the swelling crowd and reached the bench just as a group of teenagers were about to sit down.

"Would you guys mind?" She plopped the load in her arms down on the bench before they could say a word. One girl, around sixteen, sat on the bench with her legs crossed. She swung her foot as she stuck a lollipop in her mouth. Megan didn't look away. Kids these days. Another girl grabbed onto her friend's arm and pulled her up. The one who had sat on the bench pulled the lollipop out of her mouth and threw it down on the bench before she turned her back, swung her lips, and tossed her hair over her shoulder. *ARGH. Some kids . . . my girls had better never act like that when they are older.*

Settled on the bench, Megan waved to her family who were next in line. She pushed all the items on the bench closer to her. No sense in taking up the whole bench when she only needed half. She leaned forward just an inch and gazed down at the line for the Ferris wheel. It was huge. Teenagers, older children, young couples holding hands and families, just like hers, waited for their chance.

One family in particular caught her eye. An older couple. The woman wore something that reminded her of a housecoat and the older man had a worn straw hat on his head. In between the couple stood a little girl. Must be their granddaughter—how nice. Last year, Megan's mom had offered to take Hannah and Alexis to the fair. After Megan refused her, she didn't offer again. Not this year. Surprising, because she thought for sure her mom would.

She heard a squeal of delight and watched as Peter helped Hannah and Alexis climb into their seat. He sat in the middle, with his arms around each girl. Hannah held tight to the metal bar while Alexis lifted up her hands and waited for the ride to begin. Megan sympathized with Hannah. She would have gripped the bar until her knuckles went white and kept her eyes clenched shut.

Megan snapped photos of the girls. She made sure she caught the expressions on both their faces. As she was about to take another shot, a voice broke her focus.

"Would you mind if I joined you?"

Megan pulled her camera away from her face. An older woman, slightly familiar, stood before her.

Megan tried to remember where she had seen her before. Her tiny frame, bony hands, and curly grey hair made her think of someone. She smiled, moved her items tighter against her leg, and with a swift glance, looked back at the older couple with the young child who stood in line. The husband now stood alone with the little girl.

"Of course not," Megan said.

The older woman sank onto the wood bench beside Megan with a sigh. She lifted her feet about an inch off the ground before she placed them back on the dirt.

"It's so nice to be off my feet. I'm not a spring chicken anymore."

Megan gave the woman a polite smile before she picked up the camera again and searched the Ferris wheel for Peter and the girls. The girls were having fun. They were almost at the top.

"Are your children on the ride too?"

Megan turned and studied the woman beside her on the bench. Her eyes twinkled as she stared back at Megan before she gestured toward the line. Despite her elderly appearance, she exuded energy and excitement. As if she felt younger than her body looked. The soft smile she gave Megan spoke volumes. As if she had a secret to share.

"They are. My husband and two daughters. They're almost at the top now." She pointed to where Peter sat. He must have been watching her, as he waved when she pointed to him. Megan waved back.

"You didn't want to go on the ride with them?"

Megan shook her head. "I don't do well with rides. Especially when it comes to heights." She held up her camera. "I'm quite happy just taking pictures."

The woman chuckled. "I'm the same way. That's my husband over there, with our granddaughter. He's been the one to take her on all the rides tonight." She gestured toward the older man with the straw hat and the little girl in a pale yellow dress. The little girl's back was turned toward her.

Megan watched the little girl. She held onto her grandfather's hands and tried to jump high in the air. With each jump, he would lift her up, helping her jump a little bit higher every time. Megan imagined the laughter coming from the girl. Her heart cramped.

"Your granddaughter's a little cutie." Megan tore her gaze away.

"She sure is. She's the bright light in our otherwise dark world. I don't know where we would be without her."

Megan nodded her head. She reached across and offered her hand. "Since it seems we'll be on the bench together for a bit, I'm Megan," she said.

"Nice to meet you, Megan, I'm Josie." She reached across and shook Megan's hand. It was such a warm night that Megan was shocked when Josie touched her cold fingers to Megan's hot ones.

"I don't know how my husband can handle all these rides. He's not getting any younger, yet the way he's acting tonight, you'd think he was a teenager." Josie placed her purse down on the bench between her and Megan.

Megan laughed. He reminded her of Peter. She took in the two men. Peter held his hands up high as they sat at the top of the Ferris wheel. Megan's stomach lurched, again, as she watched them. Hannah was looking straight ahead holding onto the bars while Alexis not only had her hands up high, just like her father, but was also, if Megan was seeing this correctly, trying to rock the seat. What a stinker.

Beside her, Josie chuckled. Megan looked at her. She was really a beautiful woman when she smiled.

"This is my granddaughter's first time at the fair. She's so excited. Her mother is due to give birth any day and the poor little girl has been bored," Josie said as she met Megan's gaze.

Megan glanced at the little girl. Her back was still turned and she kept jumping up and down. Her pigtails were flying all over the place when she jumped, and her pale yellow dress, complete with ruffles at the bottom, floated up as she landed. Emma would be about the same age. She'd probably be just as excited too.

"I can tell." Megan couldn't take her eyes off the little girl.

"Which ones are yours again?"

Megan gestured toward the ride and waved. Peter waved back.

"My husband is up there with two of my girls. You can't miss them. One has a huge grin on her face while the other one won't let go of the handle bar."

"You have more than two?"

Megan nodded and cleared her throat.

"I have three. My youngest daughter was kidnapped two years ago." Megan's voice skipped a beat.

Josie's eyes watered as she patted Megan's hand in a motherly gesture.

"Oh dear. The little girl from Kinrich?"

Megan nodded her head.

"I remember reading about that. She was just a baby, wasn't she?" Josie's eyebrows creased together.

Megan's throat swelled as she struggled to contain herself.

"Megan? I'm sorry, I didn't mean to prod. I can only imagine the pain you and your family have gone through." Josie patted her hand again.

Megan's shoulders sank as she looked at the older woman beside her. It felt like a fist took hold of Megan's lungs and was squeezing them tight. She couldn't breathe.

"My daughter disappeared, two years ago . . ." Megan lowered her head. The fist tightened. Her body shook, light tremors that traveled from her heart to her fingers.

"I'm so sorry, dear. Losing a child is hard. But somehow, God gives you the strength to live life. Somehow. It took me years to figure that out after one of my babies died—SIDS they call it now." Josie shook her head. "But look at you—you have a beautiful family. You'll do just fine." Josie patted Megan's hand as the tight band around her heart diminished at Josie's words. The fist that squeezed her lungs let go. She could breathe again.

"Well, it looks like my dear husband has his hands full. I should go help him. It was very nice to have met you. I will pray for your daughter."

Megan smiled through her tears and grasped Josie's hand. She wished there were words to describe how she felt—Josie was an angel in disguise, her unbidden words a comfort. As Megan wiped away her tears, she heard a scream.

"Mom!"

Alexis bounded over to her. She never even noticed them getting off the ride.

"Did you get our pictures? Did you see me at the top? I wanted to rock the seat more, but Hannah was being a chicken and Dad told me to stop." Alexis grabbed her drink off the bench and guzzled it down. She threw the empty cup into the trash beside them.

Peter walked over with Hannah, his arm around her.

"I think this girl has had one too many rides." Peter squeezed Hannah's shoulder and gave Megan a wink.

"Like mother, like daughter, maybe?" Megan bent down and looked Hannah in the eyes. "Are you okay?"

"I want to go home now." Hannah's eyes were wide, her face pale.

"Can't we stay for just a little bit longer?" Alexis stuck the rest of her candy apple in her mouth.

Peter messed her hair. "I think we've done enough tonight, sweetheart. The fair is here for a few more days; we can always come back."

"Who was that you were talking to?" Peter asked Megan.

"Just a sweet old woman." Megan swiped at the remaining tears on her face and gathered the stuff on the bench together.

They walked across the fairgrounds toward the entrance. Megan kept her eyes peeled for Josie, to perhaps receive one more motherly smile, but despite all the older couples she saw, none were Josie and her family.

It shocked Megan that she'd opened up to a complete stranger about Emma. But it felt good, like a balm to her wounded soul. She'd made a promise to Peter to not focus on Emma tonight, so she kept the secret of her confession herself. A tiny seed of guilt entered her heart on their drive home. As they passed fields of corn, Megan scanned her memory. Just because she had made a promise to not look for her daughter didn't mean she was blind. What if her daughter had been there? What if she'd missed her because she didn't look?

CHAPTER TWENTY-FOUR

The house was quiet. The girls were at school and Peter had just left for work. He'd surprised her when he came on the run this morning with her and Laurie. It was nice, though. It was something they used to do together before life caught up to them. Now, Peter tended to head to the gym during lunch or after work, while Megan continued to run in the early mornings.

After her shower and her first cup of coffee, Megan took the camera into the study and opened Peter's laptop. She typed in her password for her profile and waited for the programs to load. It had been so long since she last downloaded pictures off her camera, who knew what was on there. She should probably print some of them off and add to their photo albums at least.

Laurie had tried to talk her into scrapbooking years ago when it was all the rage. Megan had gone to a scrapbooking party, made some neat cards, and even laid out a page for a scrapbook she'd bought and then made the mistake of ordering too many stickers, paper, and cutting supplies. She now had a large plastic container full of scrapbooking materials she never used.

As the photos downloaded, she caught snippets of them during the process. Alexis was so full of life, energetic, always a sparkle in her eye even though it took a lot of work to get a smile on her face.

Hannah, however, always smiled. She had a sweet look to her. Reading a book, playing a game, or drawing in her sketchbook, there was always a smile on her face.

Megan hit the delete button on the computer after the photos had downloaded. No sense cluttering up her memory card if she didn't need to. She went through the pictures, one by one. Alexis as she posed beside a clown, both with silly looks on their faces; Peter as he sneaked a piece of the girls' cotton candy; and Hannah's tight grip on the bar of Ferris wheel.

There were about sixty pictures downloaded, forty of those from the fair. The other twenty were of days forgotten, first day of school, Alexis in her gi for karate, Hannah as she posed with a cake she'd made on her own. Memories worth keeping, but forgotten as time went on. Some photos went immediately into the garbage bin. Like the one of her sitting out on the deck. Yeah, um, no.

She came across the last picture she'd taken the night before. Of Peter. They'd just walked in the door, the girls had gone to their rooms to place their hard-won prizes on their shelves, and Peter had grabbed her, pulled her in, and kissed her soundly on the mouth. It wasn't a romantic type of kiss. But it was filled with something. Excitement, maybe.

The look in his eyes caught Megan's attention. Her heart skipped a beat. She'd held the camera in her hand, about to place it on the table in their entranceway. She brought it up, turned it on, and snapped a picture of Peter just as his face was about to turn away from her.

"What was that for?" he had asked.

"Just 'cause." Megan shrugged her shoulders and turned away, about to head into the kitchen when Peter grabbed her hand and stopped her.

"I'm proud of you. Megan, you were there with us tonight, one hundred percent, and I'm so proud of you. I know how hard it must have been." He pulled her close and enveloped her in his arms. Megan stiffened, for a split-second, before she forced herself to relax. She dropped her shoulders, wrapped her arms around his, and hugged him back.

Megan leaned back in the desk chair and placed her hand on the mouse. She clicked on pictures that she wanted to send to the local pharmacy to have developed. It was a one-hour service, complete with a link on the computer. One in particular caught her eye.

It was the picture of Peter, Hannah, and Alexis. The girls held carnival prizes in their hands. The lights in the background sparkled. Megan loved this picture. She should place it in a frame and hang it on the wall in the hallway. Something in the background caught her eye. She enlarged the frame and moved in close to the computer screen.

Behind Hannah stood an older couple with a young girl. Red suspenders and a white dress stood out, prominent against the black background.

Megan couldn't quite make out the little girl. Her face was a blur. So, she enlarged the picture, enhanced it by 50 percent. The image was still a tad bit hazy, but if she looked closely, Megan could make out the little girl's features. She looked so familiar.

Megan sat back in her chair. She closed her eyes, but the image of the little girl had already been imprinted on her mind. She'd seen her somewhere. Before the fair. Megan thought back to all the little girls she once thought were Emma and tried to remember if this little girl could have been one of them.

That's when it hit her.

Megan bolted out of the chair and pulled the drawer to the filing cabinet open. She ripped the file that contained the updated pictures of Emma out. When she found the picture, she stared at it.

With slow precision, Megan backed up until the back of her knees hit the desk chair. She sank down as if a weight had dropped onto her shoulders. Her hand shook so hard that the picture she held onto wavered. Her heart stopped beating, her lungs refused to take in air.

Her daughter had been at the fair. Her daughter had stood mere yards from her and she didn't even see her. She had made a promise to her husband, she had listened to him and agreed to put him first, and she had missed seeing her daughter. Emma.

If Megan hadn't been seated in the chair already, she would have collapsed. Her daughter had been within arm's reach, and all she had was a picture.

Megan studied the picture, memorized every detail of her daughter's face. She didn't look like a boy, nor did she look lifeless, abused. She looked happy. A smile was on her face.

Her daughter. Emma. So close and yet so far away.

CHAPTER TWENTY-FIVE

Megan burst through the front doors of Peter's office. The moment her heart started to beat again, she knew she had to print off the picture and show it to Peter. Otherwise, he wouldn't believe her. Not this time. Not when it really mattered.

"Megan, how are you?"

Dana, the petite receptionist at Peter's real-estate company, smiled at her. Her French-manicured fingers were poised over top of her keyboard, held in suspended animation as Megan walked in.

"Is Peter in his office?"

Dana's eyes widened as Megan walked past her and grabbed onto the handle of the frosted glass door. She swiveled in her chair and reached her hand out.

Like that was going to stop her.

"Megan, Peter told me he didn't want to be disturbed. He's in a meeting." Dana's smile could have been labeled with a capital F. For Fake. She shrugged her dainty little shoulder, as if to say "What can I do?"

"Is he with a client?" The picture of Emma fluttered in Megan's fingers. She stilled her arm. The shock of seeing her daughter turned into anger at being kept from her husband.

"Well, no. Not exactly." Dana fidgeted with a pen in her hands. She wouldn't look Megan in the eye.

Megan sighed. Her hand dropped from the door handle.

"Is he with her?" She refused to say her name. Refused.

Dana's perfectly waxed eyebrows zigzagged on her face, her petite little button nose turned up as her lips pursed.

"Her?"

Megan closed her eyes. Seriously. As if she didn't know who. The only other person who worked in the office other than Peter. His business partner. HER.

"Yes, they are on a, um, conference call." Dana glanced at the phone.

So did Megan. The sophisticated phone system that cost thousands to install, that could do anything and everything you'd ever want a phone to do. The same phone that should have been lit up if there were an actual conference call.

"So I see."

Megan pulled the door open and stormed down the hallway. There were three offices in the back, along with a sitting room, which Megan helped to design when Peter first opened his own real-estate company. The doors to two of the offices were wide open. One was not—Peter's.

Megan's flip-flops thudded against the thick Berber carpet as she made her way to Peter's door. She hesitated. Should she knock, or just barge in? What if they were on a conference call? But what if they weren't? She closed her eyes, grabbed hold of the handle, and opened it. With force. And then opened her eyes.

She should have kept them shut.

Peter sat at this desk. But he wasn't looking at the computer. He wasn't on the phone or even writing notes down on a piece of paper.

Instead, his eyes were looking up, into the face of the only woman Megan would ever admit that she hated. With a passion.

Samantha. She was everything Megan was not. Tall, with the body of a model, she stood at Peter's desk, but her body was bent as she scribbled something down in a notebook. Her wavy blonde hair cascaded across her shoulders until it lightly touched Peter's arm. She wore a grey pencil skirt with a black silk blouse that was open at the neck offering a clear view of her eye candy.

Are. You. Kidding. Me?

As Megan entered the office, Samantha straightened with slow precision. By her height, Megan guessed she must be wearing her stilettos. If ever a woman deserved to live the life of a city woman, it was Samantha. Too bad she was stuck in a small town.

"Megan, what a nice surprise. Peter didn't mention you would be coming in today." Samantha placed her hand briefly on Peter's shoulder before she stepped back. Her voice purred with a familiar satisfaction.

Anger boiled within Megan as she forced a smile on her face.

"Am I interrupting?" She focused her gaze on Peter. His face went two shades of red as he fumbled with the papers on his desk.

"Well, actually . . ." Samantha leaned against the edge of the desk.

"No, absolutely not," Peter interrupted. He pushed his chair back and stood.

Megan stepped aside as Samantha breezed past her. She couldn't help but notice the sway of her hips. Megan refused to look her in the eye. It took all her strength just to keep her mouth shut.

Peter closed the door behind Samantha and faced Megan. She didn't say anything. Her mind swirled with unspoken questions, but Peter would need to be a mind reader today.

"Megan, it wasn't what it looked like. We just finished up a conference call and were going through the notes. I have a client wanting to move here . . ." He stared at her, a puppy-dog expression on his face. Megan wasn't moved.

The silence in the room stretched thin. Peter's shoulders flopped as he walked back to his chair.

"I don't care," Megan whispered in the silence.

She looked down at the photo in her hands. She was afraid to show him. All her steam had fizzled away. What if it was just her imagination? What if it was just a little girl at the fair with her grandparents?

She held the picture up and placed it on the desk. Peter stared at it. The worry lines on his forehead indented as he looked from Megan to the picture.

"Who do you see in the picture?"

Peter pulled the photo closer to him and picked it up with both hands.

"What am I supposed to see, Meg? Other than the girls and myself?"

Megan bit her lip. She really hoped he would see it. See her. Their daughter.

"In the background, what do you see?" Megan leaned forward.

Peter laid the picture down, clasped his hands together and leaned back in his chair. The look he gave Megan spoke volumes. Disappointment. In her. A nervous panic fluttered in Megan's chest. He didn't see it. How could he not?

"Megan, I see a blurry reflection of two, maybe three people. Two adults and one child. What else am I supposed to see?"

Megan leaned forward and jabbed the picture with her finger.

"Our daughter, Peter. You are supposed to see our daughter. These people"—Megan pointed to the couple in the background—"have our daughter."

She stared into her husband's eyes and wished with all her heart that he would see it. She needed him to make the connection.

"You see Emma?" Peter ran his fingers through his hair.

Megan stared at her husband. Was he serious?

"Yes, Peter. I see our daughter. How can you not?"

Peter stood up. Megan's gaze followed him as he walked around his desk and sat in the seat beside her. He reached for her hands.

"It's Emma." Megan's voice caught as Peter rubbed her hands. She needed him to believe her. He had to believe her. She hated the look on his face, the sympathetic smile, the soft eyes. He didn't believe her.

"It's not Emma. I know you want it to be, but it's not."

Megan wrenched her hands out from under his. She grabbed the picture off the desk.

"It is her. Peter, look"—she held the photo up—"it's our daughter. I know it!" Tears threatened to cascade down her cheeks.

Peter sighed. It was a deep sigh. She watched as his shoulders deflated and curved forward. The sliver of hope that had begun to beat in her heart when she realized it was her daughter died.

Peter took the picture out of Megan's hand and laid it back on his desk. He placed one hand on her knee.

"Meg, honey, I know how much you want it to be Emma. I do. I wish it were her. But it's not. I'm not even sure who it is. You've blown it up so much that it's all blurry. What if it's a boy? What if it's someone carrying a bag and not a little girl in a dress? Don't jump to conclusions."

Megan shook her head. Conclusions? A bag? How could he not see it? How could he not understand?

Peter leaned closer to her. His voice was velvety smooth as he spoke to her. As if she were a child he needed to comfort.

"Meg, please, would you trust me? Please? I think you need to talk to someone. I could call the counselor and make an appointment if you want?"

Megan shuddered. The tears that welled up in her eyes now overflowed and ran down her cheeks. She yanked her hand out from his and wiped at her cheeks.

"No, Peter. I won't go back to her. You know what will happen. I'm not going on medication."

"Then what about the pastor's wife at church? We could start going back, and take the girls. I know you don't like that idea, but it might be good for us." Peter handed her a Kleenex.

"The only thing good for us would be to find Emma. I'm going to take this to the police, Peter. I'll see if Detective Riley is in, give him the photo. He'll be able to find her. Hanton is only a half hour away; he can contact the local police there. Our daughter is so close. I have to do this. Please don't try to stop me." She wiped at her face.

Peter cast his eyes down. She didn't know what he thought. If he would agree.

"I'll call him," Peter said, his voice low. He didn't raise his eyes.

"You?" Megan couldn't believe what she heard. She took a quick breath. *Does this mean he believes me? Oh please God, let him believe me.*

"I need closure. I can't keep doing this. I'll call him. But on one condition." Peter raised his eyes. They pierced her own.

"I need you to promise that this will end. That if he looks at the photo and doesn't think it's her, then you'll stop. You'll stop looking for her in every face you see. That we can move on." He rubbed his face.

Megan couldn't believe the difference one sentence could make. He looked older. More tired. A stranger. She almost hated him.

"Peter, we've already discussed this."

"But you're not listening to me. I can't do this anymore, Megan. If you can't promise me this, if you can't stop, then I can't continue." He turned his face from her.

It felt like a load of bricks had fallen on Megan. She was crushed. He didn't mean that. He couldn't. He wouldn't walk away. Not from her. Not from his children.

"I would never walk away from our children," Peter said. She must have spoken out loud.

Megan stood. No matter what she did, she lost something. If she agreed with Peter, then she was giving up on her daughter. If she didn't agree, then she was giving up on her marriage. It was a no-win situation. There was nothing she could do.

Even though Peter was willing to give up without a fight, she wouldn't. If it meant she was the only one fighting, then so be it. She reached down for her purse that rested against her chair and hooked it over her shoulder.

"Call him, Peter. Just call him," she said as she opened the door to his office. Samantha stood across the hallway in her office.

"Nothing else matters to me. Not right now."

CHAPTER TWENTY-SIX

As a child, Megan loved to walk through cemeteries. She would spend hours as she meandered through the rows of graves. She loved to read the tombstones. To her, this was a way to honor those who had gone before her. Children who had died too soon. Mothers who had suffered loss too early. Grandparents who knew what it meant to survive. Her mother called her fascination with cemeteries morbid.

Today, she'd have to agree.

Somehow, between the time she'd left Peter's office and now, she had managed to drive from one end of the town to the other. But her trip was a fog. Her mind was empty, devoid of anything but disbelief. Stumped that her husband was willing to give up everything they had built together so easily. Hurt that he could cast her aside without a fight.

She opened her car door. The stillness found only in a cemetery greeted her. A lone bird chirped in the distance. Though she was close to the lake, the rush of the waves as they beat against the rocks was muffled. She took in her surroundings. The rows of white, grey, and black marble tombstones stood sentry. Being in this place soothed her. She drank in the quiet, the peace she'd always found here.

She wasn't surprised that she drove here. Often during her runs, if she were emotional or needed to really think, she would take the long route, through the cemetery, down to the lake and then back up to her house. It was worth the extra distance.

She left her vehicle parked off to the side and walked through the rows. Her gaze would caress each tombstone, as she read the few words chiseled onto the stone that someone thought embodied their loved one. She took note of the years.

Her heart broke at all the children who lay under her feet. Thank God Emma wasn't here.

Megan reached a large tree that stood alone on top of a hill and sagged against it. Weariness infused her body. At the bottom of the slight hill stood a group of people dressed in black. A hearse with its back door open waited on the other side of the crowd.

A casket was being pushed out of the hearse and into the hands of the four men who stood waiting for it. The moment the casket appeared, a woman in the crowd let out an anguished cry and would have crumpled to the ground if it wasn't for the man who stood beside her. He caught her in time.

Megan's gaze reverted back to the casket. To the small child-sized casket.

This is what Peter wanted. For her to accept Emma's death and move on in life.

Her body slithered down the tree as a sob tore through her throat. Her fisted hand covered her mouth as she tried to remain silent. She imagined Emma in that box. She watched the woman down at the grave site. Her face was turned as the casket made its way past her. When it rested on the lowering device above the empty hole, the woman broke away from the man's hold and draped herself over the casket. Her cries echoed through the cemetery.

Megan turned her gaze. It was as if her heart had been ripped out of her, thrown to the ground, and trampled on. Tears flowed freely down her face. Her silent cries echoed the woman's sobs.

It was time to admit Emma was gone.

❦

Megan returned to her car and drove to the nearest building where she could hide until she had calmed down after the scene at the cemetery.

Unfortunately, it was their old church.

It had been two years since she'd last crossed through the front doors. After Emma disappeared, she couldn't handle the looks of sympathy she knew she would receive, the tiny pats on the hand along with the whispered words, *sorry for your loss*. In their minds, Emma was already dead.

The worst was when the pastor had dropped by their house one night and told them that God didn't give more than a person could handle. If Peter hadn't escorted him out of the house, Megan would have killed him. Literally.

The reserved parking spots for the pastors and administration staff were full, but other than that, the church that should have been open to all people was empty. Megan had no doubt that the doors would be locked, even if she had wanted to enter the church and spend some time on her knees. Which she didn't.

Megan drummed her fingers on the steering wheel. She never quite understood the concept of a locked church. Why do people have to make an appointment to pour out their hearts to a man, when the altar should be open and available for anyone who needed to feel the hand of God upon their shoulders?

At the end of the street, Megan watched the funeral procession pull out of the cemetery. It was a small group; a total of six cars followed the large black limo as it snaked its way down the street.

A sharp pain shot through her chest, and she put her hand up to where the pain originated and struggled to breathe. What was going on? This used to happen to her at the beginning, when her nightmare first started, about a month after Emma was kidnapped and they'd received no word about her whereabouts.

Panic attacks, the counselor told her. Worry pains, her mother insisted. Just give it to God and you'll be fine. If Megan had a dollar for all the times her mother told her to just give it to God, she'd be a rich woman.

The funeral procession passed and faded into the distance as Megan focused on breathing through the pain. At the count of twenty, she was able to breathe without issue again. She massaged the back of her neck where a bubble of pressure had formed. She should head home before a full-blown migraine hit.

Megan reached into her purse to pull out a tissue and instead her fingers found the little candle Johnny had given her at the ice cream parlor. She pulled it out and rolled it in her hand. Such an innocent little thing. As a child you believe that making a wish is all it takes for all your dreams to come true. As an adult, you know wishes go unheard.

But she had made a promise. What could it hurt?

She reached across to the glove box and clicked the little lock. She should have some matches in there somewhere. After pushing aside her insurance papers and the Jeep's owner's manual, she found them.

Her fingers trembled as she broke off a match and struck it against the black edge. A flame leaped to life and blazed brilliantly. She dipped the flame to the wick and watched as it burned brightly.

She shook the match and watched as a plume of smoke drifted toward her open window. She flicked the match out the window and stared at the lit candle in her hand.

She ignored the taunting in her head that teased her, called her weak and fainthearted. Who but a child would believe in wishes from a candle?

Hot drops of wax burned her fingers as the flame continued to burn.

There were no wishes left to whisper. It was time to face reality.

With a soft burst of air, she blew out the candle.

She dropped the candle into her cup holder and flicked the small ball of wax off of her finger before driving past the parked cars in the church lot and heading home. In her rearview mirror, the white cross on the church steeple diminished the farther away she drove.

"Where were you, God, when my daughter was taken away from me? Where were you when we waited for word of her return? Why did you let her die alone?"

A gentle breeze caressed her cheek through the open window.

CHAPTER TWENTY-SEVEN

Butterflies and fireflies danced together in the garden beds in Megan's backyard. As she rinsed the dinner dishes in the kitchen sink, the scene at the cemetery filled her mind. The mother draped across the little casket.

Peter's footsteps alerted Megan to his presence. She wished he would go away. The girls were in the family room playing a game on the entertainment unit, and despite their fervent pleadings, Megan had begged off from the game. Peter took her place instead.

"Done so soon?"

Peter's arms encircled her body. She stiffened her back and stilled her hands in the hot sudsy water. The last thing she wanted right now was to be touched. By him.

"Yeah, the girls are getting pretty good at the game. They whipped my butt in a matter of minutes." His arms withdrew from around her body and she breathed a sigh of relief. A small one.

She rinsed another dish and placed it in the dish rack to dry. Hand-washing dishes soothed her. She could have used the dishwasher, but they had had takeout tonight, so there wasn't much to wash.

"Listen, about today . . ." Peter headed over to the island and leaned against it.

Megan clutched the dishcloth in her hand. "It's okay."

"No, I . . ."

She bit her lip before turning. "I said it was okay. I heard you, Peter. And you were right." Tears dripped down her face as she stared at her husband.

"What do you mean?"

"It's time to say good-bye." The air shattered into a million pieces.

Peter shook his head. "No, no. That's not what I was going to say." He dropped his gaze and hunched his shoulders. "I spoke with Riley."

Megan's hand shook. A jolt of energy fluttered through her stomach. She drained the sink and wiped down the counter.

"Does he think it's her?"

She didn't want to look at Peter, afraid of what she might see in his eyes. Afraid to hope again.

When he didn't answer her, she turned. That was answer enough.

"Meg . . ."

He'd crossed the slight distance between them and reached out.

"We need to be prepared that it's not her."

Megan fisted her hand against her mouth, silencing the sob that welled deep within from escaping. Tears welled up in her eyes and it was all she could do not to let them spill. Everything ached inside of her. Her heart. Her mind. Her soul.

"Dad?" A small voice broke the silence that had formed in the kitchen. Both Peter and Megan turned to face their daughter who stood in the doorway.

Alexis's eyes darted back and forth between Megan and Peter. "Um, it's your turn, Dad," she said. The uncertainty in her voice spoke volumes.

"He'll be there shortly, okay, hon?" Megan tried to keep her voice calm. She gave a tentative smile, which apparently reassured her daughter since she nodded her head and left.

"Peter . . ."

Peter shook his head and reached for her hands. Again. This time, she didn't pull away.

"Riley doesn't know if it's her or not. It's not a clear picture. He'll follow up, though, and let us know." His fingers caressed her hand. "I know you want it to be her. I want it to be her. But it's not. We have to accept that." Peter's eyes shone with unshed tears. "I can't keep doing this, I'm sorry. I know you think I'm a monster. That I'm uncaring and selfish. That I've given up on our daughter. But that's so far from the truth. I just wish you could see that. Waiting for Emma is hurting our family. Don't you see that? It's killing us, Megan. We need to say good-bye to the little girl who was ripped from our arms. We need closure. I need closure." His eyes searched hers. She could see the need there, the need for her to believe him.

If she wanted her marriage to survive, the next words she spoke would determine the outcome.

"Okay."

"Okay?" She heard the doubt in his voice.

"Okay. But I can't . . ." Her voice broke. "I can't be the one to plan the ceremony. You'll need to. Or my mother. But I don't want to be a part of it."

Peter gathered her into his arms, held her close to his body. She stiffened before relaxing and drawing her arms up against his chest. She buried her face into the crook of his neck.

"Thank you," Peter said.

"What if she comes home, though? What then?"

"If," he said as he rubbed his hand against her back. "No, Megs, when. When she comes back, we'll welcome her with open arms.

But she'll be a different girl than the one we knew. And we'll be a different family. A stronger family. I'm not saying to give up, Megan." He pulled away and took a step back. "Just that this will help us move forward until she comes home."

He leaned forward and placed a kiss upon her cold lips before heading back toward the living room to continue playing games with their daughters.

Something had changed between them. It began a long time ago. A little crack that widened on its own. She wasn't sure if it could ever be fixed.

CHAPTER TWENTY-EIGHT

Do I get to pick my very own donut, Papa?"

Jack glanced down at Emmie. She sat in the middle of the truck cab, the seat belt buckled across her waist, with her hands in her lap and a smile on her face. Her eyes danced with excitement.

"Whatever kind you want," said Jack.

When Dottie had been about to bring out ice cream for their dessert, Jack stopped her and said they should go to town for a donut. Emmie, wide-eyed, waited for Grandma to agree. Jack had a feeling she would. Today had been a good day. Going to the fair last night seemed to perk Dottie up.

Emmie twisted in the front seat to look out the back window of the old pickup truck.

"What's taking Grandma so long?" She placed her chin in her hands as she stared at the back door.

Jack looked at the watch on his wrist. What was taking her so long? All she had to do was grab her purse—wasn't like she had to get all dolled up or anything. They were only going to the donut shop.

"Will your friends be there, Papa?" Emmie tilted her head to look at him.

"Oh, I'm sure they will. They've wanted to meet you for a very long time." Jack winked. Too long.

He looked out the window and saw that the grass on the side of the house needed to be cut. That side always grew faster than the rest of the yard. Dottie had wanted him to dig up a plot in the spring and let her plant some sunflowers there. Maybe he should have done it. Less grass to cut.

The door to the back remained closed. What was Dottie doing in there? If she didn't hurry up, the sun would set and she'd be telling him Emmie needed to go to bed. He nudged Emmie in the shoulder and honked the horn. Her eyes widened to twice their size, her mouth shaped into a big O. Jack chuckled. Yep, Emmie knew Grandma didn't like to be rushed.

"Emmie, why don't you go over and play with Daisy for a couple of minutes while I see what is keeping Grandma?"

Jack opened the door and cringed as it squeaked on its hinges. He knew he forgot to do something today. Dottie mentioned the noise last night when they headed into the fair. He waited for Emmie to scoot across the seat and then he helped her to jump out of the cab.

"Daisy, Daisy," Emmie called as she ran into the backyard.

Daisy poked her tiny head out of the large doghouse Jack had built. He waited to ensure Emmie could open the gate he'd rigged to keep Daisy enclosed whenever they were out and about. Which wasn't often.

Jack headed to the back door, cupped his hands over his eyes, and peered inside. He couldn't see Dottie in the kitchen. He opened the screen and stuck his head inside.

"Dottie, hurry up, woman. What's taking you so long?"

"I can't find it," Dottie yelled. Jack found Dottie in the front room tearing apart the closet.

"What can't you find, love?" Jack stood behind her and peered into the closet. She was pushing shoes and boots aside on the floor.

"My purse. I can't find my purse." She leaned back and blew a strand of hair out of her face. Jack leaned down to grasp her hand and hauled her up so she was back on her feet.

"Where did you last see it?"

Dottie rubbed her face. "I don't know. I don't remember. I just can't find it."

Jack glanced around the room. "Are you sure you looked everywhere?"

It was obvious she'd already looked for her purse in the living room. It had been torn to shreds. Pillows that would sit in the corner of the couch were now on the floor. Wool had been dumped out of her knitting bag and some of the balls had rolled off the chair. Yards of yarn now crisscrossed on the floor.

"What about the kitchen?" He pulled Dottie along behind him.

"I've already looked. I just don't know where it is!"

Dottie's hand fisted while Jack held it. Not good. He made Dottie sit at the kitchen table and with gentle pressure he massaged her neck. Her head dropped as he worked his magic. Maybe if she just relaxed for a few minutes she would remember.

"Things were busy last night when we came home. Emmie was pretty hyped up from the fair and Daisy made a mess in the kitchen. I'm sure you just set it down somewhere. You've just forgotten, that's all," Jack said.

Dottie's head shot up and she pulled her body forward, out of Jack's hands.

"I don't just forget, Jack," she said. Her mouth had set in a straight line as she twisted her head to look at him. He backed away while holding his hands up.

"Yes, Dottie. You do. Lately, you've been forgetting more and more. Remember this morning, when you asked me if we were going to the fair today? We did that yesterday," Jack said.

Dottie shook her head. "No we didn't. We're going now. That's why I need my purse. You gave me the tickets to hold on to, and they are in my purse."

"No, love, that was yesterday," Jack said.

Maybe it was time to go back to the doctor.

Dottie's shoulders slumped. Jack took a quick peek out the kitchen window. Emmie sat on the grass with Daisy in her lap. He started to open the kitchen cupboards. Maybe Emmie hid the purse as a joke. When he looked back at the kitchen table, he saw Dottie's head hung low and her shoulders shaking. He walked over, sat in the chair beside her, and took her hands.

"I miss her, Jack. So much so that it hurts. I'm empty without her." Tears ran down Dottie's face. Jack leaned forward and wiped them away.

"I miss her too." Jack knew she was talking about their daughter.

Dottie lifted her tearstained face. The sorrow written in her eyes broke Jack's heart.

"I never told you. I always meant to tell you." She reached up and stroked his face. "I'm so sorry."

Jack covered that hand with his. These little trips into the past were happening more frequently. It worried Jack. She was becoming more enmeshed in the life they once had then the one they were now living.

"I know you miss her, it's okay." He was at a loss anymore how to help his wife, and it really bothered him.

Dottie shook her head. "No, Jack. You don't understand."

"Understand what? What don't I understand?"

Dottie pulled her hand away and fiddled with the basket of Emmie's stuff on the table. She looked everywhere but at him.

"I know we promised to never keep secrets from each other. I didn't mean to. I just . . . my mind gets all muddled . . ." Dottie's body trembled.

Jack's heart broke. He knew the secret Dottie carried. He knew, but he never confessed it to her. Some secrets are better left unsaid.

"It's okay, love. It is okay. You don't have to say any more," he said. He took a deep breath. "I already know."

"How do you know? How?" A glazed look filled Dottie's eyes, her brows furrowed. Jack knew she didn't understand what he was saying.

"Why don't you tell me, love? Tell me your secret."

Dottie's voice could barely be heard as she confessed. With each word she whispered, the crack in Jack's heart widened until the pain became so intense he thought it would shatter.

"She's dead, Jack. Our Mary is dead."

A small cry filled the room. Jack's head whipped up. Emmie stood at the screen door.

With a speed he didn't know was possible in his old age, Jack rushed to the door. He gathered Emmie in his arms, crushed her to his chest as the tears ran down his cheeks. She didn't need to hear this. Not here, not now. Emmie's arms tightened around Jack's neck.

"It's okay, Papa. I know my mommy's in heaven," Emmie whispered in his ear.

Jack's eyes closed as he held on tight. Dottie's quiet sobs filled the kitchen, but all Jack saw in his mind's eye was his daughter at Emmie's age, as she danced in their front yard. Emmie reminded him of his daughter in so many ways. As he held her close, he whispered a silent prayer that if he couldn't have his daughter, at least he could have his granddaughter.

"Why don't you run up to your room, okay? Let me talk with Grandma for a few minutes and then I'll be up and we can talk."

Jack kissed the top of her head and set her back down on the floor. He watched her give Dottie a hug and then climb the steps to her room. It wasn't until he heard her bedroom door close that he sat back down at the table.

"I already knew, Dottie. I called the halfway house and they told me."

The memory of that phone call hit Jack full force. When he found out that his daughter was dead, his heart just about broke. The only thing that kept him going was Emmie.

"They told you? Why did you call them?" Fear filled Dottie's eyes. There was something she didn't want him to know. What could be worse than keeping their daughter's death a secret?

Jack explained with painful patience why he called the halfway house. He confessed the ache in his heart for Mary and the thought that if he could just hear her voice, or even leave a note letting her know he cared, that the ache would diminish. The counselor at the home told him that Mary had been very sick. Whether from the drugs or disease, Jack didn't think to ask. She'd been dead for over two years now. At Mary's request, they didn't contact any family until after her cremation. They used money Jack had sent to cover the cost.

"You must hate me," Dottie said once Jack fell silent.

"How could I hate you? We've been through too much, Dottie-mine, for me ever to hate you. I wish you had told me, I wish that you could have confided in me. You shouldn't have had to deal with that all on your own," Jack said. No, he didn't hate. He never could.

"Why didn't you tell me, Dottie? Why didn't you tell me when you brought Emmie home?" He tried to wrap his mind around that, but he couldn't. No matter the various scenarios he thought of, none of them made sense.

Dottie's head shot up. A horror-stricken look covered her face.

"Because I couldn't remember. I couldn't remember, Jack. I couldn't remember . . ." Dottie's fist hit her head over and over as she said the words.

Jack grabbed at her fists and struggled with her. She pulled away from him.

How could she not remember? Her memory wasn't that bad back then. That's when it hit Jack. That was at the time Dottie's memory started to slip. They had gone to the doctor and they began to play around with the various medicines and dosages to help her. There was one point where things were really bad, when her memory wasn't there at all. The doctor readjusted the dosage until she was back to normal. That was right around the time Dottie brought Emmie home.

"Of course you do, Dottie. You remember the day you brought Emmie home, right? How happy you were when you walked in the door? I'll never forget that day. Emmie held onto your hand so tight, but your face, ah, your face was aglow. You remember that day, don't you?" Jack needed her to remember.

Dottie nodded her head. "I remember being so happy. When I found her, alone on the street, all it took was one look for me to know she was Mary's daughter. She looks so much like her, doesn't she?" A soft smile settled on Dottie's face. She retreated, back into the past, to the day that Emmie came home. Jack couldn't let her. He couldn't lose her, not now. Now when she was so clearheaded.

"On the street?" Jack prodded her. He needed her to focus, to stay with him in the present. Jack needed her to remember.

"Dottie, you said you found her on the street? Was that in front of the halfway house where Mary stayed?"

Dottie didn't answer. Tears shimmered in her eyes, her lips pursed as her fingers clenched together.

She twisted her hands together and closed her eyes. Jack gave her a minute. He needed her to remember.

"Then where did I get Mary?" Dottie asked, her eyes still closed.

"Emmie, you mean Emmie."

Startled, Dottie gasped. "Of course I mean Emmie. Jack, what are you thinking?"

Jack stared out the window. His world crumbled all around him and he felt helpless to do anything about it. He wished the blinders were still on, that he didn't see what was before him. His heart broke as he struggled with the truth that stared him directly in the eyes.

"I think . . . I think you're struggling with your memory more and more each day and that we need to go back to the doctor. It's been a while. You missed your last few appointments. You promised you would reschedule, but you haven't. Do you have any pills left or are you empty?"

Dottie's head twisted back and forth, as she denied what he was suggesting. He knew she would. She hated going to the doctor. She always had.

"I don't need a doctor. I'm fine." She looked into his eyes, and he knew he'd lost her. She was gone.

"Come on, let's get Mary and go to the fair. You know how she loves the fair," Dottie said as she pushed her chair back to stand. Jack grabbed onto her hand and wouldn't let go.

"Emmie, Dottie. Emmie. Our granddaughter. We took her to the fair yesterday. Right now, she's up in her room. She heard about Mary, Dottie. Emmie knows that her mom is dead."

A wave of sadness flowed out of Jack as he said the words. His granddaughter. The weight of the world had crashed down upon his shoulders. He was afraid. More afraid then he'd ever been in his life—more afraid even than when he had been in the army, facing the enemy.

Dottie sank in her chair. Her body shook with force as a sob tore through her throat. If Jack had been anywhere but next to Dottie, he would have thought the feral sound to be something from a horror movie.

"I'm so sorry, Jack. I'm so sorry."

Jack stood in the doorway and watched his granddaughter. His heart swelled with love, heartache, and a sadness he couldn't understand. He wasn't a stranger to death, in the war it had become a constant companion. But not like this. This he wouldn't wish on his best friend.

Emmie was hunched over her little table. She'd placed her stuffed animals all around her in a circle. Jack couldn't see what she was doing, but he imagined she was coloring a picture.

Jack coughed and Emmie looked up. A sad smile settled on her face.

"Hey, princess," Jack said. His voice croaked out the words.

"Hi," Emmie said. She bent her head again, focused on whatever she was doing.

"Can I sit down?" Jack took a step into the room. He wasn't sure what to expect. He had just left Dottie in their room after convincing her to lie down for a bit. He just hoped it would help her calm down.

Emmie moved a stuffed animal off the chair that sat beside her. She didn't say anything. He peered over the animals to see what she was doing. A piece of paper lay before her. On it she had colored a large castle sitting on a sparkling white cloud.

Emmie watched him as he took in her picture. When he glanced up, he noticed the unshed tears in her eyes. He swiped at his face, erasing any evidence of his own tears.

"It's okay, Papa. I'm just a little sad." Emmie's quiet voice soothed the ache in his heart.

He didn't understand this gift that God had presented to him. He had come upstairs to help comfort his granddaughter, not for her to comfort him.

"I'm sad too," Jack admitted. More sad than he would ever have imagined.

"Do you like my picture, Papa?" Emmie's hand hovered over the picture, a pink crayon cradled in her fingers.

"It's very beautiful. I think that's the best castle I've seen yet."

"It's Mommy's castle in heaven. She loves flowers, so I made sure I drew lots. And here's the swing, Papa, just like the one you made when she was a little girl. Grandma told me how much she used to like to swing in it." Emmie drew another flower beside the castle.

Jack couldn't answer. He didn't know what to say.

Silence reigned over the room. A whisper of a breeze fluttered through the window along with the soft chirps of the robin nestled in the tree outside of Emmie's room.

"Papa?" Emmie's voice broke through the quiet.

"Yes, princess?"

"Are my sisters with her?" Emmie's brow furrowed together.

The question shocked Jack. This wasn't the first time Emmie had brought up these imagined sisters. He didn't know how to answer her.

"What sisters, Emmie?"

"My sisters. Grandma doesn't like me to talk about them. She said that it's foolish talk. Does she not like me talking about them 'cause they're in heaven with Mommy and Daddy?"

CHAPTER TWENTY-NINE

I f we had paid as little attention to our plants as we do our children, we would be amazed at the jungle we found ourselves in.

It was a saying Dottie's mother loved to repeat while she shadowed her children in the garden. Dottie muttered it to herself now as she crouched among the rows in her own garden and plucked at the tiny weed sprouts that grew beneath the plants.

She poked her head above the plants and checked on Emmie. She couldn't help but smile. Emmie threw a stick and tried to get Daisy to chase it, but no matter how hard she tried, that little dog was determined not to learn to fetch. Dottie chuckled. At least it kept the girl occupied.

She bent back down and reached for another bundle of weeds, when she heard a pop. She'd reached too far, and her back cracked. With a groan, Dottie struggled to stand. A sharp pressure built up on the one side of her back. She twisted to the side in an attempt to crack her back again. It took a few minutes, but the moment she heard another pop, the pressure released. She sighed. Old age wasn't all it was cut out to be. Retirement wasn't as relaxing as she thought it would be either.

As she stood up, she noticed Emmie wasn't where she had played a few minutes ago. Dottie took a deep breath, but it was difficult. Emmie had to be around, she couldn't have gone far. She wouldn't lose her too. As she stepped over her plants to reach the far side of the garden, Emmie's giggle, along with Daisy's bark, sounded to her right. With a hand raised over her eyes, she searched the hill that led to the neighbors' house. *I should have known.*

Emmie stood at the fence while Daisy jumped around.

"Emmie," Dottie called. She knew she was scowling, but the girl knew better than just to take off.

"Over here, Grandma." Emmie waved her hand.

Dottie took a few steps toward the hill. Her knees creaked. Even though it was only a small incline, she wasn't sure she could make it up. She stopped at the bottom of the hill, and was just about to call her granddaughter to her side when Sherri, the neighbor, came to the fence. She waved. Dottie waved back. It was the polite thing to do, after all.

"Can Emmie play with the girls?" Sherri shouted down to her.

Dottie closed her eyes. A sudden wave of dizziness hit her. She wobbled on her feet. Jack, where was Jack? She looked behind her, but the truck was gone. Where was he?

"Grandma?"

Dottie's eyes widened. Emmie. Where was she? Her head whipped back and forth, but she couldn't see her.

"Grandma!"

Dottie glanced down. There she was, at her feet. She closed her eyes as another burst of dizziness sent the world spinning around her.

"Can I go play, please?" Emmie pulled at her hand.

Dottie made an effort to listen to her. Play? Play where? She looked up and noticed her neighbor waving at her. Dottie waved back and then dropped her hand. She'd already done that, hadn't she?

Dottie nodded her head. All Dottie wanted was to sit down in her chair and close her eyes. Maybe then the world would stop spinning. Emmie let go of her hand and ran off. Dottie watched as Sherri walked to the gate on her side of the yard and took Emmie's hand.

"Thanks!" Sherri called down.

Dottie brought her hand up to her waist and gave a half-hearted wave. She took a step forward and the gravel driveway pitched to the left. Her arms went out, for balance. She brought her foot back down and waited for everything to go back to normal.

A wave of dust appeared on the road out front. With the dry weather and lack of rain, their country dirt road was dry. Whenever a car drove down their side road, a trail of dust announced its presence long before you actually saw the vehicle.

Dottie hoped it was Jack. She needed Jack. He'd run down to a neighbors' house down the way for a tool he needed. But he'd been gone too long.

Dottie crossed her arms as she waited to see if it were Jack's truck. She shielded her eyes with her hand when the vehicle approached. But it wasn't Jack's truck. It was a dark car. It slowed as it neared her house.

A nervous flutter overtook Dottie's stomach. She stepped backward. Something about the car . . . didn't police cars look like that?

She felt a moment of fear. As the car slowed to a crawl, Dottie knew that something was wrong, very wrong. Her nostrils flared as she fought the panic that threatened to overtake her. She could feel it bubbling up. Her hands shook first, then her arms.

"No, no . . ." Dottie said as she turned and hurried toward the house.

She didn't understand this sudden flight of panic. All she knew was that she needed Jack. The vehicle on the road stopped in front of Dottie's driveway. Dottie edged away, so that if whoever was in the vehicle were to look, they wouldn't see her.

She turned her back and was hit with a pain so fierce in her head that she stumbled over the gravel under her foot. She held her arms out for balance and realized she was seeing double. She glanced back to the road. The car had moved on, still slow, but now at her neighbors' driveway. Maybe they were looking at the mailboxes. She should tell Jack. He would know what was going on.

CHAPTER THIRTY

Dottie managed to move her shaky limbs into the house. She grabbed hold of a kitchen chair and sank her weary body down. When she closed her eyes, things stayed still. She took a few deep breaths to calm herself. She didn't understand why she was so dizzy. If everything would just stay still, in one spot, she would be okay. She had too much to do today. With that thought in mind, Dottie rose from her seat and glanced around her kitchen. There was something she was supposed to do.

A bowl sat on the kitchen counter with a tea cloth over top. Dottie stared at it for a few moments before she remembered that she had left the bread dough to rise earlier. She took a few tentative steps to the counter, unsure if she would get dizzy from the movement or not. She felt odd. She couldn't put her finger on it, but she'd never felt like this before.

Dazed, Dottie repeated a process she knew by heart. She placed the dough on the counter and worked the air out of it. She didn't pay attention to the rhythmic motion; instead, she glanced around her kitchen. Something was wrong. Something was missing. Emmie. Emmie was missing.

A squeal of laughter sounded outside. It was Emmie. Dottie's heart pounded. Where was Emmie? She searched her yard through the window and remembered that Emmie was with the neighbor. A wave of relief flowed through Dottie as the initial panic wore off. Emmie was okay. Emmie was okay. All that mattered to Dottie was Emmie.

Dottie's fists crushed the dough, over and over. Tears drifted down her face. Her hands start to hurt from the repeated motion, but she couldn't stop. She tried to stop, to step away, but it felt like something had taken over her body and was controlling it. A sharp pain pierced through her head. She cried out in anguish and crumpled to the ground. She tried to stand, but her legs wouldn't work now.

⚜

Jack pulled into the driveway, parked the truck off to the side, and looked around the yard. All was quiet. Dottie must be inside with Emmie and the dog. Jack picked up the treat he'd picked up in town and headed toward the house. He hoped the little cupcakes he had found at the downtown bakery would put a smile on Emmie's face.

When he entered the house, he heard mumbling. The radio must be on.

"Dottie?" he called out.

The low mumble continued. He dropped the bakery box on the table along with his keys and walked into the front room. It was empty. He stood at the front door and opened the heavy wooden door. A nice breeze whisked through the house. Why hadn't Dottie opened this earlier? She always did.

He headed back toward the kitchen. Maybe she decided to have a nap while Emmie either did the same or played in her room. He walked around the corner into the kitchen and was about to head up the stairs when he heard his name.

"Jack."

He turned. Dottie lay on the floor, almost in a fetal position, with her head angled to the side. Her legs were curled up underneath her while her one arm was tucked under her body.

He rushed over and pulled her into his arms.

"Dottie!"

The weight of her body as she lay in his arms shocked him. Dead weight. Yet, she was alive, breathing fine. Her eyes were glazed over and her mouth was slack on the right side. Stroke. Dottie was having a stroke. With a gentleness normally reserved for babies, Jack laid her back on the ground and searched the kitchen for the cordless phone.

"Emmie?" Jack called out while he searched for the phone.

It was over on the desk. He rushed to grab it and dialed 911 as he ran back to where Dottie lay on the ground. Her eyes shot him a desperate look. His heart wrenched while the love of his life lay there helpless.

Assured that the ambulance was on its way, he cradled Dottie in his arms and shouted for Emmie again. She must be sleeping. *Please God, don't let her come down here. Not yet.*

"Jack . . . dust . . . up," Dottie whispered. Her voice was agitated. She mumbled words he couldn't understand, words that didn't make sense.

"Shh, sweetheart. It's okay. Shh."

Jack struggled to keep his composure as he comforted his wife. The drive from town to their house took about twelve minutes. He hoped the ambulance could make it in five. He'd never been so scared before. Nothing compared to this. Nothing.

Dottie struggled to move. He swept her arm from beneath her waist and Dottie sighed. It must have been hurting her. Why hadn't he noticed earlier? He kept an eye on his watch while he continued to try to soothe Dottie. She moaned and mumbled, her words no longer distinguishable. It scared him. Slight tremors would travel along her body, from her legs up to her head. The moment she began to shake, he'd tighten his hold on her. The sweat that beaded on his forehead trickled down.

Through the windows, Jack heard the siren of the ambulance as it approached. He breathed a quick prayer of thanks for their swiftness. He wiped Dottie's drool and rocked her back and forth. A sense of dread hung over him.

When the ambulance arrived, Jack felt like he was stuck in a nightmare. He took his arms from around his wife and stood to the side and watched helplessly as the medics took care of his wife better than he could. He didn't take his eyes off of Dottie. Her pale complexion worried him. *Please don't let her die, God, please, I'll do anything.*

He was startled out of his prayer by one of the paramedics.

"Sir, is your wife on any type of medication?" The man waited with pen in hand as Jack forced his eyes to leave his wife's frail body.

"Um, yes. Namenda, Zyprexa, and Aricept. Sometimes she'll take . . ."

Jack searched his memory for the name of the sedative their doctor prescribed. He only gave it to Dottie when she was really agitated. He didn't like its effects, how it changed her. He turned and opened the upper cupboard where he kept her medication. Where Emmie couldn't reach. He searched the pill bottles until he found the one he wanted, at the very back. He looked at the label . . . Ativan . . . and handed it to the medic.

"Sir, we'll have to ask you to follow us to the hospital; is that all right?"

Jack nodded his head. He needed to grab Emmie first and explain what happened. Then he'd need to pack some items for Dottie. She wouldn't appreciate waking up in the thin hospital gown and she'd need her slippers. Maybe even her knitting.

As the medics loaded Dottie in the ambulance, Jack crumpled. He grabbed onto the table for support before he stood up straight, squared his shoulders, and gave himself a stern talking-to. His family needed him to be strong. If he fell apart now, he'd be ashamed of himself forever.

About to head up the stairs to find Emmie, Jack stopped when a knock sounded at the door.

"Jack, is everything okay? I wanted to wait until the ambulance left until I came over, I didn't want Emmie to see and get worried." Sherri wrung her hands as she stood there.

"Emmie's with you?"

Shocked that she wasn't up in her room like he'd thought, it took a moment before he realized that if she was at the neighbors', then Dottie must have known. Maybe that's what she was trying to tell him.

"Jack, is everything okay? What happened to Dottie?" Sherri's voice shattered the confusion that reigned in Jack's mind.

He opened the door for her to come in, while he pulled out the desk drawer to find Dottie's medical information. The last time he looked in the drawer for Mary's phone number, he remembered seeing a clear plastic bag that held all the information they received from the doctor they last time they visited.

"She had a stroke. I think. I need to get a bag made up for her. And Emmie. I need to get Emmie."

In a rush, Jack pulled the desk drawer out instead of pushing in it, and everything fell to the floor. Sherri bent down to gather up all the loose papers, pens, and keys that emptied onto the floor while Jack stood there and watched. The drawer reminded him of something. He couldn't quite place his finger on it, but he knew it was something best left forgotten.

"Jack, let Emmie stay the night with me. She can have a sleepover with my daughter. The girls will love it. All she'll need is a nightgown and her favorite stuffed animal. Okay?"

Jack didn't know what to say. A neighbor in the disguise of an angel. Right when he needed a miracle, one had knocked on his back door. Too shocked to reply, he grunted before heading upstairs, not only to pack essentials for Dottie at the hospital but also for Emmie. She'd want her pink lion.

A thought entered his head as he stuffed everything into a bag. What if the neighbor wasn't the angel she appeared to be? What if having Emmie over at her house is what caused Dottie's stroke? The worry, the stress of not having her granddaughter near could have put Dottie over the edge. Dottie's fear at losing Emmie had grown stronger the past few days.

CHAPTER THIRTY-ONE

Sherri rushed back home. She'd left the girls giggling together over a bowl of popcorn while the latest My Little Pony movie played in the background.

Both girls looked up from the movie when she opened the front door. She quenched her concern for Dottie as she held up the bag Jack had thrust into her arms before he left.

"I have a surprise," she announced. Grins covered the girls' faces as they looked at her. Marie, her daughter, jumped up in anticipation.

"We're going to have a sleepover!"

Sherri placed the bag on the chair by the door and held out her arms. Her daughter slammed into her, excitement all over her face as she squeezed Sherri's breath out of her. Sherri glanced at Emmie. She doubted the little girl had ever been away from her grandparents for longer than an hour, let alone overnight. Emmie's face was scrunched and her eyes darted to the bag on the seat. Sherri opened the bag and took out the stuffed animal Jack had stuffed in the bag. Emmie leaped up and grabbed the pink lion. She held it close to her chest as a tentative smile crept on her face.

"What do you say, Emmie? Want to have a sleepover?" Sherri asked.

Marie pulled away from Sherri, placed her hands on Sherri's cheeks, and smiled.

"Sleepover?" Sherri asked her daughter. Marie nodded her head.

Sherri chuckled and gave her daughter a quick hug. If there was one thing her daughter loved, it was sleepovers. She struggled to suppress her grin as her daughter jumped from her arms over to Emmie. She flung her arms around her friend and squeezed tight. Emmie's eyes opened wide until she giggled.

"Fort, Mama?"

She needed to make this night a happy one for Emmie. It might be her last one for a while. She held up her one hand and began to list off everything the girls would do tonight. Make a fort. Bake cookies. Have a bonfire and roast marshmallows, then read a bed-time story.

Her daughter jumped high in the air, and her yell bounced off the living room walls until Emmie was forced to cover her ears with her hands. Marie grabbed Emmie's hand and pulled her upstairs. Sherri knew the bedroom was going to be a mess as the girls attempted to make their fort. She would need to remember to take pictures.

As she prepared to make dinner, loud thumps and peals of laughter drifted from her daughter's bedroom upstairs. It's so good to hear the laughter. Sherri uttered a small prayer for Dottie. A stroke. What would that mean for Jack and Emmie? Where was Emmie's mother and why wasn't she taking care of her daughter? Sherri knew she shouldn't judge or allow her thoughts to grow in an exaggerated form. Many elderly couples took care of their grand-children these days. It was just sad. Grandparents were there to spoil small children, not raise them.

With a pot of water on the stove to boil, and a tray of chicken nuggets in the oven to bake, Sherri poured herself a glass of iced tea and started to clean her kitchen table. Her husband wouldn't be home until after dark tonight. Matt managed the car dealership in town and often worked the night shift. An easy dinner tailored specifically to the girls would make it an even easier night for Sherri. It was a win-win situation for everyone.

Once everything was ready, Sherri called the girls down. When there was no reply, she had a sneaking suspicion, so she climbed the stairs and stood outside the bedroom door. She couldn't believe her eyes. Not only was the fort built and the room surprisingly clean, but the girls were inside the fort and only muffled giggles could be heard. They had managed to empty the bed of all blankets and sheets, and with the help of Marie's desk chair, dresser drawers, and desk, they had created a large enough space to sleep under.

On tiptoes, Sherri snuck into the room and lifted a corner of a bed sheet draped over the chair and peeked inside. She was smashed in the face by a pillow. With a growl, she launched her body inside the fort and grabbed a nearby pillow. After a few minutes of blows to the body and a pain in her side from laughing so hard, Sherri persuaded the girls to join her downstairs for dinner.

As Sherri dished out the plates of homemade macaroni and cheese and chicken nuggets, Marie took milk out of the fridge and poured herself and Emmie each a glass. Before Sherri could bring the plates over to the table, her daughter had already downed one full glass of milk and was in the midst of pouring herself another. Emmie just sat there, wide eyed as she watched Marie chug the milk with superhero speed.

Emmie waited until Sherri had sat down before she reached for her milk and took a big gulp of it. Sherri smiled at her, reached for her hand, and waited for her daughter to say a simple prayer of thanks for the meal. Silence reigned in the kitchen as they ate their dinner. Any time Marie would speak, Sherri marveled at how quickly Emmie recognized the need to look her daughter in the eye before she answered. Children were able to adapt and accept what adults often struggled to even notice. Her daughter's hearing disability didn't even seem to faze Emmie.

Emmie started to giggle and Sherri noticed the reason why. Marie's face was covered in sauce and she had strings of cheese hanging off her chin. If there was one thing her daughter wasn't, it was a clean eater. Sherri pushed her chair back and reached for the napkin holder she'd forgotten to place on the table earlier. She overreached and knocked a stack of flyers to the floor.

"Mama? Why is Emmie on that paper?" Marie asked

Sherri glanced down. What? Marie pointed to a flyer that rested just below her dangling feet. Sherri reached down and picked the paper up. It was one of those missing children advertisements. Sherri had never really taken much notice of them before.

"I'm not," said Emmie as she continued to spoon her macaroni and cheese into her mouth.

Sherri looked at the picture and back to Emmie. There was a resemblance. It was uncanny.

"It's not me," Emmie said again, with a shake of her head. "See, my hair is longer and I have all my tooths." She opened her mouth wide to display her teeth.

Sherri glanced back at the picture. With her two front teeth missing and her hair in a ponytail, now that she really looked at it, that little girl didn't resemble Emmie at all. Emmie was older as well, plus where were the dimples?

"Okay," said Marie before her attention returned to her dinner. Sherri didn't say anything.

⚜

Sherri stood at the foot of the stairs and sighed with relief. It had taken a while, but she had finally managed to get the girls to settle down and go to sleep. She had kept the excitement level high for Emmie. First sleepovers were always difficult, but the brave little girl only asked for her grandparents a few times.

She checked to make sure the porch light was on for Matt. He should be home soon. She needed to talk to him about the photo on the flyer. The campfire smoldered in the fire pit outside in the backyard. It had become a habit to sit and enjoy the quiet night in the country once their daughter was in bed. She poured a tall glass of iced tea from the pitcher she'd made earlier and was about to head outside when the slam of a car door caught her attention. She looked out her window, but Matt's silver truck wasn't there.

With her iced tea in one hand and cordless phone in the other, Sherri nudged the screen from the patio door open. A warm red glow emitted from the fire pit. The girls had so much fun out here earlier as they had toasted their marshmallows. Sherri's stomach turned at the thought of all those sugary treats. Emmie wouldn't eat any of the ones that caught on fire, so rather than waste them, Sherri had engorged herself.

The night was still. The crickets' soft melody carried in the warm summer's night breeze as a cow in the farmer's field called out to the herd. Sherri loved the quiet nights of country life. She didn't miss living in town at all. Sherri sank back in one of the white-washed Adirondack chairs that encircled the campfire and closed her eyes. The scuffle of rocks sounded to the right. It was a quiet sound, but Sherri shot up and looked around.

A vehicle was parked outside of Jack and Dottie's house. Sherri walked over to the fence that separated their properties. Maybe Jack was home already, although he drove an old Fold pickup, not a Jeep.

Sherri could barely make out the silhouette of the person who banged on her neighbors' back door.

"They're not home," Sherri called out during a lull in the pounding.

The figure turned and took a few steps away from the porch and into the small light.

"They're not home," Sherri called out again. She didn't want to make her voice too loud. Her daughter's window was open and the last thing she wanted was for either one of the girls to wake up.

"Do you know when they'll be home?" A man's voice carried in the wind.

Sherri was about to call out again when she realized the person was headed toward her.

"I'm sorry, there was an emergency and they had to go to the hospital."

"Is everything okay, ma'am?"

As the man approached, she noticed something in his hand. A badge. It was a cop. Why would a police officer be looking for Jack and Dottie?

Should she say anything about Emmie and the photo of that missing girl?

"I'm sorry, but I'm sure Jack will be home tomorrow. Do you want me to let him know you were here?" An awkward silence hung in the air.

The officer walked up to the fence until he stared Sherri right in the eye.

"Ma'am, can you confirm if they have a little girl who stays with them?"

Sherri hesitated. The image of the missing child photo flashed before Sherri's eyes.

"Yes, their granddaughter. Is everything okay?" Sherri was about to ask if anything had happened to Dottie at the hospital, but recalled that the officer hadn't known anything about them being there in the first place.

"I'm sorry. Jack is at the hospital with Dottie."

"Thank you, ma'am. I'll head up to the hospital to see Mr. and Mrs. Henry myself. I hope you have a good night. Sorry to have bothered you." The officer took a step backward.

Sherri glanced behind her and thought about the two girls sleeping in the upstairs.

What if Emmie was that missing little girl?

"Officer?"

CHAPTER THIRTY-TWO

Megan's hand rested on the doorknob to Emma's room. She never thought she would do this—say good-bye. Not like this. It didn't feel right.

She should be in here tidying up the room, fluffing the pillow and comforter, dusting the picture frames. Getting it ready for when Emma came home.

Except she wasn't. Ever. And it was time to accept that.

A heavy shroud blanketed Megan.

She opened the door and she surveyed the walls, bookshelves, and bed. Peter was right. This room was a shrine. Her life had been on pause all these years.

This room would never be anything other than Emma's room. A coat of paint and new furniture couldn't change that.

The phone rang downstairs. Megan's heart stopped for a brief moment before she remembered it no longer mattered. She had to accept that the likelihood of anyone sighting Emma now was slim. She needed to stop expecting the phone call.

Still, she rushed out of Emma's room and down the stairs, only to stop dead in her tracks. Peter stood there. The phone in his hand.

Peter cleared his throat. She stared at the phone in his hand. She raised her eyes to look in his face, and her heart dropped. His eyes were red.

"Detective Riley." The weary anguish in his voice shattered what few shards of hope Megan still held on to.

"It's not her, is it?" she cried. She went to move past him but he blocked her. His hands settled on her shoulders and he forced her to stay still.

"Detective Riley found the couple in the picture. But they were at the hospital. The woman, a grandmother"—Peter shook his head—"had a stroke. The child you saw in the photo is their granddaughter. The mother passed away almost three years ago. She's lived with them ever since."

Megan's body froze. Granddaughter. The little girl wasn't Emma. Her body shuddered as the realization swept over her.

"We sent a police officer to the hospital to speak to a man whose wife just had a stroke based on a grainy picture that I told you wasn't Emma. Why?" Peter turned from her. His back was rigid. Anger rippled through his muscles.

Megan's heart seared as if poked with a hot iron. Pain, heartache, despair was forever branded upon her heart. She was gone. She was really gone.

"I had to try. I would have always wondered," Megan sobbed. She wanted to curl up in a ball and block everything out. She couldn't do this anymore.

"I know. That's why I sent the image to Riley. But we can't do this anymore, Megan. Don't you see that? We can't hurt anyone else. Not like this." Peter's voice cracked. His body convulsed from the sobs that tore through him.

"Peter?" She didn't like the distance between them.

A haunted look entered his eyes. He stepped away from her, only one step, but to Megan it might as well have been to the moon, that's how far the distance between them felt.

"It's late. I'm going to bed." The stoop of his shoulders and the way his head hung spoke volumes to her.

"Peter," Megan repeated as she reached out to him only to stop.

She couldn't handle losing him too, not tonight. The realization hit her. It was his strength, his love, his laughter that she needed. She couldn't do this alone. She needed him to help her live again. Live without Emma.

"Come to bed, Megan. I just want this day over with."

Megan followed him up the stairs. She stopped at Emma's bedroom. She closed the door, but not before her eyes drank in the sight of the frilly princess bed, a room where only sweet dreams should reside. This wasn't a room full of dreams anymore. Not for her.

Peter had disappeared into their bedroom by the time Megan turned around. She hoped she wasn't too late. That he hadn't shut her out yet.

Megan crawled into bed beside Peter and snuggled up to his cold body. He just lay there. With her head on his shoulder and her hand on his chest, she closed her eyes and prayed. Prayed that there was still a chance for them to repair the cracks in their marriage, that their family would be able to heal and move forward and that Emma, no matter where she was, would be happy. A tear slipped past her eyelashes as she thought about Emma.

God, please let my daughter be in heaven, happy with you. Megan couldn't bear the thought that she could be anywhere else, with anyone else.

"We can't do this anymore," Peter said. His voice was heavy with emotion and rumbled deep within his chest.

"I know." Megan rubbed her hand gently across his chest. As much as it hurt, she knew she couldn't do it anymore either. Her heart splintered into minuscule pieces.

"Saying good-bye is going to be hard," she whispered.

Peter's arm tightened across her shoulders as he pulled her closer. Megan closed her eyes. Words didn't need to be said tonight. Tomorrow was a new day, with new decisions to be made.

Megan gave a deep sigh and burrowed into Peter's now warm body. She listened to the rhythm of his breathing, matched her breath with his, and worked at clearing her mind. Sleep beckoned and she welcomed it.

The shrill ring of the phone jarred her awake. Her body buzzed with excitement the moment the phone rang. Peter reached across to the table beside the bed, and answered the phone.

"Okay, see you then," he said after a few moments.

Megan held her breath.

"Detective Riley wants us to meet him at a farmhouse near Hanton."

"Why?" *That didn't make sense.* Megan sat up to look at Peter.

His right shoulder shrugged.

Megan's chest felt like it was going to explode; the heart palpitations increased until she felt acute pain. She bit her lip to contain the cry that ripped through her throat.

Peter's eyes met hers. The pain she experienced in her chest equaled the pain in his eyes.

"Maybe he wants to show us personally that it's not Emma. Maybe he wants to help us let go."

Megan turned and lay on her side, away from Peter. She curled herself into a ball and stuffed her hand into her mouth to stifle the sobs that racked through her body.

CHAPTER THIRTY-THREE

The antiseptic smell bothered Jack's nose. He scrunched it up in distaste. He rested his hand on the cold metal rail of Dottie's bed. He'd just finished tucking the thin hospital blanket around her body. He should have brought one of the afghans she'd knitted to cover her. She was always cold, even in summer, and loved to have an array of blankets on her body as she slept. He hoped she wouldn't notice.

Jack stroked Dottie's age-spotted hand. Its coldness bothered him, but the nurse had assured him it was normal. He checked her face for any signs of life, but she lay as still as she had before he'd stepped out of the room fifteen minutes ago.

Jack glanced over his shoulder. The detective had finally left. It bothered him how long the man had stood just outside Dottie's door after Jack had excused himself. The hour was late and his wife was lying in a hospital bed unconscious from a stroke. The man shouldn't have even been here.

But his words, the questions he asked, wouldn't leave Jack alone. Questions about Emmie. Questions that Jack wanted to be able to answer but couldn't. Not until he spoke with Dottie.

He leaned back in his chair and shifted his hips. He was glad Emmie was at their neighbors' house tonight. Jack would have been lost otherwise. Hospitals were not a place for little girls. He could have called Doug to take Emmie if he needed to. He would have been here in a heartbeat. But it had been a year since Doug last stood in a room with Dottie, and he didn't think now was the time to break the promise they had made him.

Jack reached into his back pocket and pulled out the business card the detective had given him. He agreed to call if he ever saw the missing child named Emma. Emma. Not Emmie. Or was it?

He held the card in his hand. He pictured Emmie when she first came to the house. How quiet she had been. He remembered the nights she would call out for her mommy, how it tore his heart that she'd been ripped from Mary's arms at such an early age. He remembered the anger he felt toward his daughter, that she couldn't take care of her own child. Jack shook his head. What if that had been all a lie? What if Dottie hadn't taken Emmie out of a hopeless situation where her mother had just died, but instead, took her out of the arms of a mother who loved her?

Detective Riley had painted a picture earlier of a woman who refused to give up searching for her missing daughter. A woman who believed that daughter was Emmie.

Only Dottie could answer the question the detective raised. Except Jack wasn't even sure Dottie could answer. She claimed to have no memories of that day. With the drugs she'd been on, Jack wasn't surprised either.

As the heart monitors continued to beep in the corner, Jack closed his eyes. Memories replayed in his mind. Memories of when Emmie first came home. Memories of his own daughter. Memories of Dottie and how she would react to certain things when it came to Emmie.

He snapped his eyes open and sat up straight. As much as it broke his heart, he had a phone call to make.

Two wrongs don't make a right. Isn't that how the saying goes?

CHAPTER THIRTY-FOUR

Megan drummed her fingers on her knees.

"Can you please stop?"

Her fingers stilled. Her leg bounced instead.

"We need to talk."

Megan glanced over at Peter. His jaw jutted out and his lips tightened.

Megan kept silent. Whatever he had to say, she couldn't hear it right now.

"I called your mother before we left. She's going to make all the arrangements for us."

Megan stared out the window and watched the corn rows streak by in the early morning light. Miles of corn stretched out before them, dotted with farmhouses and barns. She wondered how life in the country would be any different than life in town, apart from the obvious smells.

"Are you listening to me?"

She took in a deep breath and forced herself to count to five. He wanted to do this now? Now, when they were almost at the farmhouse? She reached into her purse and fingered the candle she'd wished upon. Was it only yesterday? It felt like a lifetime ago.

"Yes, I heard you." Megan heaved a sigh and turned in her seat so she faced him. "Don't you think it's too soon? Can't you wait till tomorrow? Or maybe next week?"

"I also booked an appointment with the counselor," Peter whispered.

Megan sat back in her seat. Her heart wrenched and her throat tightened as she processed what he'd just said.

"Why?" Her breath carried the word as she exhaled.

Peter reached across and laid his hand on hers. He gave it a small squeeze.

"Because I think we need to figure out what we want, what we need. All we've done is accuse each other lately. We need to rebuild the trust between us."

He was right about the lack of trust. The accusations they'd been throwing at each other proved that.

"I don't want to lose you." Her heart shattered into minuscule pieces at the thought. What about the girls? What would it do to them to have Peter leave?

"I'll always be here." Peter's grasp tightened.

Megan didn't respond. They'd reached the farmhouse where they were to meet Detective Riley.

⚜

"We're here." Megan choked on the words.

Peter slowed the Jeep and turned into the driveway.

A light blazed from inside the quaint farmhouse windows as they drove down the gravel driveway. It reminded her of an old farmhouse her grandparents used to live in. She thought about the people who lived there, what they were like, who they were. *I hope it's a happy house.*

"Why are we here anyway? Are you sure Riley didn't say anything?" Megan muttered the question. It wasn't the first time she'd asked it, and she didn't expect to hear an answer from Peter.

She had hardly slept last night. She tossed and turned. Her mind would play tricks on her, a childish giggle would fill the room, and she'd dissolve into tears again. It was hard to say good-bye when there was no closure, when your heart didn't believe it. She'd finally headed down to the kitchen where she made herself a cup of tea. She'd pulled out the family photo albums and thumbed through them. Wistful thoughts of the way things had been when they were newly married and then as new parents. A light in their eyes had reflected a happiness settled deep within. A happiness that was now missing.

Detective Riley leaned on his black car as he watched them drive up. Megan couldn't read the expression on his face. She wasn't sure she wanted to even try.

The Jeep crawled to a stop. Peter grabbed Megan's hand and squeezed. She glanced down at their hands entwined together. There had to be hope. Hope for them. Hope for their family. She glanced up into Peter's eyes. He stared back. Once upon a time, she'd garnered strength from this man she married. She thought she'd lost that strength, but it was always here. Why did she think she didn't need it? Why did she think she had to do it all on her own?

Riley straightened and took a step toward them.

Peter released her hand and opened his door. Megan did the same. Despite her nervous energy, her body reacted as if on automatic. One foot in front of the other until she stood in front of Riley. Peter held out his hand to her. She reached for it and squeezed. She needed a lifeline to hold on to, an anchor to steady her. Her skin tingled.

"Why are we here, Riley? What is going on?" Megan bit her lip. She wanted to ask more, to demand more answers. She couldn't handle the secrecy, the unknown.

Riley jerked his head toward the house and crossed his arms.

"Just a few more minutes."

Megan's mouth dropped. A few more minutes, for what? What was he talking about?

Peter squeezed her hand. She looked at him. He shook his head.

"You asked us to meet you here. Why?" Peter's voice was low, hard. Megan knew he was struggling to rein in his emotions.

Riley let out a long breath and unfolded his arms. He stood straight and faced them.

"Because I knew you needed closure. Your lives have been ripped apart the past two years. I'm hoping that today will help you move past the nightmare you've lived. It's not how we normally handle things, but . . ."

Megan tried to read his eyes to see if he was telling them anything, but they were guarded. She glanced to the farmhouse. The house she hated. It gave off the persona of a quaint old farmhouse, but for Megan, it would forever be branded in her nightmares. It's the house that she thought would answer her dreams, but instead shattered them.

A figure stood in the doorway.

Riley glanced over his shoulder. "Listen. The older gentleman you're about to meet, his name is Jack, and his wife . . ."

The screen door edged open and Jack stepped through it. He stopped and stared at Megan. Tears streaked down his face. Megan's heart stopped. He took another step past the door and turned. Time stood still for Megan. The seconds it took for Jack to reach his hand inside the door seemed like an eternity.

A small figure with curly blonde hair in pigtails stepped out of the door. Her gaze was fixed on Jack as she held his hand.

Peter's arms encircled Megan as she took a step forward. He made her wait.

Jack reached inside the door again. This time he withdrew a large suitcase.

Megan's eyes darted from the suitcase to the little girl whose head was turned enough that she couldn't get a full view.

Jack bent down to the ground and opened his arms. The little girl rushed into them, her eyes clenched tight as her little arms squeezed his neck. His lips moved as he whispered words into the little girl's ear. She nodded her head, leaned her head on his shoulder, and uttered the words that froze Megan's heart.

"I love you, Papa."

Megan choked back a sob as the voice of her daughter reached her ears.

Detective Riley threw his arm out in front of Peter and Megan.

"Wait, please just wait," he whispered.

Megan's head turned. Riley's eyes shone bright with unshed tears. She glanced up at Peter and realized that his tears were flowing freely down his face as well. His eyes remained fixed on their daughter.

Jack stood up. Emmie's arms were still wound tight around his neck. He gathered his arms around her and held her close to his body. He took a tentative step forward. Emma cried out. He stopped. Megan's heart fluttered as she waited for him to carry her daughter to her. Her daughter. Emma.

Jack whispered more words into Emma's ear. Megan wished with all her heart she knew what he was telling her daughter. Seconds stretched into a lifetime for Megan. Her heart ached as she struggled to hold back the tears that threatened to overwhelm her.

"Who do you see, Emmie? Open your eyes, princess." Jack's gruff voice broke every inch of self-control Megan had.

"Momma?" Emma whispered. Her voice was hesitant, unsure almost.

The tears Megan tried to withhold overflowed and ran down her cheeks. She let out a loud sob and broke free of the hold of Peter's arms. With speed she didn't imagine possible, Megan rushed across the driveway. Mere inches from her daughter, she stopped and dropped down to her knees. She didn't care that the gravel sank into her skin.

"Emma," she whispered. Her voice cracked.

"Momma? Papa told me that you weren't in heaven. He said you were lost. But you found me."

Megan opened her arms wide. She needed to feel her daughter's body tight against her own. To ease that ache her arms felt constantly for over two years. She couldn't wait to enfold her daughter in her arms.

Emma took the three steps that kept them apart. Her tiny little arms encircled Megan. Megan cried out in relief. Emma. Her daughter. *Thank you, God, thank you, God.* She brushed her hand against her daughter's hair and rubbed her back. She stood up on shaky legs but kept a tight hold on her daughter.

As she turned to face Peter, he rushed over and gathered them both in his arms. Her husband, usually so calm and collected, was speechless, but his face beamed with joy. Emma scrambled from Megan's arms to Peter's. Megan's arms were bereft, empty. She wanted to gather her daughter back up, but she stopped herself.

Instead, she leaned her head against Peter's body and marveled at the changes in Emma. No longer the pudgy almost three-year-old, Emma had sprouted up into the most precious little girl Megan had ever seen. Those other girls she'd thought looked like Emma were nothing like her. Nothing.

When Emma twisted in Peter's arms and stared at the man she called Papa, Megan did the same. Detective Riley had walked over and laid his hand on the older man's arm.

"You need to come with me," he said. Jack nodded his head, a sad smile on his face. Megan wanted to be angry with him, desired to lash out at him, but she couldn't. The words wouldn't come.

Jack followed Riley to the black car, but stopped when he stood in front of Megan. He hung his head, his shoulders stooped as he clasped his hands in front of him.

"I'm so sorry. I had no idea," he said. He didn't look up as the words seemed to empty his soul.

"Papa?" Emma twisted in Peter's arms and reached her hand out to him.

"It's okay, princess." He winked at Emma, but Megan noticed the sad smile that crept across his face. "Remember, we talked about this. It's all going to be okay." Jack leaned forward and planted a kiss on Emma's head. She buried her face into Peter's neck. Megan reached up and rubbed her back.

Megan was at a loss. Her heart broke for her daughter. She called this man Papa. She wouldn't call him such an endearing word unless she had been loved by him. Her throat, swollen from the sobs she fought to contain, whispered words she never thought she would ever say.

"Thank you. Thank you for giving my daughter back to me."

Jack's head shook at her words. Heartache and despair filled his eyes.

"I didn't know. Not until last night. If I had known . . . little girls, they need their mamas." Jack's head dropped. He looked old. Old and frail.

She held her arms out to her daughter, who was sobbing into her daddy's neck. When her little girl turned and held her arms out for her mommy, Megan grabbed her and held on for dear life. Nothing mattered to Megan at this moment but Emma.

Peter walked away from his family and shook Detective Riley's hand. He ignored Jack.

"Thank you. Thank you for finding my daughter," he said.

"Don't thank me. It was Megan who found your daughter," Riley said. He opened the car door and held it as Jack sank down in the backseat.

Megan, with Emma still in her arms, joined Peter as he stood beside Riley. Peter placed his arms around her.

"So, what happens now? She called him Papa?" Peter turned his face away from Emma and lowered his voice. Megan had to lean closer to hear him.

Detective Riley shut the car door. Megan winced at the sound.

"We'll take him in for questioning. Jack called me this morning and explained what happened two years ago. His wife is ill and in the hospital. Your daughter wasn't hurt, but there will be extensive interviews and consultations with doctors and psychiatrists." He gave them a smile.

"This is one story that can only be called a miracle," Riley said.

Megan tightened her arms around her daughter. She thought about the candle and the wish she'd made.

A miracle indeed.

CHAPTER THIRTY-FIVE

Jack shuffled down the driveway and kicked some of the large rocks out of his way. He needed to lay fresh gravel before the snow. Hard to believe it was already fall.

He shielded his eyes against the glare that glistened off his mailbox. The red arm was up, which meant only two things. He prayed it wasn't more condolences. He had nowhere else to place the cards.

Without glancing through the stack of mail he pulled out of the box, Jack tucked the bundle beneath his arm and headed back toward the house. He cut across his front lawn and grimaced as his tread left an imprint in the overgrown grass. Maybe he'd cut the grass today. Something he should have done weeks ago. If Dottie were here, she'd bite his head off for neglecting the yard.

If Dottie were here, things would be different.

Jack rested against the porch railing and gasped for breath. Not too long ago he'd had enough energy for a man half his age. Now he felt his age plus some. One step at a time Jack climbed the stairs and sank down in his wicker chair. He dropped the bundle of mail on the little table beside him, leaned back, and closed his eyes.

The stillness around him suffocated him. The birds didn't even chirp. Since the funeral, the death song of silence had draped his property like the heavy winter's snow that he knew was coming soon enough.

He missed Dottie. Some days he didn't think he could go on. Most days he couldn't. The only thing that kept him going were the little pink envelopes he received in the mail.

Three weeks after his little girl left him they arrived in his mailbox. The first one was covered with flowers and rainbows. One after the other they would arrive. For a while, he got one every day.

The first one made him cry like a baby. He kept it in his pocket; its creases were stained with his tears.

She still called him Papa. He hadn't been sure if she would. Each card that arrived was a gift. One he wasn't sure he would have given if the roles had been reversed.

A week had passed since the last envelope. Walking to the mailbox to return empty-handed was hard. The condolences were thoughtful and caring, but meant nothing compared to Emma's letters.

Jack reached for the mail and fingered through the envelopes. No pink ones. He rubbed his whiskered jaw and cleared his clogged throat. The echo of Emma's giggles whenever Jack had given her a whisker rub tickled his memory. He'd give anything to hear her laughter again.

Anything.

There were no words for what Dottie had done. No excuses. But he would never trade the days he had with Emma. Never. Jack swiped at his face and sniffed. He'd change how, though. No parent should have to go through that nightmare. Poor Dottie. She had no idea the horror she had escaped while in her coma. Jack was thankful she had slipped away silently without having to say good-bye. It was easier that way. For her.

Not for him. He would relive that day for the rest of his life.

The handwriting on one of the envelopes stood out. Childish letters carefully drawn.

Jack ignored the tears that ran down his face. No one was around to see him wear his foolish heart on his sleeve. He carefully slit open the envelope and took out the folded paper within.

Pink and purple flowers covered the edges of the paper.

Dear Papa,

I lubs you Papa. I have a new dress for school. It's yellow. Like Daisy. Daisy says hi. She misses you. So do I.

A NOTE FROM THE AUTHOR

Did you fall in love with Jack and Dottie as much as I did? Want to know more about their story? You're not the only one! *Dear Jack . . .* a Finding Emma novella is out now!

Be sure to sign up for my newsletter over at www.steenaholmes. com so you don't miss out on any new releases.

Emma's story doesn't end now that she's reunited with her family. Keep an eye out for *Emma's Secret* coming spring 2013.

If you enjoyed *Finding Emma*, I would appreciate it if you would help others enjoy this book, too.

Lend it.

This e-book is lending-enabled, so please, share it with a friend.

Recommend it.

Please help other readers find this book by recommending it to friends, readers' groups, and discussion boards.

Review it.

Please tell other readers why you liked this book by reviewing it at one of the following websites: Amazon or Goodreads.

If you are part of a book club, please turn the page for the reader's guide for *Finding Emma*. If you would like to have *Finding Emma* as part of your next book-club meeting please email me at steena@steenaholmes.com for more information.

Book list for Steena Holmes
~ *Dear Jack* . . . a Finding Emma novella
~ *Emma's Secret* (coming spring 2013)
~ *Chocolate Reality*
~ *Unknown*

Enjoy a bit of romance?
Check out other titles by Wynne Holmes that might whet your appetite:
~ *Hot for Cowboy*
~ *Cabin Fever*

Like paranormal suspense? Check out my titles under the name J Mann.
~ *Fallen*—Book 1: Nephilim Arise Series
~ *Sanctuary*—Book 2: Nephilim Arise Series

1) In the beginning of the story, Megan is a tired mother, overwhelmed by the daily tasks of her life and her children. Were you able to relate to her when you first met her?

2) After Emma's disappearance, Megan started up the Safe Walk program. What do you think was the underlying reason for Megan starting up this program?

3) When you first are introduced to Peter, what is your initial reaction to him? Do you see him as a man trying to be the glue keeping his family together or does he come across as more selfish?

4) Losing a child is every mother's worst nightmare. Do you think you would react the same way as Megan does or differently? Do you know anyone who has gone through this?

5) When Megan first thought she'd seen Emma at the coffee shop drive-thru, what was your first reaction? How would you have reacted if you were in her shoes? What if you were that child's mother and a stranger came up to your child like Megan did?

6) As the story progressed, how did your attitude toward Megan change? Was she a woman you felt you could sympathize with? Did you agree with Peter and everyone else in her life who felt she'd been so focused on finding Emma that she's forgotten about everyone else?

7) When you are first introduced to Jack, Dottie, and Emmie, what was your initial reaction? Were you drawn to them as characters?

8) Dottie is a strong woman with a conflicted past. It becomes evident early on that Dottie has some memory loss. When did you start to wonder that things weren't as they seem at the farmhouse?

9) Emmie believed that her mommy was in heaven. How did that make you feel? Do you think that Jack and Dottie handled everything correctly when it came to Emmie wanting to read stories about heaven, drawing images of her and her mom in heaven?

10) The scene where Peter showed his journal to Megan was crucial, not only to their storyline as a couple but also at showing how Peter was handling Emma's disappearance. Did that change the way you looked at Peter at all? Did it affect how you viewed Megan and her thoughts about her marriage and her husband?

11) Why do you think that Jack never fought Dottie on the issue of Emmie never leaving the farm? When Jack finds out the truth about Mary, his own daughter, how did you react?

12) Hannah carried a lot of guilt on her young shoulders regarding Emma's disappearance. Why do you think that was? Why do you think she never let go of that guilt?

13) When Peter asked Megan to "let go" of Emma, what was your immediate reaction? Was it right of Peter to give Megan the ultimatum of "Emma or me"?

14) When the subject of preparing a memorial service was brought up, how did you feel? Do you think you could go through preparing this type of service for a child you believed was still alive? Do you think having a formal way of saying good-bye to Emma was necessary for the family to move on?

15) The scene Megan witnessed at the cemetery was instrumental in her decision to say good-bye to Emma. How did you feel at that point?

16) A small county fair is always fun to attend. Have you ever been to one? Did you agree with Peter that it was time for the family to finally go? What were your thoughts when Megan sat down on the bench and watched an elderly family with their young child? Did you think that maybe Dottie/Jack and Megan/Peter would run into each other while there?

17) When Megan realized that the image she took was her daughter, what were your thoughts? When she brought the photo to Peter, did you agree with his reaction?

18) When Jack finally admitted to himself that he'd been ignoring the obvious, what were your thoughts? Do you think he purposefully turned a blind eye? Do you think he knew all along that Emmie really wasn't his granddaughter, or do you feel that Jack really thought this was his second chance?

19) What was your favorite moment of the final scene?

20) Now that you are finished with the story, what are your overall thoughts? What was your favorite scene? What character did you resonate with more? What character did you like least? If there was one thing you would change in the story, what would it be?

ABOUT THE AUTHOR

S teena Holmes grew up in a small town in Canada and holds a bachelor's degree in Theology. She is the author of one previous novel, *Chocolate Reality*. In 2012 she received the Indie Excellence Award. Holmes was inspired to write *Finding Emma* after experiencing a brief moment of horror when she thought her youngest daughter was missing. She wanted to write a story other mothers of young children could relate to. She currently lives in Calgary with her husband and three daughters and loves to wake up to the Rocky Mountains each morning.